CONTENTS

The
Choking
Doberman

Other books by Jan Harold Brunvand

THE VANISHING HITCHHIKER
THE STUDY OF AMERICAN FOLKLORE
READINGS IN AMERICAN FOLKLORE
THE MEXICAN PET

The Choking Doberman

and

Other "New" Urban Legends

JAN HAROLD BRUNVAND

UNIVERSITY OF UTAH

W·W· NORTON & COMPANY
New York · London

Published simultaneously in Canada by Penguin Books
Canada Ltd, 2801 John Street, Markham
Ontario L3R 1B4
Printed in the United States of America

The text of this book is composed in Baskerville, with
display type set in Isbell Medium Italic. Composition and
manufacturing by The Haddon Craftsmen, Inc.
Book design by Jacques Chazaud.

First published as a Norton paperback 1986

Library of Congress Cataloging in Publication Data

Brunvand, Jan Harold.
The choking doberman and other "new" urban legends.

Bibliography: p.
Includes index.
1. Urban folklore—United States. 2. Legends—
United States. 3. Legends—United States—History and
criticism. I. Title.
GR105.B687 1984 398.2'09173'2 83–22031

ISBN 0-393-30321-7

W. W. Norton & Company, Inc.
500 Fifth Avenue, New York, N.Y. 10110
W. W. Norton & Company Ltd.
37 Great Russell Street, London WC1B 3NU

7 8 9 0

PREFACE

Hooked on the American Urban Legend

In 1981 W. W. Norton & Company published *The Vanishing Hitchhiker,* my book about recent American folk stories. It contained the results of some twenty years' study of many highly captivating and plausible, but mainly fictional, oral narratives that are widely told as true stories. We folklorists call them urban legends, although modern legends might be a more accurate term.

The book set forth the history, variations, and possible meanings of some popular belief tales found in contemporary storytelling, such as those about hitchhikers who vanish from moving cars, alligators lurking in New York City sewers, rats that get batter-fried along with the chicken in fast-food outlets, convertibles filled with cement by jealous husbands, housewives caught in the nude while doing laundry, hairdos infested with spiders, pets accidentally cooked in microwave ovens, and so on. This is my second book of modern American folklore of the same type; it contains "new" urban legends that are Americans' favorite false-true tales.

Calling urban legends "folklore" requires an explanation. The usual definition of verbal folklore is material that gets orally transmitted in different versions in the traditions of various social groups. Proverbs, riddles, rhymes, jokes, anecdotes, and ballads are among the folk forms that circulate in oral and usually anonymous variants, comprising the folklore of the people among whom they are known. Urban legends, despite their contemporary sound, display the same characteristics as older verbal folklore. They pass from person to person by word of mouth, they are retained in group traditions, and they are inevitably found in different versions through time and space. If an urban legend at first seems too recent to have achieved the status of folklore, further study often reveals its plot and themes to be decades or even centuries old. And even a new story partly disseminated by the mass media soon becomes folklore if it passes into oral tradition and develops variations.

The Vanishing Hitchhiker dealt with classic American urban legends, those that have been the most studied by folklorists. Stories like "The Death Car" (smell of death permeates upholstery), "The Runaway Grandmother" (Granny's corpse nabbed from auto roof-rack), and "The Hook" (maniac's hook-hand caught in car-door handle and wrenched loose) have been long collected, and have been subjected to a certain amount of scholarly analysis. This book takes up stories that have been relatively ignored by folklorists.

I became hooked on American urban legends when I was in high school hearing and telling them myself. Later, as an undergraduate at Michigan State University, I learned in a folklore class that "The Death Car," for one, was a traveling tale, not something that had really happened in my hometown. During graduate studies at Indiana University I recognized the traditional status of several other familiar stories; for example, in 1959 in Bloomington, Indiana, I clipped for my files a local newspaper's report of "The Dead Cat in the Package" legend (package shoplifted, with comic results). As an instructor at the University of Idaho beginning in 1961 I became interested in tracing the legend about "Red Velvet Cake" (recipe sold to unwitting customer for outrageous price by famous restaurant), because several students swore that it had really happened to a relative. (Of course, it had not.) When I came to my present position at the University of Utah in 1966 I was told that "The Hook," "The Killer in the Backseat," and "The Spider in the Hairdo" were all Salt Lake City occurrences—just as they had been told to me as actual happenings before in Michigan, Indiana, and Idaho. All of this and more went into *The Vanishing Hitchhiker,* where I sampled versions of widespread urban legends, summarized available published materials, and offered some analysis of the legends' meanings.

The reaction to my book was gratifying, and one result of the wide notice it received is this sequel. Hundreds of readers sent me different versions of familiar urban legends, as well as their favorite stories not included in the book. Journalists telephoned me long distance to inquire about hot new local rumors or tales. Radio and television interviewers put me on the air and invited listeners to call in with stories. I even made *People* magazine (23 August 1982) as an instant scholar-celebrity. Suddenly, it seemed, the urban legend, which had long been second in popularity only to the joke in American oral folklore, was also becoming famous in the print and broadcast media.

I raised many a reader's consciousness about his or her own folklore, and thus I contradicted the first sentence of *The Vanishing Hitchhiker:* "We are not aware of our own folklore any more than we are of the grammatical rules of our language." With awareness, for some, came a new sophistication. For example, a letter from a Midwestern teacher of high-school English for students with attitude or behavioral problems who had used my book in class described one result: "I've so upgraded their vocabularies that instead of loudly exclaiming 'bullshit!' in response to others' statements, they now come through with 'hyperbole!' or 'urban legend!' "

People wrote me to say that my book had settled longstanding arguments between friends, co-workers, or spouses, whether or not a particular bizarre but believable story was an old one and whether it was true. I found myself repeating in numerous interviews and letters that not all folklore has to be generations old, and that part of every legend is true. Therefore, we should expect new urban legends to spring up eventually, and we can trust that each of these repeated stories contains some credible core that may be at least partly based on fact. But "new" or not—"true" or not—they are all *folklore* (i.e., oral, traditional, usually anonymous, and varying stories).

I imagined at first that with *The Vanishing Hitchhiker* I had written the definitive work on American urban legends for some time and possibly had even contaminated oral tradition and caused some urban legends to die out. But I remained hooked on the subject, and I kept on collecting and filing variations. Then I realized that while I had got the record of past urban legends more or less completely documented, I would soon see my book outdated as new versions and new stories quickly emerged. People didn't stop telling and believing urban legends—even temporarily—just because some folklorist could show that they were doubtful as reports of completely verifiable events. Of course, I should have anticipated this better, remembering the truisms of folklore research that no tale remains static once it enters oral tradition and that modern folklore is extremely fast—aided by the mass media—to reflect current events.

This book carries my research onward to more and different urban legends. Yet—probably not surprisingly—the story categories in both books are much the same, even if the casts of characters vary somewhat. Here you meet the Doberman pinscher that is choking (on what?), the mysterious living lump in the newly laid carpet (what's under there?), the elephant that sits on a Volkswagen (why?), the corpse of a relative (found where?), the unaware owner of a sabotaged Cadillac (how and by whom tampered with?), and so on. The themes and motifs in these stories will be immediately familiar to readers of *The Vanishing Hitchhiker:* there are automobile legends, horrors, dreadful contaminations, sex scandals, big business ripoffs, and repeatedly the quintessential urban-legend plot twist—the poetic justice, or got-what-he- (or she-) deserved, ending.

I could not have brought together the far-flung examples upon which this book is based without a great deal of assistance from professional colleagues, willing correspondents, and other helpful friends. Since most of my "fan mail" consists of one-shot letters containing stories that many others sent as well, I have not given specific credit to most individual unpublished sources. For the few that I quote directly and at length, the names are cited; for the rest I simply say, "Thank you, and I hope you like this book." However, six particularly energetic and helpful letter writers deserve special mention: James Able of Tampa, Florida; John Dunphy of Alton, Illinois; Ann Jarvis of Racine, Wisconsin; Thelma C. Johnson of Sioux City, Iowa; James Oberg of Houston, Texas; and Dr. T. Healey of Barnsley, South Yorkshire, England.

I have cited journalistic sources of urban legends in full directly in the text. The scholarly books and articles referred to concisely in the text are identified fully in the Bibliography. Individual scholars and correspondents are credited directly in the text for their contributions to my research, but the following academic colleagues and good friends require special mention here in thanks for the particular help they gave me in securing texts or verifying references: Reinhold Aman ("Uncle Maledictus"), Louie Attebery, Ernest Baughman, Jerome Beatty, Jr., Ervin Beck, Bob Bethke, Simon Bronner, David Chaston, Xenia Cord, Rodney Dale, Mihai Dimiu, Eílís Ní Dhuíbhne, Nancy Faber, Sandy Hobbs, Randall Jacobs, Bengt af Klintberg, Carl Lindahl, Alan and Barbara Meyer, William Nicolaisen, Don L. F. Nilsen, Ethelyn Orso, Pamela Ow, Donna Parsons, Lutz Röhrich, Neil Rosenberg, Doc Rowe, Stewart Sanderson, Cynthia Scheer, Jacqueline Simpson, Paul Smith, Karen Spear, Barre Toelken, Don Ward, Gary Warne ("The Answer Man"), Roger Welsch, John O. West, John Widdowson, and Tom Zaniello.

My family, as always, has been supportive of my research

and writing, and I appreciate this more than words can say. However, neither wife nor children, secretaries nor assistants, students nor colleagues, had to take any part in preparing, typing, or proofreading the manuscript of this book. For these tasks I relied on my trusty Kaypro II computer, used with the Perfect Writer and Perfect Speller word-processing programs, and a Daisywriter 2000 printer. The University of Utah provided travel grants that allowed me to attend the California Folklore Society annual meeting in April 1982 and the seminar "Perspectives on Contemporary Legend" at the University of Sheffield in July 1982 during which I presented papers based on the material in Chapter 1.

Have I missed your favorite urban legend? Please send your variants of these or texts of "new" legends to me:

Professor Jan Harold Brunvand
Department of English
University of Utah
Salt Lake City, Utah 84112

The
Choking
Doberman

1

"The Choking Doberman" and Its Ancestors

"New" Urban Legends

What is more welcome on a routine day than a new and intriguing true story or rumor told in the first person? The very opening sentence of such a story makes our ears tingle and draws our attention sharply away from the workaday world: "Did you hear about what happened to a neighbor of mine?" or "My aunt just had the most amazing experience," or "I was told by my hairdresser about this terrible thing that happened to another customer of hers."

All of us hear "urban legends," and we retell them eagerly at home or at parties, work, school, and everywhere we meet other people. The advice and opinion columns of the daily press pass on such stories too, as do some radio and television broadcasters. The media both pick up rumors and legends from the oral stream and feed them back into it again.

Is a dog biting a man not news? It is if it has the right twist. Here is a "Dog bites man" urban legend that recently got into the pages of *Woman's World* magazine (20 April 1982):

> A weird thing happened to a woman at work. She got home one afternoon and her German shepherd was in convulsions. So she rushed the dog to the vet, then raced home to get ready for a date. As she got back in the door, her

phone rang. It was the vet, telling her that two human fingers had been lodged in her dog's throat. The police arrived and they all followed a bloody trail to her bedroom closet, where a young burglar huddled—moaning over his missing thumb and forefinger.

It matters little that Philip Brennan, Jr., the author of the article in which that legend appeared as a teaser, titled his piece "Rumor Madness" and emphasized the completely un-true nature of such narratives. Hundreds of thousands of read-ers will have read the story, and a goodly number of them will have found it so gripping that they discussed it with or retold it to their families and friends; finally, the legend of the watch-dog in convulsions began to return from whence it first came to the author's ears—back to modern American folklore.

But where did the story come from? What other familiar stories are merely legends? Who tells such stories, and why are they believed by so many tellers and listeners? It is their status as folklore, and their behavior and meaning as part of modern oral tradition, that this book about new urban legends deals with.

From the start there are problems with the idea of new urban legends in folklore. First, these "legends"—which are by definition *believed* oral narratives—are not necessarily taken as literal truth by all of their tellers all of the time. Sometimes they are told, or printed, merely as jokes or (as with the *Woman's World* text) as typical examples of recent popular falla-cies. Furthermore, some are really more *rumor* (plotless un-verified reports) than *legend* (traditional believed story). Sec-ond, though the stories are modern, they are not just "urban" in their circulation or subject matter. They are often, but not always, city stories. Third, and most important, urban legends (as I continue to call them, following folkloristic tradition) often appear to be "new" when they begin to spread, but even the newest-sounding stories may have gone the rounds before.

A "new urban legend," then, may be merely a modern story

told in a plausible manner by a credible narrator to someone who hasn't heard the story before, at least not recently enough to remember it. And this sort of thing happens to folklorists just as well as to any other folk.

No sooner had I finished *The Vanishing Hitchhiker* * in 1981 than people started telling and mailing me strange and funny stories of all kinds, many of which sounded like urban legends. Some stories, people claimed, were authentic, though peculiar, real-life occurrences—and they seemed so. But these stories eventually also showed up in the supposed experiences of many other people and had the scent of legend rather than truth. An example of this is "The Stolen Specimen" in Chapter 4. Other stories were old ones not told much lately, and I had forgotten about them; these included "The Rattle in the Cadillac" (Chapter 2), "The Licked Hand" (Chapter 3), and "The Poison Dress" (Chapter 4). Still other stories turned out to be genuine instances of modern folklore that American folklorists had not taken notice of, such as "The Elephant That Sat on a VW" (Chapter 2), "The Bump in the Rug" (Chapter 3), and "The Double Theft" (Chapter 7).

The most fascinating ones I received were the stories that incorporated throughly up-to-date references and thus might represent actual new urban legends. Mentions in these stories of Superglue, jogging, butane cigarette lighters, automobile cruise control, and the 911 emergency telephone number all suggested the possibility of uniquely modern legends; but in most such narratives only the details proved to be new while the structures or ideas were definitely old.

The particular story that came most often to my attention shortly before *The Vanishing Hitchhiker* got into print was the one about the choking dog. It had a plot that sounded as fresh as this morning's headlines, and plenty of true believers passing it along as gospel. The story of the dog—usually a Dober-

---

*For a sampler of the legends in *The Vanishing Hitchhiker*, see Appendix, p. 210.

man—that was choking on fingers bitten off an intruder turned out to be a fine example of a "new" urban legend sweeping the country, but its apparent newness just thinly masked much older folklore elements.

In order to expose this new legend as the old story it is, and also to demonstrate how folklore research sometimes works, I give in this chapter the history of the choking dog plot, insofar as it can be written, plus an account of my detective work that established its sources. Unlike most other new urban legends that spring up, for this one a fairly complete genealogy can be traced.

"The Choking Doberman"

The earliest reliably dated complete American version of "The Choking Doberman" story that I have found introduced most of the elements that are characteristic of this new tradition. From the Phoenix, Arizona, *New Times,* 24 June 1981:

Gagging Dog Story Baffles Police

It happened in Las Vegas. A woman returned from work and found her large dog, a Doberman, lying on the floor gasping for air. Concerned over the animal's welfare, she immediately loaded the pet into her car and drove him to a veterinarian.

The vet examined the dog but finding no reason for his breathing difficulties, announced that he'd have to perform a tracheotomy and insert tubes down the animal's throat so he could breathe. He explained that it wasn't anything she'd want to watch and urged the woman to go home and leave the Doberman there overnight.

When the woman returned home, the phone was ringing off the hook. She answered it, and was surprised to discover it was the vet. Even more surprising was his message—"Get out of the house immediately! Go to the neighbor's and call the police!"

It seems that when the vet performed the operation, he found a very grisly reason for the dog's breathing difficulty —three human fingers were lodged in its throat. Concerned that the person belonging to the dismembered fingers might still be in the house, he phoned to warn the woman.

According to the story, police arrived at her house and found an unconscious intruder, sans fingers, lying in a closet.

New Times learned of the story from an employee of a large industrial plant in the Valley. He said he had gotten the story third hand from another employee who in turn had heard it from a woman whose relatives in Las Vegas knew the dog's owner. As of Friday, *New Times* was not able to nail down the identity of the Doberman's mistress.

According to a spokesman at the *Las Vegas Sun,* that paper, too, was very interested in breaking the story. Unfortunately, even though the story was all over Vegas last Thursday, the paper—and police—weren't able to dig up one shred of evidence to prove the incident ever occurred. "The police are baffled," the *Sun* spokesman said.

Besides the telltale signs of a vigorous oral tradition in this news story, two details remind us of other urban traditions: one is the *suffering pet theme* (as in "The Poisoned Pussycat at the Party" and "The Pet in the Oven" legends); the second is the *urgent warning given over the telephone* (as in "The Baby-sitter and the Man Upstairs" legend). The conclusion of "The Choking Doberman" story also calls to mind not only the killer who is hidden upstairs in the baby-sitter's house, but also "The Killer in the Backseat," yet another American urban legend, in which a would-be killer lurks in the back of a woman's car. (Legends not discussed in this book appear in *The Vanishing Hitchhiker.*)

"The Choking Doberman" legend—and legend it had to be —was evidently being told all over the country during the summer of 1981, judging from newspaper accounts. The same week the Phoenix, Arizona, story was published, columnist Ron Hudspeth of the *Atlanta Journal* discussed the same story under the headline "Don't bet your life on 'gospel' truths" (25

June 1981): "A half-dozen people have called me with that story in recent weeks," Hudspeth wrote, and "each is dead serious [though] none can identify the woman involved." In Nebraska the *Lincoln Journal* ran a similar article on the Fourth of July: "Police can't put finger on story." Numerous calls had come in, both to the newspaper and the police in Lincoln, and *Journal* staff writer Tom Cook made manful efforts to follow up the fruitless leads for possible verification of "The Choking Doberman," supposedly having been told on the popular Paul Harvey radio show or learned from "reliable" informants in Iowa. Cook finally decided that he was barking up the wrong tree, that this was "the stuff of which legends are made."

Meanwhile, in the Northwest, Associated Press writer Jim Klahn in Seattle (as reported in the *Portland Oregonian,* 19 July 1981) concluded a lengthy job of research on the Doberman story by writing "It's nothing more than a transcontinental rumor—so far." He mentioned that the story had crossed his news agency's General Desk in New York months before, besides being rampant by word of mouth in his part of the country.

In August "The Choking Doberman" made the news in Florida; "You'll find this story pretty hard to swallow," read the *Tampa Bay Star* headline (19 August 1981) for an article that featured a cartoon version of the legend. The *Star* quoted a St. Petersburg Police Department spokesman as saying, "I think it started at a cocktail party where a bunch of newsmen were." Journalists, at any rate, found "The Choking Doberman" irresistible and kept coming up with witty headlines like "Reporter's dogged search reveals some hard-bitten truths" (*The Spectator,* Hamilton, Ontario, Canada, 1 December 1981), "Weird story makes rounds" (*The Herald-Palladium,* Benton Harbor and St. Joseph, Michigan, 31 December 1981), and the inevitable "Did you hear the one about . . . ?" (Los Angeles *Herald Examiner,* 3 February 1982). This L.A. version, in a column by Digby Diehl, gives a nice example of how such

REPRINTED WITH PERMISSION OF
THE *Tampa Bay Star/Times*.

stories spread in different versions, and how even a seasoned journalist at first might be fooled by one:

An astonishing story was told to me by my friend Judy Riley at a dinner party a few weeks ago. One day a woman she knew had returned to her Brentwood home from a shopping spree to discover the family dog, a German shepherd, choking and unable to breath. She rushed the dog to the veterinarian's office; the vet was so busy she was told to leave her pet for observation. When the woman returned home, her telephone was ringing; the vet was on the other end and spoke in a calm but firm tone: "Set down the receiver and run out of your house immediately. Go to a neighbor's house. I'll be right there." Puzzled, and a bit frightened, the woman followed instructions.

Minutes later, four police cars arrived, and hiding in the bedroom closet of the house the officers found a large, menacing burglar who was bleeding to death and terrified. The veterinarian arrived on the scene and explained to the homeowner that when he examined her dog to determine the cause of the choking, he had found three human fingers lodged in the dog's throat. He called the police and then called her.

Everyone at the dinner party was stunned by Judy's story. We marveled at the veterinarian's cool; we speculated about our own dogs' ability to attack an intruder; we agreed that urban crime was coming too close for comfort. I re-told the story several times during the following week and thought no more about it until, at a party in Santa Barbara, another friend recounted almost precisely the same story about her friend in Montecito who had a boxer. Subsequently, I heard the story repeated—each time as second-hand truth—about friends in Palos Verdes, Long Island, and San Francisco.

Judy Riley was not lying, of course; she was passing on a bit of urban mythology as I had. And part of the power of this folklore is that at the time of the telling we believe the story to be true.

Diehl had exactly caught the nature of urban legend transmission in this account. A trusted friend at an ordinary social gathering passes on a story in good faith that describes something that supposedly happened to a third party; listeners accept this plausible anecdote as truth and discuss its pros and cons. There is no immediate reason to question such a narrative, since it deals with current concerns, like crime, pets, police, and punishment. Only later, having by then told the story to others, might one hear a varying version and suddenly perceive it as probably apocryphal.

Actual tellings of "The Choking Doberman" in oral tradition—of which I have collected examples virtually from coast to coast—usually dramatize the dog owner's shock, especially at the point of her hearing the vet's surprising commands over the telephone. In the following selection from a version told in Louisiana, for instance, we get this imagined dialogue:

So, she went back on home, and when she entered, the phone was ringing. And he said, "Leave your apartment immediately and call me back." And she said, "What are you talking about?" "Who is this?" And he said, "This is Dr. So-and-so, the veterinarian." He said, "Get out of that apartment. Go to another telephone. Go to a neighbor or friend or something like that." She said, "You must be out of your mind!" So he said, "Alright, if you won't leave any other way," he said, "would you like to know what was choking that dog? Two black fingers!"

And she panicked, and she dropped the phone, and ran over to a neighbor and called him back, and said, "Alright, I'm over at the neighbors. Did you say two black fingers?"

"Yes," he said. "Call the cops." So she called the cops.

The mention of black fingers in the story, with the subsequent discovery of a black intruder hiding in the house, injects a negative racial stereotype into most oral versions of "The Choking Doberman" that is seldom mentioned in published accounts. Providing a striking example of how such themes enter urban legend tradition, a Salt Lake City man told "The Choking Doberman" to a woman in his bowling league, and she happened to be a University of Utah folklore student who then told the story to me. The intruder, her friend said, was black; he had read all about it in the March 1982 issue of *Shooting Times* magazine. "Fine," I said to her, "Can he show us the story in the magazine?" So he gave *her*— and she gave *me*—a photocopy of the page from *Shooting Times,* but it was *not* a black man mentioned there—no definite race was either specified or implied. The storyteller just understood the story that way, and his attitude was typical, for the "black fingers" (occasionally "Mexican fingers") motif has been a standard feature of the oral tradition of this urban legend since it surfaced in the United States.

Core elements of "The Choking Doberman" remain consistent in hundreds of versions I have gathered: the dog is choking, some fingers are extracted, and an injured intruder is found. The points of variation in the story are fairly predictable: the number of fingers, the breed of dog, the race and the hiding place of the intruder, and the exact words of the characters. But widespread folk dissemination of the tradition has introduced an occasional imaginative element into the tale. Sometimes, for example, the bitten burglar leaves the house, but he is caught when he goes to a hospital for treatment; in other versions the FBI is able to trace the escaped intruder by means of fingerprints taken from his severed fingers. (Both of these variations suggest trust in law enforcement officers to get their man.) Several graphically gory versions mention blood dripping from the wheezing watchdog's mouth, or blood seeping from the intruder's hiding place. One veterinarian treating the pet warns the dog's owner, in a curious bit of unnatural natural history, that once a guard dog has tasted blood it has to be killed, since it would forever lust after more and more blood.

I heard of one version of the story in which the dog's owner at first thought the Doberman was choking on a frozen hot dog, and with this in mind we might speculate whether a phallic symbol should be understood by the consistent reference to the intruder's fingers; after all, why didn't the dog go for the throat? And, if fingers could symbolize the penis, would their severence then imply a castration motif? Supporting such a possible reading—besides sexual interpretations of other urban legends (see "The Hook" in my first book)—are related stories to be discussed later in which various male intruders (or supposed intruders) come at their female victims through (symbolic?) windows or doorways with their fingers or hands sticking in at the terrified targets first. Often the intruder is found hiding in a bedroom or a closet therein, probably suggesting that his purpose was rape. Also encouraging a sexual meaning for the legend is this version I received from a reader who heard it in the Midwest:

A husband returned home from his bowling night and found the family's Doberman choking horribly in the bedroom while his wife was in hysterics. Reassuring her, he got down on the floor to see what he could do for the dog, but noticed a trickle of blood running from under the bed. Peering under it, he discovered a half-naked man holding a handkerchief over his badly bleeding hand. His wife tearfully confessed that she and the man had been having an affair. She had always locked the bedroom door to keep Rover out, but this time she had forgotten, and the dog had entered. Apparently he had mistaken their affection for an attack upon the woman, and had sought to defend her by taking a rather sizable chunk out of his hand.

Considering this sexy version of "The Choking Doberman," we should ponder why with the phallic reality in range this dog went so directly for the mere symbol. Maybe it was an English major at obedience school.

While published versions of "The Choking Doberman" have consistently suppressed the racial and the possible sexual overtones of the legend, with but one exception known to me they have at least clearly stated that the story is untrue—calling it rumor, legend, myth, and the like. The only unqualified firsthand report of "The Choking Doberman" I have found was published in the 10 November 1981 issue of the scandal tabloid *Globe,* printed there as the day's twenty-five-dollar prize "Liveliest Letter":

My Neighbor's Dog Fingered Intruder

When my neighbor's only son went into the service, he gave her a sleek black dog called Tiger to keep her company.

One day, she was working on her old treadle sewing machine when she heard strange sounds coming from Tiger. It was as if he was gagging on something.

She quickly bundled him off to the vet, only a short distance away. After a brief check, the vet told my neighbor

MY NEIGHBOR'S DOG FINGERED INTRUDER

WHEN my neighbor's only son went into the service, he gave her a sleek black dog called Tiger to keep her company.

One day, she was working on her old treadle sewing machine when she heard strange sounds coming from Tiger. It was as if he was gagging on something.

She quickly bundled him off to the vet, only a short distance away. After a brief check, the vet told my neighbor to go back home. He wanted to keep Tiger there for a few more tests and would call her later.

The moment she arrived home, the phone rang. It was the vet.

"Get out of the house," he yelled excitedly. "Come back here."

My neighbor was completely mystified, yet she complied with the unusual, but urgent demand.

Back at the vet's, she was told Tiger was fine, but, added the vet: "He had two human fingers lodged in his mouth.

"I've already called the police."

When the police later checked the house, they found a man in a severe state of shock, cowering in the closet. He had two fingers missing. Apparently, he had broken in through a back window.

Tiger had really proved himself worthy of his name.
— *Gayla Crabtree,*
Lansing, Michigan.

to go back home. He wanted to keep Tiger there for a few more tests and would call her later.

The moment she arrived home, the phone rang. It was the vet.

"Get out of the house," he yelled excitedly. "Come back here."

My neighbor was completely mystified, yet she complied with the unusual, but urgent demand.

Back at the vet's, she was told Tiger was fine, but, added the vet, "He had two human fingers lodged in his mouth.

"I've already called the police."

When the police later checked the house, they found a man in a severe state of shock, cowering in the closet. He had two fingers missing. Apparently, he had broken in through a back window.

Tiger had really proved himself worthy of his name.

—Gayla Crabtree
Lansing, Michigan

Now we have a dog with a name, plus the charming detail of "her old treadle sewing machine," and—best of all—the signed testimony of the neighbor of the victim. Our suspicions arise, however, not only from the doubtful nature of much of the "news" in publications like *Globe,* but also from the fact that a man providing the female victim with her guard dog is not an uncommon motif in the larger tradition, and it preserves the familiar cultural stereotype of protective male/helpless female that is also projected in other American folklore.

Sometimes, for instance, a father gives his daughter the dog for protection when she goes off to college in another city alone. Or a divorcée may acquire the dog, following her lawyer's advice, shortly after she has shed her husband and is living alone again. And in one version the choking dog is discovered by a female dog-sitter who is watching over a boyfriend's Doberman while he is out of town. But these similarities to oral tradition aside, can we give any credence at all to the Gayla Crabtree/Lansing, Michigan/*Globe*/happened-to-my-neighbor version?

Conveniently, a Michigan journalist did the research on this story that a folklorist might have done. Dan Poorman, a reporter for the *Lansing State Journal,* spotted the letter in *Globe* and went in search of Gayla Crabtree and her neighbor. He quickly learned that there was no one by that name in Lansing who knew anything about the incident and no police or veterinarian reports on the case, and that rumors of such an occurrence had been floating around southern Michigan for some time. Poorman also extracted from the *Globe* offices in New York City the comment, "It's easy to make up a story." After some more digging, Poorman located a Lansing woman who, using the pen name Gayla Crabtree, had sent *Globe* a story she had heard in a beauty parlor, retold as her neighbor's actual experience. So much for our first-person report.

But the important question to students of folk legends is not "Are they true?" but "Why are they told?" And what do they mean? The consistent themes in variants of "The Choking Doberman" point clearly to fearful current concerns about threats of burglary and violent crimes, especially as these take place in private homes and are directed against women by men. The woman living alone is perceived, according to the legend, as a likely victim for the male intruder. As I have already suggested, this may be understood as an intended sexual assault.

The principal shock in the conclusion of the story—as in several other urban legends—comes from the fact that the intruder is discovered to be hiding right on the premises, and that he was there all the time. Inclusion of a veterinarian and of the police in the legend provides supposed validation, as does reference to friends, relatives, or neighbors who allegedly know the facts behind the case. Specific details—such as the number of fingers, the breed of dog, the dog's name, the hiding place, and so forth—all contribute to the plausibility of the story, which is, after all, no more unreasonable than many news items one reads or hears nowadays. The negative racial reference in oral versions of the story simply reflects the racism in our society in general, as it is also echoed in many versions of "The Killer in the Backseat" legend, in which the driver of the pursuing car is said to be a black man.

What about the dog in the story? Bruno Bettleheim's suggestion in *The Uses of Enchantment* (1976) that ferocious dogs in fairy tales "symbolize the violent, aggressive and destructive drives in man" might be applied to "The Choking Doberman," perhaps, only in the sense that the dog as the man's alter ego vigorously protects the woman. But let us consider further the Doberman pinscher in particular in these current stories. Dobermans (or is it Dobermen?) are traditionally used as guard dogs, sometimes trained as attack dogs, and always look rather lean, hungry, and active. The Doberman's very demeanor, then, suggests something sinister, and if it isn't specifically a Doberman in the story, it's always some large and threatening-looking dog.

Not surprisingly, the Doberman pinscher has an image problem as well as a similar role in other folk stories. Recently (28 December 1982) Ann Landers published a poignant and revealing letter that began:

> I am a Doberman pinscher, 8 months old. My master says I am the most gentle, friendly dog he has ever had.
> Now for my problem: Everywhere we go, I hear people say, "That Doberman is friendly now, but wait three or four years. He will go berserk and rip your son's arm off." They say my brain is too big for my skull and that is why I will become vicious one day.

This dog seems to have heard the legend that describes a young couple with a pet Doberman and a new baby; one day when they have been out briefly, leaving the dog to guard the child, they return to find that the dog in a fit of misdirected sibling rivalry has leapt into the crib (or overturned it) and killed the baby (or chewed off its legs or arms). In another legend, told to me over the telephone from Regina, Saskatchewan, a man has accidentally cut off a finger while working in his home shop; he is rushed to the hospital, where an attendant says that a surgeon might be able to reattach the finger if it is brought in right away. The man's wife hurries home, but she arrives just a moment too late: their Doberman has chewed the severed finger to bits. Or how about the Doberman left in a parked car with the window slightly open for air while the driver stops briefly to shop? Returning to the car, this dog owner, according to the story, finds a finger lying on the seat nearest the open window, while the dog is moving about in the car in an agitated manner. One recent offensive riddle-joke in oral tradition makes a racial/dog connection that is also relevant to our story: "What's brown and black and looks good on a nigger?" Answer: "A Doberman."

But our quest for the history and meaning of "The Choking Doberman" does not end on this sour note. This is only the beginning, since it turns out that several other legends—some new, some old—include many of these same themes. First there is the recent apocryphal one about the ladies on the elevator in New York—or did you *believe* that one when you heard it?

"The Elevator Incident"

This new American urban legend that has been going around simultaneously with "The Choking Doberman" for the past few years also deals with frightened, isolated, white women, a supposedly threatening black man, and a dog. The strong emphasis on such themes probably shows how scared people really are, though in this story the fright is shown to be a foolish overreaction, and the black man is both genial and generous.

The story's variations and rapid spread can easily be traced through press reports and writers' accounts of where they picked it up. Let's begin with a column by Jack Jones of the Rochester, N.Y., *Democrat and Chronicle* (5 January 1982):

> . . . three unidentified Rochester women . . . recently visited New York [City].
>
> The women were on an elevator. A black man got on the elevator with a dog.
>
> The elevator door closed.
>
> "Sit!" the man commanded.
>
> The three women sat.
>
> The man apologized and explained to the women that he was talking to his dog.
>
> The women then nervously said that they were new to New York, and asked the nice man if he knew of a good restaurant.

The women went to the restaurant recommended by the man. They had a good meal, and called for their check. The waiter explained that the check had been paid by Reggie Jackson—the man they had met on the elevator.

Journalist Jones of Rochester managed to get ball player Jackson, formerly of New York—now California—on the telephone. And Jackson, after delivering himself of "a depressing sound—a cross between a groan and a laugh," flatly denied the report, saying, "I've heard the story a thousand times. . . . I would never own a dog in New York. It would be cruel to have a dog in New York. Whatever you've been told isn't true."

Two days later, Bob Minzesheimer, another *Democrat and Chronicle* staff writer, revealed under the headline "Reggie's 'story' still going strong" that columnist Frank Weikel of the *Cincinnati Enquirer* had beaten the Rochester paper to the nonstory by one day; Weikel's "metro today" column for 4 January 1982 had credited "The Elevator Incident" to "a businessman who says it was a friend of a relative." Weikel added, "The guy's been an impeccable source." Well, nobody's perfect.

On 29 January "The Editorial Notebook" column of the *New York Times* discussed the Reggie Jackson anecdote. "It's this season's quintessential New York story," writer Robert Curvin declared, "though . . . it may be next season's quintessential Los Angeles story." In the *Times* version the women were four doctors' wives from York, Pennsylvania, the black man with the Doberman rode *down* on their hotel elevator with them, and he paid for their breakfast rather than dinner. Curvin also referred to "a Bob Newhart story" (presumably a TV skit) in which a black man had a white dog, and his command to it was "Sit, Whitey!"

Another enterprising reporter, Leigh Montville of *The Boston Globe,* researched the same story; the column containing his results, headlined "The cold facts of a winter tale," ran on 11

February 1982, along with a photograph of Reggie Jackson in civilian clothes more or less fitting the description given by storytellers of "a giant bearded black man, wearing a cowboy hat and jeans." This time the three elderly white ladies were staying in "an exclusive Park Avenue apartment" owned by the son of one of them; he warned them, "Never resist a mugger . . . do whatever he wants. It's better than dying."

In the conclusion of the *Boston Globe* story, Reggie Jackson sent champagne to their table and smiled at them from where he was dining across the room in "a fashionable hotel restaurant." Judging from Leigh Montville's summary of his sources for the story, mothers may be a major influence in spreading the legend. (Is this a mother lode of urban folklore?) The summing up:

> My mother has told me this story.
> "It's true," she said. "I know a woman who knows a woman who was on the elevator."
> . . . I heard two passengers on a plane to Baltimore tell the story to each other. One guy said it was his mother from Peabody who was involved, swore it was true. The other guy said *his* mother in Atlanta had told him the same story. She said her best friend was on the elevator.
> . . . A sportswriter from Philadelphia told me the story. He said a woman in his office had told him the story. She said it was *her* mother who was on the elevator.

Montville's and others' mothers notwithstanding, Reggie Jackson's agent, Matt Merola ("in charge of confirming and denying these Reggie rumors"), told the *Boston Globe* sports writer over the telephone, "I tell everyone it's true. It's a nice story, a good story, if you want it to be true, it's true. Whatever way you heard it, that's the way it happened." Then he admitted, "I've had maybe 50 calls on this thing. It's been going on for six months now. . . . No, it's not true. . . . The part about his looks—he goes around town wearing jeans and a cowboy hat all the time—might fit, but the rest doesn't."

So the details of the legend don't fit Reggie Jackson, and the impeccable sources closest to the baseball superstar—plus the star himself—deny the story as it was told by the impeccable sources known to journalists. Did the story, then, die out? Of course not; instead it grew and spread. Why? Because, as Reggie's agent himself said, "It's a nice story."

Mike Harden of the *Columbus* [Ohio] *Citizen-Journal* fell for the story, and published it in his "One for the Road" column of 13 February 1982. Local variation: the dog is a *small* one, and the ladies hadn't noticed it; but again, Reggie sent them champagne. Two weeks later Harden confessed in another column that he had published it as a secondhand story, one "which thrived on the Columbus cocktail circuit the way mesquite thrives in cow flop." On 12 June Nora McCabe of the Toronto *Globe and Mail* wrote about the "Three little old ladies from Hamilton [who] decided to ignore all the horror stories they'd heard about New York City"; would you believe who they met on an elevator there? Jackson himself, in Toronto with the California Angels, told reporter McCabe, "It's completely erroneous. I've heard it a thousand times—two dogs, two people, whatever. . . . It started about 2 1/2 years ago but I dunno how."

Meanwhile, back in Ohio, Steve Love of the *Akron Beacon Journal* had heard a new version: Three couples from Canton, Ohio staying in a Manhattan hotel that had a rooftop restaurant, boarded the elevator to go up for dinner, and they met boxer Larry Holmes and his huge dog in the same elevator. That's scary except that reporter Love both knew the Reggie Jackson version already (happened in Las Vegas) and also recalled the old Bob Newhart skit. (See "Last laugh belonged to fearful," 14 July 1982). Wilt Chamberlain, "Magic" Johnson, O. J. Simpson, and "Mean" Joe Greene have also been mentioned in versions of "The Elevator Incident," though Reggie Jackson still leads the league in comical elevator episodes. Besides this variation in personal names, another typical folkloristic development for the story is that sometimes there are *three* warnings to the women about dangers they face in the big city: from the travel agent, an airline stewardess, and a taxi driver.

My favorite journalistic report of "The Elevator Incident" appeared on 25 February 1982 in a twittery gossip column published in the *Detroit Free Press* called "Darling." It starts like this:

> Darling can't get over the story of four Cottage Hospital Pink Ladies who wanted to go to a convention in New York. Their husbands agreed only if the little women promised not to visit Times Square or any other nasty areas.
>
> The first evening, as they were boarding the hotel elevator, a large hand reached in and held the door open. Then the rest of a large, muscular man, accompanied by a big dog, got on the elevator . . .

But, of course, that nice Reggie Jackson paid the dinner tab, and the Detroit columnist promised, "The next time Darling hears someone say sit, she'll be much more obliging." But really, Darling, he meant the dog!

Two weeks later (18 March 1982) "Darling" was somewhat chagrined, and she knew she had been had; as the headline stated it, things stood like this, "Score: Reggie 1, Darling 0":

> *C'est dommage*—blame it on Darling's cabin fever—but *deux faux pas* appeared here recently. There was that item about the four timid ladies who sat, when Reggie Jackson commanded his dog to sit in a New York elevator. . . . It seems the tale has appeared in newspapers across the country, the result of unverified phoned-in tips. Darling has friends, however, who *swear* they have friends who know those ladies. . . .

Marty Kohn, the *Free Press* writer who sent me these two columns, added his own variation; he had heard that it was "these three bubbies [old Jewish women] who decided to go to New York from Toronto." Kohn added that he also remembered the related skit from the old Bob Newhart series and thought it might have been soul singer Isaac Hayes who had appeared in it as a guest star.

The possible specific religious affiliation of the hapless ladies in the lift is an interesting motif, since "The Elevator Incident" also acquired a strong Mennonite (occasionally Amish) tradition in the Midwest, in Pennsylvania, and in Canada. Folklorist Ervin Beck of Goshen College, Indiana, called my attention to this development, passing on a story concerning three Mennonite women from eastern Pennsylvania who spent a weekend in Manhattan. They were riding an express elevator to the upper-floor restaurant in their hotel when "Just before the elevator door closed, they saw a pair of hands grab the doors and open them again. There stood a big, black man —and his equally big dog." Summary: "Sit!" sat, then saved by the superstar. This was a pretty conventional version, except that one of the ladies was positively identified by name as the wife of a Mennonite pastor in the Bronx and the mother of one of Beck's own students at Goshen College. The trouble with such details, of course, is that they only make it easier for a folklorist to disprove the tale. The student's mother denied everything.

Closer to home, Professor Beck found the elevator story attached to Esther Diener, wife of an Ohio Mennonite pastor and herself proprietor of Das Essen Haus restaurant of Pettisville, Ohio. Mrs. Diener became so well known as an alleged participant in the Reggie escapade that she put on a two-day "Reggie Jackson Hog Roast" in her restaurant to capitalize on her fame. The big event was held on 28 and 29 July 1982. Mrs. Diener, who actually denies the elevator story, called Reggie Jackson's agent for permission to stage the event, and she told Ervin Beck that he gave it grudgingly—"just this once"—and he also told her that the elevator story was true. I figure she must have got Matt Merola on the phone (see *Boston Globe*, above). The centerpiece of the Essen Haus celebration was a big cake with Reggie Jackson pictured on it giving his dog the command "Sit!" via a cartoon balloon. It's too bad, I think, that Reggie wasn't there to eat his own word.

Meanwhile, in Canada, the nationally distributed *Mennonite Reporter* of Waterloo, Ontario, passed on in its 26 July issue the familiar story of three Mennonite women from Lancaster, Pennsylvania, visiting New York. Recognizing a fishy tale when they heard one, the editors invited readers to submit other versions. This drew a letter printed in the 23 August issue from a Scottdale, Pennsylvania, reader. The way he understood it was that early baseball hero Jackie Robinson had been the one who scared the three women, but later the reader had heard other versions and had begun to detect a folk legend tradition in the making. Jackie Robinson is a nice touch, though; the name has just the right possibilities for confusion with the mainstream Jackson tradition, and the reference falsely pushes the date of the tale back several decades. Eventually (20 September 1982, to be exact), the *Mennonite Reporter* got onto my *Vanishing Hitchhiker* and ran a squib relating the Reggie tale to other urban legends.

But where was Brunvand and his book when he was needed at home? Unfortunately, in the summer of 1982, I was off on vacation during the exact week when both hometown newspapers in Salt Lake City picked up "The Elevator Incident." First, columnist Maxine Martz of the *Deseret News,* on 27 July, wrote (probably tongue in cheek) about "three prominent Salt Lake doctors, accompanied by their wives, [who] went to Philadelphia for a convention." The ladies continued on to New York, staying overnight at the Waldorf-Astoria, where nice-guy Reggie Jackson joined them, as usual, on an elevator, leading his Doberman pinscher that was "snarling and tugging at its leash." Well, wouldn't *you* sit down when the big man commanded "Sit!" and wouldn't you be relieved the next morning to find the bill paid and a nice note of apology from the baseball star? "The storyteller," Ms. Martz wrote, "a friend of a friend of a friend of one of the doctors, insists the women have the note." How I would love to see it, but I don't suppose Maxine Martz even bothered to ask.

Just around the corner in the editorial offices of Salt Lake City's morning newspaper, sports editor John Mooney of the *Salt Lake Tribune* (who evidently doesn't read the *Deseret News*) gave us the Reggie Jackson legend, complete with a smiling mug shot of our hero, on 29 July. "To get back to the good aspects of sports," wrote Mooney, "I'm happy to reprint this little story from the Camarillo (California) newspaper." The ladies were from Colorado Springs; the man was huge, bearded, and black; the dog was "equally huge and mean-looking," and Mooney was so edified by the story as to comment: "Now doesn't that make you feel better this morning, realizing that most of the athletes are really decent folks underneath all the bickering and scandals?"

Herb Caen of the *San Francisco Chronicle,* an old hand with urban legends and not likely to be fooled by a new one, gave "The Elevator Incident" a nice wrap-up in his column of 6 August 1982:

> The story arrives in the mail about once a week, always from a person who heard it secondhand. Or it happened to "my cousin," or an aunt. It is the kind of story told above the clatter of dice in bars, or around luncheon tables. Columnists all over the country have printed it as gospel. It must be a good story, because it has been making the rounds for a year now, and seems to be gathering momentum.

Caen concluded, after telling the standard version, "Even Reggie can't figure out how this fable got started, but since he comes out the hero, who cares."

It's not crucial, I'll admit, to know exactly where or how the story of the Reggie caper originated, but I surely would like to gain at least a little insight into the matter. The Bob Newhart references are especially intriguing, since they raise the question whether a TV sitcom might have given rise to an urban legend, or conversely, whether one of Newhart's writers might have based a script on a story he had heard. All Bob Newhart himself can recall about the show is that "When the large black man told the dog to 'Sit, Whitey!' it was one of the largest laughs we ever got."* But I have been unable to trace the episode further, though every now and then I hear from a friend of a friend of someone who has just see it on rerun.

As recently as the summer of 1983 "The Elevator Incident" continued to appear in newspapers. On 7 July, for instance, the *Augusta* [Georgia] *Herald* front-page columnist John L. Barnes included it in his popular feature "Our Town"; with perhaps a hint of the Bob Newhart version, the black passenger in this one says to his dog, "Sit, Lady!" Then on 18 August the *Los Angeles Times* columnist Jack Smith wrote up the first of three installments about his "discovery" of the legend. In his original version, told by an acquaintance of Smith's from Huntington Beach, California, concerning a friend of a friend from Lincoln, Nebraska, Reggie Jackson has two Doberman pinschers and leaves the familiar "You made my day" note. In Smith's second reference to the story one week later (25 August) he reports six letters from readers giving different "true" versions of the story, and he also quotes a telephone conversation with an alleged firsthand source of the story. (It was, she told Smith, the Bonaventure Hotel in Los Angeles, but she was not sure who the black man in the elevator was, and there was no later payment of a bill or a note.) Finally, in his 1 September 1983 column, Smith was able to report two earlier printed versions of the story plus this similar yarn from Britain told three years previously:

In Parliament, the equivalent of our Speaker of the House is called the Keeper of the Woolsack; at the time of the story this gentleman was Sir Quentin Hogg, Lord Hailsham. Parliament has just adjourned, and his lordship, resplendent in the gold and scarlet robes of his office, topped by a ceremonial wig, emerges from the great hall into the

---

*Letter from Bob Newhart dated 23 March 1983.

corridor on the way to his chambers. The corridor is crowded with an American tour group, beyond which Lord Hailsham sees an old friend, the Hon. Neil Matten, MP, with whom he would like a word.

"Neil!" his lordship shouts. "Neil!"

"There followed an embarrassed silence . . . as all the tourists obediently fell to their knees."

Wherever and whenever the story sprang up, there does seem to have been a much nastier prototype of "The Elevator Incident" circulating in the Midwest some twenty years before the story was sanitized and attached to Reggie Jackson. This legend, much more graphic and sexually explicit than the current version, was collected by folklorist Xenia Cord of Indiana University at Kokomo; she heard it in Cleveland, Ohio, in the early 1960's:

A woman went shopping in downtown Cleveland, properly attired in dress, hat, and gloves. Although she was somewhat hesitant to go alone into the downtown area, because the black population had become more obvious and more aggressive of late, she felt that her proper attire would somehow armor her against insult. Arriving downtown, she went to the May Company, an aging but still elegant department store. She entered the ornate self-service elevator. Just as the doors began to shut, two large black men got on. Instead of facing the front of the car, they faced her and approached, forcing her to move to the back corner of the car. Slowly and deliberately they both unzipped their pants, and urinated all over her!

If we seem in tracing "The Elevator Incident" to have moved far away from "The Choking Doberman," bear in mind that both legends draw their effects from racial stereotypes, fear of crime, and people's efforts to thwart or mollify a potential assailant. To state the similarities more directly, both legends are specifically about white women frightened by black men who they think might want to rob or even rape them. In either plot, the woman may be the wife or the mother of a husband or a son who offers helpful advice or even practical aid toward the woman's defense. (In a way, the elevator story is a bit more like "The Killer in the Backseat" legend than "The Choking Doberman," in that the black man who frightens the woman or women is really a gallant benefactor in the end.)

Besides the general symbolic and psychological affinity of "The Elevator Incident" with "The Choking Doberman," both legends situate the woman or women in a restricted space where escape may be difficult (a hallway or elevator), both may include the son's help or warning, and both may involve a dog. In *some* of the elevator stories (as in *all* of the choking-dog stories) special emphasis is put on the fingers of the black male character in the story. While it is true that simply grabbing the closing elevator door is a natural way to stop it for entry, it seems odd that exactly this tiny detail is preserved in several tellings.

As interesting as these two recent legends are, however, with their similar emphasis on analogous themes and details, neither one can clearly be said to be the original of the other. They seem to be coexisting independent oral-narrative traditions that deal with related material, but there must be some other ancestors for them both. This brings us, now, to Wagger's little tale.

The "Wagger" Story

For clearer historical ancestors of "The Choking Doberman," and some that tie its themes to those in "The Elevator Incident," we must look further back in time to folk stories collected before these "new" legends were told. One such story from at least the early 1960s is the following, sent to me by folk-narrative specialist Ernest Baughman of the University of New Mexico. This legend has several features reminiscent of "The Choking Doberman," yet it also seems to represent a definite link to older folk traditions. And in a couple of details it is even a bit like "The Elevator Incident" as well.

This "Wagger" story was collected by a student of Baughman's in 1964 in Albuquerque; the teller was a housewife, sixty-two years old, who had heard it as a child in West Virginia:

> An old lady who had lots of money had a son who lived with her. The son had a dog he called "Wagger." There were reports of a robber around the neighborhood. The son was going out one night and he told his mother to keep Wagger in the house and if anyone bothered around, all she would have to do would be to say, "Take him, Wagger," and he would get the intruder.
>
> After the son had been gone a while, the mother noticed that the dog was uneasy. He prowled around the room, growling, listening, the hair rising on his back. Then the mother heard the sound of someone raising the window stealthily. She saw black fingers reaching in to pull the fellow up and through the window. As he leaped into the room, the mother, terrified, remembered what her son had said to do. "Take him, Wagger! she screamed.
>
> Wagger leaped up, grabbed the fellow by the throat, and dragged him down to the floor. It seemed to the mother that the robber was saying, "Wagger, Wagger," but ever more faintly as the dog kept on choking the life out of him. After the fellow lay there lifeless, the woman gathered courage to examine him closely. She found that it was not really a black man but a man blacked up, and finally that it was her own son who had come to rob her.

There are obvious similarities to "The Choking Doberman" in Wagger's tale: the woman, a mother it happens, is home alone with a dog to protect her, and specifically it is the son's dog; the would-be robber appears to be a black man, and his fingers in particular are singled out for mention. (The fingers come into view first, just as those of the man on the elevator sometimes do.) The choking motif is reversed here, with dog choking man rather than man's fingers choking dog. The ending of the "Wagger" story is a bit peculiar, but my feeling is that the storyteller may have forgotten to explain, or failed to understand, that the son was in reality testing Wagger's guarding abilities by coming home incognito. His choice of a blackface disguise clearly draws from a negative racial stereotype, and it heightens suspense as the story is told.

It may be significant that the dog's name—Wagger—is rather close to the only other named dog in this whole series of stories—Tiger—the old lady's dog (a dog also given to her by her son) in the Lansing, Michigan, *Globe* version. (On the other hand, the name "Rover" is fairly close to these names too!) In both stories, the woman is alone at home with her son's dog when it becomes excited, and in neither of these stories is the dog specifically said to be a Doberman pinscher; that detail may be a later refinement in the plot. As we shall see, the woman alone at home threatened by an intruder and without a dog is another, even earlier, form of the story.

While the "Wagger" story and the "Tiger" story were told some eighteen years apart, there is no reason why they could not be instances of the same older folk subtype of a tale being retained by different narrators. Baughman has another story in his unpublished collection that seems to represent an even earlier version of the plot without a dog in it. It was collected in New Mexico in 1959 from a woman who remembered hearing it in Texas in 1920. Here a man and his partner have a great deal of money (implied to be ill-gotten) that one man keeps in his house. One night he leaves his wife home alone, saying that she should guard the money. She kindheartedly allows a tramp to spend the night sleeping on the porch, and during the night, hearing someone trying to enter, she shoots the intruder with a gun that the tramp has with him: "The lady took the gun and shot the man who was coming into the house. After shooting him, she discovered that it was her husband dressed in old clothes with blackened face and hands. The man had wanted all of the money for himself and had thought that this would be the best way to get it."

Going further back in time, to yet another layer in this odd history of a legend, we come to the similar story of Prince Llewellyn of Wales and his faithful dog, Gellert.

"Llewellyn and Gellert"

There is a much older legendary dog named "Gellert" (another two-syllable dog's name with an "-er" in the second syllable) that ties into our modern legends. The famous Welsh story about Prince Llewellyn and his dog is summarized in *The Motif-Index of Folk-Literature* (1955–58)* under the number B331.2. as follows: "Dog has saved child from serpent. Father sees bloody mouth, thinks the dog has eaten the child, and kills the dog." Many older tales and legends, especially those from Europe, are classified, summarized, and cross-referenced in this manner in the *Motif-Index,* giving the folklorist a convenient tool to trace and compare variants.

More often in the British tradition of "B331.2." it is a wolf rather than a serpent that the prince's huge hunting hound has killed. Here is the scene from a Welsh version of the legend, dated 1800, when the prince comes home, where he had left his dog guarding the infant, as given by Joseph Jacobs in his book *Celtic Fairy Tales* (1892): ". . . when the hound came near him, the Prince was startled to see that his lips and fangs were

---

*Motifs, in folklorists' jargon, are traditional narrative units—such as characters, objects, or actions—that serve as the building blocks of folk stories. The *Motif-Index* compiled by folklorist Stith Thompson is the standard classification and bibliographic guide for older traditional motifs, but new ones (like a maniac with a hook in place of a hand) are frequently introduced into modern folklore. See the Bibliography for the full reference to Thompson's important work.

dripping with blood. Llewellyn started back and the grey-hound crouched down at his feet as if surprised or afraid at the way his master greeted him."

In the conclusion of the Welsh story, as the quoted motif summary revealed, rather than being comforted in its distress and rushed to the vet like the modern suffering pet, poor Gellert is slain by the prince, who afterwards finds the cradle overturned, his baby alive, and a great wolf that had been killed in a fight with Gellert.

That version from 1800, however, is the first one to locate the scene of the story and even the grave of the dog at the village near Mount Snowdon in Wales, which is still called Beddgelert ("Grave of Gellert"); you can go there today, hear the story, and be shown the grave, all allegedly dating to the tragic event of centuries ago. The basis of the legend is not native to Wales, and the story is probably much older than even the Middle Ages. Or, as Sir George Webbe Dasent, a nineteenth-century translator of Norwegian fairy tales, put it, "Let [not] any pious Welshman be shocked if we venture to assert that Gellert, that famous hound upon whose last rest-ing-place the traveller comes as he passes down the lovely vale of Gwynant, is a mythical dog, and never snuffed the fresh breeze in the forest of Snowdon, nor saved his master's child from ravening wolf."

Two other English folklorists of the same period, Sabine Baring-Gould (in *Curious Myths of the Middle Ages,* 1866) and William A. Clouston (in *Popular Tales and Fictions,* 1887) traced the ancestors of the Welsh story back through many other helpful-animal legends in Ireland and England, on the Conti-nent, and thence to fables of the Middle East and the ancient Orient. They showed that although the Llewellyn and Gellert story had been popularized for a century or more as part of the ancient lore of Wales, it was not known there at all before about the sixteenth century, and it was obviously imported from abroad, then simply attached (around 1800) to a popular hero of the thirteenth century and to a particular place. The international variants of the story involved various animals and many different kinds of rescues that were similarly misunderstood; that is, the faithful guarding animal in the fable always lost its life at the hands of a rash master. Clouston also explained the name "Gellert" as an alteration of "Killhart" (meaning "Deerslayer"), a traditional hunting dog's name.

But my concern here is not with the wider range of other older helpful animal stories, but rather with the possible New World offshoots of the English or Celtic version of the story about the misunderstood dog.

Here Professor Ernest Baughman is helpful again. His monumental reference work *A Type- and Motif-Index of the Folktales of England and North America* (1966) documents the presence of thousands of story types and motifs in published English and Anglo-American sources.* But Baughman lists only one version of Llewellyn and Gellert outside of Great Britain, a somewhat puzzling one related by the popular author Rex Beach as "The Trapper and His Dog" in the July 1942 issue of *Reader's Digest.* Beach introduced his version of the story with this useful information: "For years animal lovers have repeated this story of the North Woods, and although some of them declare that they had read it, nobody seems to remember who wrote it or where it was published."

In Beach's version the hero is a young trapper named Peter Dobley. Peter lives alone except for his huge, part-wolf sled dog, Prince. Then Peter marries, but his wife dies soon after giving birth to a son, and the dog must be left behind guarding the baby while his master is out trapping. One day, caught in a blizzard, Peter Dobley is hours late returning home. Approaching his cabin, he sees the door standing half-open, and he rushes inside:

---

*In this instance Baughman uses only the motif number, although the Aarne-Thompson Index assigns tale type number 178 to "The Faithful Animal Rashly Killed" and Type 178A specifically to "Llewellyn and his Dog."

The baby's crib was empty. The blankets were red with blood and there were great smears on the floor. As the father stood rooted in horror, Prince crept from under the bed; his muzzle, too, was red and the fur of his neck was matted. He did not look at the man or try to approach him, but lay there, head down, silent, eyes averted.

In a flash Peter understood. Once wolf, always wolf! ... With a cry the man raised his axe and struck with all his strength, burying it in the dog's massive head.

Following this thoughtless act, Peter steps further inside the cabin, sees the baby, safe under the bed, and a dead timber wolf with a piece of Prince's bloody fur clenched in its teeth.

Although the conclusion of this story is different, the opening scene in both the Welsh and the North American versions —with the suffering pet, the helpless victim home alone, and the injured intruder lying, so far undiscovered, in the house— is very close to "The Choking Doberman." Even the idea of a guard dog's instinctive lust for blood is found in versions of our new legend, as is the description of blood clinging to the dog's mouth. And the specific recent Doberman legend about the dog attacking the new baby in its crib must certainly be a direct descendant, reduced in length, of the Gellert story, possibly via the trapper story (or something like it) as Rex Beach related it from "the North Woods."

But, still, there are no fingers here. Where are the fingers?

"The Severed Fingers"

If we turn to the severed-finger theme that is so characteristic of "The Choking Doberman," we open another line of inquiry. The English folklorist Stewart Sanderson summarized an English urban legend he called "The Severed Fingers" in his article "The Folklore of the Motor-Car" (*Folklore,* vol. 80, 1969). Sanderson reported six versions of this story that circulated in 1961 and 1962, paraphrasing them as follows:

A man is driving his rear-engined car home at night. While stationary at traffic-lights, he is attacked by a band of youths who try to overturn the car. He drives rapidly off. Next day he discovers four fingers which have been amputated by the fan in the air-cooling system. In some versions he hears that a youth has been given emergency treatment for a corresponding injury at the local Infirmary.

At least three other urban legends may be related to this one. The threat to a lone driver reminds us again of "The Killer in the Backseat," the hand-part pulled off by a moving car is reminiscent of "The Hook," and the youth's treatment at a hospital parallels the similar detail in some "Choking Doberman" variants.

Of course, we have "The Severed Fingers" legend in the United States as well. Usually it is said here to be a tough-looking hitchhiker who angrily swings a chain he is holding, striking it against the side of a man's car who refuses to stop for him. When the man arrives home, he finds a piece of the chain with one or two fingers stuck into it hanging from his car-door handle or caught on a piece of the chrome trim. Similar stories have been reported recently by folklorists in both Scandinavia and Germany, and the writer of a letter to the editor of *Folklore* (vol. 84, 1973) reported a chain version of the car-and-finger story told at a Christmas party in England in 1972.

There is more involved here, however, than just a recent legend about some young toughs pestering a solid-citizen driver and getting accidentally injured themselves in a rather grotesque way. Yes, it is plausible; and sure, they merely "got what they deserved." But isn't it also a little hard to believe that just such a sequence of events—so much like several other legends—really happened more than once on the highways of Europe and the United States? Again, there is an earlier prototype that shows us clearly how story lore repeats itself, which is, after all, much more likely than such bizarre history repeating itself.

Our parallel this time appears in a rare book titled *La Nou-*

velle Fabrique des Excellents Traits de Vérité, a French collection of ninety-nine tall tales probably first published in 1579, and attributed (pseudonymously) to "Phillippe d'Alcripe." Here is Philippe's tale number thirty-eight from Gerald Thomas's annotated translation of the Renaissance original:

About a Thief Who Had His Hand Cut Off

One day a man of the world, vigorous, alert, pleasing and as brave at least as Richard the Lion-Heart, was travelling along a narrow forest path when he saw a thief on the look-out, in among the trees, and he came out at him, putting his hand on the horse's bridle and saying: "Hold! Your money or your life!" The traveller, who was not easily frightened, immediately seizes his sword and gives him such a blow on the hand holding his horse that he cuts it clean off. Having done this, he spurs his horse and rides off so swiftly that he arrives home very soon after. His servant took his horse and led it to the stable; but when he came to unharness it, he noticed a hand hanging from the bridle, which gave him a nasty fright; surprised as he was, he dashed off into the house where, all a-tremble, he told him how he had found a severed hand still holding the horse's bridle. At first the master did not seem at all moved by his account, but after thinking about it for a while he recalled having hit out with his sword at a highwayman who had stopped his horse; whereupon he went to fetch the said hand, which he detached from the bridle with great difficulty and then nailed it on to his front door as a trophy.

I like the "new" in the book's title (translation: "The New Fabrication of Some Excellent Truths"); evidently, a good "new" story was as prized four hundred years ago as it is now. The "Truth" of the story is another matter, since the surrounding narratives in the book are mostly unabashed jokes and lies that were told strictly for entertainment. Yet, in the context of miscellaneous entertaining storytelling (like a contemporary coffee break), this old version of a new urban legend fits right in. Furthermore, the servant's horrified reaction to finding the hand is very much like how modern drivers are said to feel (in either "The Hook" or "The Severed Fingers") when they discover the accidental amputation. The nailing of the hand to the door may be compared to—not *Beowulf,* I believe—but rather to some other rural and urban legends about would-be robbers, intruders, and other assorted rascals who lose or injure a finger, fingers, or a whole hand while on the prowl for victims or loot. Robbers seem often to get hurt in their hands near doorways, it seems.

"The Robber Who Was Hurt"

Another English folklorist, Jacqueline Simpson, writing in a recent issue of *Folklore* (vol. 92, 1981) called attention to a neglected urban legend that she proposed to recognize with the title "The Robber Who Was Hurt." Already it sounds familiar!

Simpson's sample story, originally told to her in 1974, involved a woman living alone in "a good block of flats" in London. One day she happens to have a red-hot gas poker in her hand from igniting fuel on the grate when the doorbell rings. The text continues in typical breathless urban legend style: "Well, she opened the door, and there was a man with a stocking mask on his face! But when he saw the poker he must have thought it was a gun, because he grabbed hold of it, and of course he screamed and turned and ran away."

When the woman hurries to a downstairs flat to use the telephone in order to report the incident, the neighbor woman who answers the door cannot let her in because, as she explains, her husband has just come in with his hand terribly burnt.

While there is no dog and there are no severed fingers in this story, there *is* a woman living alone, a male intruder (in disguise), and a severe injury to the hand of said intruder, plus

a telephone to summon help, and a neighbor to run to. Simpson did not mention "The Choking Doberman," but she did call attention to Stewart Sanderson's "Severed Fingers" story, pointing out further that some traditional witches in older rural folklore were said to have had the power to immobilize carts, and that the countermeasure—cutting into the spokes of the cart's wheel—could inflict harm on the witches' fingers. In the witchcraft lore, then, it was a matter of what is called "sympathetic magic" (like affects like—cutting spokes magically injures fingers). In modern folklore this supernaturalism is rationalized as the act of aggression directed against a car that leads to the torn-off fingers of the aggressor.

To get further with an explanation of "The Robber Who Was Hurt" story, Simpson cited the interesting English legend titled "The Hand," as summarized from a 1914 source in Katharine Briggs's *Dictionary of British Folk-Tales* (1970):

> Small shop attached to house near great heath infested by robbers. . . . One of the robbers went down to rob the shop one winter evening.
>
> Younger girl heard the shop bell, went in, saw shop door on the chain, and a hand groping. Terrified, took the bread knife and cut off the hand.

The robbers lurking in the heath (a wasteland or wilderness area) call to mind the robber in the forest of the old French story, where also a hand is cut off during self-defense. (In the "Wagger" story too "there were reports of a robber around the neighborhood.") Since the intruder in the English legend returns later in the story wearing a false hand, and he again threatens the shop girl, and in the French tale a whole hand is caught on the bridle, we seem to have in both of these narratives some anticipation of the modern legend "The Hook." Even the minor detail of the door chain in the story may point ahead to the finger-severing chain caught on the car in some versions of the "Severed Fingers" legend as we now know it.

This English legend, "The Hand," and some other stories somewhat like it in which shop girls defend themselves against intruders, are, as Simpson points out, related to a traditional folktale that appears in our standard indexes of fairy tales ("The Clever Maid at Home Kills the Robbers," Type 956B). In all of these, "a solitary woman, usually a servant, realizes the presence of a disguised robber in the house and contrives to wound him, kill him or put him to flight." (For the published index of tale types, see Aarne and Thompson in the Bibliography.) But Jacqueline Simpson's major point about "Rationalized Motifs in Urban Legends" (her article's title) is that older stories about the witch who was hurt have probably been updated and turned into a new urban legend.

Her argument goes like this. In witchcraft lore a witch may be wounded while attacking someone with magic means (as in the disturbance of carts) or while in the form of an animal; the witch herself is recognized later by a similar wound to the corresponding part of her anatomy. If a magically stopped cart wheel was cut, as we have already seen, the witch may suffer cut fingers. If a paw is cut off a malevolent cat or dog, a hand may be missing later from the witch in the neighborhood. The burning wound given to a modern intruder (with a hot poker), and the recognition of the attacker as one's own neighbor (the man in the downstairs flat) both match specific details of older witch legends.

Simpson concludes, "For the modern town-dweller, especially women living alone, the burglar is a dreaded figure who may be lurking at any time and in any guise, just as the witch once was in rural communities." She asserts that "The Robber Who Was Hurt" is "a clever transformation of an old rural, supernatural, motif into modern, urban, rationalized form."*

Jacqueline Simpson's analysis is convincing, and (combined with the other legends discussed here) it allows us to regard "The Choking Doberman" as a new combination of recently popular American urban legend themes (suffering pet, in-

---

*An apparent American version of "The Robber Who Was Hurt" was reported as a true crime-victim narrative by folklorist Eleanor Wachs (see Bibliography) who collected it in Brooklyn, New York, in 1977. The storyteller in this instance was a young social worker who understood that this was "an incident which happened to one of her clients, an elderly [blind] woman who lived near the social services agency where [she] worked." The older woman's doorbell rang, and she opened it partly, without undoing the protective chain. The man who had rung grabbed her arm, pulled it through the opening, and began scratching it with sandpaper, threatening to injure her severely unless she unfastened the chain. But the woman summoned all her energy, grabbed hold of her assailant's fingers, and broke them—"all his fingers broke like spaghetti." The man ran away, and the woman called the police. Later the assailant was recognized when he went to a hospital emergency room for treatment of his five broken fingers. It is not clear in Wach's discussion whether her informant had in fact heard about the alleged incident directly from the participant or if this is another friend-of-a-friend situation. In any case, the structuring of the narrative as well as several of its details strongly suggest the direct influence of traditional versions of "The Robber Who Was Hurt."

truder hiding on the premises, telephone warning, etc.). These themes have in their background certain older stories well known in Europe about brave women at home alone attacked by a robber; and underlying these are even older supernatural accounts of magic-working or shape-shifting witches who are injured, sometimes while in animal form, in their fingers or hands. Related to these individual legends are others involving hands or fingers torn off would-be assailants, or guard dogs caught in distressing and misunderstood circumstances. Modern lore about the Doberman (though it may be another breed of dog), plus racial prejudice lore, and possibly phallic/castrative lost-finger lore of various kinds, also interacts, at least in the United States, with these baseline narrative traditions. So there is nothing new in all of this except the selection of particular details, the emphasis on certain themes, and the updating of the settings for the story.

Since "The Choking Doberman" surfaced first as a "new" legend in the United States, I was inclined to think of it as my research progressed as an American folk story, based on European prototypes, which might eventually work its way back to where all of its major elements seemed to have come from. The next thing I wanted to know, then, was whether "The Choking Doberman" legend as such had been collected in England.

"The Choking Doberman" in England

As soon as I recognized the significance of Jacqueline Simpson's contribution to understanding this legend cycle, I wrote to her asking whether she knew "The Choking Doberman." She replied in a letter dated 7 March 1982: "I was about to tell you that I knew no example of The Choking Doberman, when lo & behold! Yesterday I received a letter from a stranger (presumably, a reader of *Folklore* . . .) named Eric C. Binns, of

Watersfield, Pulborough, West Sussex. He is writing to tell me of a story which he suspects to be a legend, although his informant, the landlord of the 'Three Crowns' pub in Watersfield, told it to him as a true tale.''

Let us call this one the West Sussex version:

> An Alsatian dog was kept for protection against robbers. Late one night, a commotion was heard, and the inhabitants of the dwelling went down to investigate. Signs of a break-in were found, and the dog was seen to be distressed. The dog was violently sick, and it was assumed that the invaders had administered a drug to subdue the dog to aid their entry. Despite the lateness of the hour, the vet was summoned and, on opening up the throat of the dog, three severed fingers were found—three severed black fingers.

This sounds very much like an imported American story simply cast in language and given details to fit the English setting. The Alsatian breed of dog (a German shepherd, or police dog) also appears in some American texts, as does the incident happening downstairs while the couple sleep upstairs (although this is rather rare). The idea of the dog being drugged is unique, but sometimes a suspicion of food poisoning or of the dog choking on a bone or a piece of food is mentioned in the United States. The lack of conclusion to the story (that is, not actually finding any intruder hiding in the house) suggests that this version is an imperfect derivative of the American plot, while the mention of black fingers seems to indicate retention of a characteristic American detail.

The notion of a veterinarian (or any doctor, for that matter) making house calls is somewhat uncommon in recent American experience, although I do have a few versions in which a vet, very conveniently, lives just down the street from the suffering dog's owners. Occasionally in American versions the vet comes to the house along with the police.

In a similar vein, two English texts told in February and March of 1982 supplied to me from the University of Sheffield Folklore Archive are very typical in content and style: in one,

an Alsatian chokes on four fingers, and a robber with four
fingers bitten off is found hiding in the upstairs bathroom; in
the second, a couple's dog is found choking on two fingers,
and the intruder is found collapsed in the upstairs bedroom.
In both tellings collected from the Midlands the narrators
referred to anonymous oral or printed sources supposedly
verifying the truth of the story. All of this sounds very much
like the growth and development of "The Choking Doberman" in the United States the year earlier.

The same may be said of the version published in the London *Times* later in the spring ("The Times Diary," 27 May 1982):

> A Highgate colleague, who walks his mongrel in Park-
> land Walk, a former railway line become a meeting place for
> dog-owners and their mutts, encountered a couple who
> proudly told him about their doberman pincher [*sic*].
>
> Returning home one night they found a round hole in
> the kitchen window and the young dog writhing and chok-
> ing on the floor. They rushed to the vet who, to their sur-
> prise, extricated three human fingers from the doberman's
> throat.
>
> They telephoned all the hospitals to say that if anyone
> was missing three fingers they could be reclaimed from the
> vet, but no one reported his loss to the casualty depart-
> ments.

In common with so many American journalists before him,
"P.H.S.," the writer of "The Times Diary," had to withdraw
his belief in the story within the week. In the same column on
4 June 1982, we find this:

DOG'S BREAKFAST*

My horrifying tale of the doberman found choking on three
fingers bitten from a would-be-intruder's hand, will not
have been entirely new to all of you. There is a hitherto

*In English slang "dog's breakfast" means any kind of a muddle
or mess.

unreported crime wave of canine assault going on, and more mutilated burglars about than the police can hope to trace.

I have been inundated with reports of similar cases from various parts of Britain, and as far away as San Jose, California. In all instances, save one aberrant version which cited a Scottish terrier, the dog involved has been a doberman. In some the burglar has lost only two fingers. In one or two the detail has been added that the fingers were black, and an improved version has the burglar discovered, in a collapsed condition understandably, in the dog-owner's bedroom.

And so we are pretty much back where we began with "The Choking Doberman": a lively current oral tradition centers on a stock plot but incorporates varying details as it spreads rapidly from person to person and occasionally appears in the press.

England was buzzing with choking-dog stories when I was there in July 1982 attending the first international seminar "Perspectives on Contemporary Legend" at the University of Sheffield; participants at the seminar were interested to learn of the widespread circulation of virtually the same legend in the United States a full year earlier. I set my theory before them that certain British and Continental themes of much older folklore had recombined in the United States to form this "new" urban legend tradition.

But then a Scottish scholar called my attention to an article by Sandy Hobbs of the Department of Social Studies, Paisley College of Technology; the intriguing title of Hobbs's essay was "The Folk Tale as News." I eventually dug out a copy of the scholarly journal involved—*Oral History* (vol. 6, 1978)— published by the University of Essex in Colchester, England, and I found this shocker as Hobbs's first example:

Case One: Fingers

In September 1973, whilst talking to a joiner who was working in my home, I happened to mention that the house had recently been burgled. He told me that dogs are useful for preventing entry by burglars. He said he had a friend "down Dumbarton Road" (i.e. a mile or so away) who had a boxer dog. One night his friend came home and found a finger behind the door, presumably the finger of a potential burglar, bitten off by the dog.

Now I had to come up with a slightly different scenario than before. This early version—taken together with the recent ones from West Sussex and from Highgate in London—suggests that "The Choking Doberman" may have taken shape as a legend *not* in the United States, but perhaps in England, and *not* in 1981, but perhaps several years earlier. In all three of these 1970s–80s English versions a dog, not always a Doberman, chews off an intruder's fingers, but the injured intruder is not found. In the 1973 version the dog is not even choking on the finger; the finger is simply lying there "behind the door." In the Highgate version the would-be intruder has evidently reached in through a hole in the window, had his fingers bitten off, and fled. It is as if certain predecessors of our new urban legend—namely, "The Robber Who Was Hurt" and "The Severed Fingers" (the car story), both considerably older in English folk tradition, had not yet quite become the full "Choking Doberman" story as we now know it, although (judging from the two Midlands versions and the proliferation of versions in London and beyond in 1982) this older cycle of intruder-and-dog legends had quickly assimilated elements of the American folk story (i.e., black fingers and finding the intruder).

Sandy Hobbs, in fact, mentioned "The Severed Fingers" legend as he remembered it in oral tradition from the 1960s. But he also quoted an even more interesting, and much older, related Scottish story from Robert Chambers's *Traditions of Edinburgh,* first published in 1825:

> . . . Mrs. Campbell remembered residing in an Old-Town house, which was one night disturbed in the most intolerable manner by a drunken party at the knocker. In the morning, the greater part of it [that is, the door

knocker] was found to be gone; and it was besides discovered, to the no small horror of the inmates, that part of a finger was left sticking in the fragments, with the appearance of having been forcibly wrenched from the hand.

The core story I had been tracing is all here in "The Drunk at the Knocker," as, indeed, it also is in the Renaissance French version: first there is an intruder (or intended intruder); second an injury to his hand; and third the subsequent discovery of severed fingers or hand. All the other details in all the many variants of this baseline tradition are little more than enlargements and enrichment of the basic plot. And, clearly, there seems to have been a strong and, we might say, archetypal legend tradition in urban Britain possibly leading up to "The Choking Doberman" there before it existed as such in the United States. Note that even the disturbance to the house in the Old Town of Edinburgh in the middle of the night matches the nocturnal intrusion in the West Sussex version, and that the discovery of a finger left behind by the intruder matches that same detail in the 1973 story told to Sandy Hobbs.

History repeated itself with this legend in Australia in early January 1984. First, "Column 8" in the *Sydney Morning Herald* made this report:

> The December issue of NSW Police News reports that a veterinarian in Ferntree Gully, Victoria, was confronted by a pair of distraught dog owners who had returned home to find their beast gagging on an obstruction in its throat. When the vet operated he discovered two human fingers. A search of the dog owners' house uncovered a burglar with eight fingers, collapsed under a bed from loss of blood.

One day later, in the same paper:

> Column 8 is thunder-struck. Yesterday we printed a macabre story from the NSW Police News about a vet who found two fingers lodged in a dog's throat. We said the owners of the dog searched their house and found a burglar

collapsed under a bed suffering from loss of blood. Yesterday a voice chortled over our line saying that the story had been invented two years ago and was now a great urban myth. There is one redeeming factor. Police News was fooled too.

Folklorist Bill Scott of Yeerongpilly, Queensland, Australia, who sent me these clippings, added another version told to him by a friend from Adelaide, South Australia:

An Adelaide couple were off on a fortnight holiday but decided to leave their fierce Alsatian dog behind to deter burglars. They left the dog free inside the house and arranged with neighbours to throw food in for the dog every day. When they got home they were distressed by an awful stench inside the house. Investigation showed a dead burglar with half his hand bitten off who had taken refuge on the top shelf of a cupboard and there bled to death.

Notes toward the Life History of a "New" Urban Legend

One thing that folklorists have sometimes tried to do is to write a "life history of a folktale." While I cannot do this fully for "The Choking Doberman" and its ancestors at this point, I have developed a clear outline of the story's probable historical development. It looks something like this:

A. *The oldest level of the tradition* (tales of magic; fables)

Rural witchcraft lore in which supernatural intruder, possibly a neighbor in disguise, is injured severely, often in hand or fingers. (Sympathetic magic)
Stories in which a helpful animal is misunderstood and killed in a fit of anger (Motif B331.2.), evolving to "Llewellyn and Gellert" and then to "The Trapper and his Dog."

B. *The median level of tradition* (supernatural is rationalized)

"The Thief who had his Hand Cut Off," "The Hand," (Type 956B), "The Robber Who Was Hurt," etc.

Injured intruders more generally: "The Drunk at the Knocker," etc.

"The Severed Fingers" (the car legend).

C. *The recent level of tradition* (the latest urban legends)

Helpful animal injures intruder's hand or fingers (The "Wagger" tale, the "Tiger" tale, and "The Choking Doberman")

Introduction of racial details, an implied sexual threat, male's dog protecting a female, veterinarian, suffering pet, police, telephone warning, etc.

Cross-influence with "The Hook," "The Assailant in the Backseat," "The Elevator Incident," and miscellaneous Doberman lore.

This is not exactly an airtight genealogy, but it does account plausibly for all the facts so far uncovered, and it opens the door for studies of how modern legend narrators accept, repeat, vary, and interpret "The Choking Doberman" and its offshoots. So, in the prideful flush of bringing all of these different threads together, I yield to the temptation to quote the nineteenth-century English folklorist Sabine Baring-Gould in the conclusion to his own research on the legend of Prince Llewellyn: "There is scarcely a story which I hear," he wrote, "which I cannot connect with some family of myths, and whose pedigree I cannot ascertain with more or less precision."

But questions remain—too many and too important for me to remain smug about my findings. Nagging queries like these keep occurring to me:

1. Are there other versions of a legend—English, Scottish, Canadian, American, or whatever—similar to the "Wagger" story?*

---

*A possible prototypical "Wagger" story, with overtones of other legends in this cycle, was discovered by Professor Simon Bronner of

2. What further prototypes of dog-burglar-finger (or hand) stories exist that folklorists have missed?

3. Can "The Choking Doberman" story as such be found in full form earlier than spring 1981?

4. Why did the story seem to become popular so suddenly and so vigorously in the United States in 1981 and in England the following year?

5. Where are the other "Trapper and His Dog" stories—either printed or oral—that Rex Beach mentioned in 1942?

6. Could a dog—even a Doberman or an Alsatian—neatly nip off a finger or two or three, and why would it?

The case of "The Choking Doberman" cannot be closed yet, and the study of its oral-performance styles, contexts, and meanings in contemporary folklore are just ready to begin in earnest, based on this foundation of historical background. But to conclude my present findings—however incomplete—I am ready with a motif number that other folklorists may use in the next edition of the *Motif-Index* for this story. It's a start.

We should number it K982, or "the legend of the canine that ate two fingers."

The Pennsylvania State University (Capitol Campus) while this book was going to press. In the 22 July 1876 issue of *Harper's Weekly*, Charles Reade described the supposed experience of two women, keepers of a toll gate at the edge of a village in Yorkshire. Fearful of thieves, they mention an inheritance they recently acquired to the wife of the village blacksmith. Then a passing tradesman leaves them his huge mastiff as overnight protection. In the middle of the night they are awakened by the sound of the dog choking the life out of an intruder who had tried to enter at the window; it turns out to be the blacksmith himself, whose wife had mentioned the inheritance to him earlier. An illustration shows how "The great mastiff had pinned a man by the throat." Besides the familiar folk motifs in this account, Reade's conclusion lends further support to its legendary nature: "I have tried to learn the name of the village, and what became of this poor widow [i.e., the blacksmith's wife], but have failed hitherto."

2

More Automobile and RV Legends

The Foaf at the Wheel

"How do you know that these stories you have collected did not really happen?" People keep asking me this, often claiming to have access to some indisputable evidence of the truth of one. I usually reply, "If you know that one of them is true, then please get me the proof; I'd be delighted to have it." Frequently it is some classic automobile story floating around in oral tradition, like "The Killer in the Backseat" or "The Death Car," that people are absolutely sure "really happened."

So these people try very hard to remember who told them, and exactly when it was, and where they were living at the time that a fine sports car was advertised for sale by a wronged wife at an extraordinarily low price; or when someone accidentally was sold an experimental car with a carburetor that got 200 miles per gallon; or when a jealous husband filled an unfamiliar new car parked in his driveway with wet cement.

Unfortunately, the believers in legends like these—"The Philanderer's Porsche" "The Economical Car," and "The Solid Cement Cadillac"—always conclude eventually that they cannot unearth any firsthand information on the stories they thought were true or locate anyone else who can vouch for them. It usually turns out instead that they only heard them from other friends; and so it went through legions of friends and relatives beyond counting who had always *heard of* but had never *seen* the cars in question. Those who accept urban legends as true, then, have for verification not personal experience, nor even a friend's own experience, but only an unnamed, elusive, but somehow readily trusted anonymous individual—a "friend of a friend" [f-o-a-f]—or, we might say, a "foaf." And it is amazing how many foafs have had odd experiences with automobiles.

Rodney Dale, an English collector of apocryphal stories, coined this useful term "foaf" for the most commonly alleged urban legend source. In his amusing book *The Tumor in the Whale* (1978), Dale explained that while first-person accounts or named second-person accounts of even the most bizarre incidents do have some probability of being true, the third-hand report of a friend-of-a-friend's experience has every likelihood of being merely what he called a "whale tumor story," or a "WTS." (He refers to a legend about some whale meat bought in wartime England when other meats were scarce; it was found "gently throbbing" on a plate, since it contained "a live tumor." When you try to verify a wild story like that, Rodney Dale found, you end up searching for a nonexistent foaf.)

I have not heard that particular WTS in the United States —the category, yes, but never the specific legend—but I have met plenty of people who tell equally wild stories about things that supposedly happened to foafs. In fact, there is enough evidence of this sort of thing to encourage me to think seriously about founding a new science of foaflore. Seldom is it possible to bring together the amount of evidence I found to show that "The Choking Doberman" is an old legendary theme, but at least the oral tradition of different variants for other stories can establish that they are present-day legends.

Actually, foafness—attributing urban legends to third-hand unnamed sources—is only one of the two common ways that such stories are said to be validated by their tellers. The other spurious method of proving them true is to claim in a general way, "I read it in the paper," a gambit we might designate as "ritp," or just plain "rip" for ease of pronunciation. Just as when the person whose friend's friend had the experience, the friend cannot be tracked down; also, the person who "read it in the paper" never has the clipping in hand or the exact reference available.

Between the foafs and the rips, then, there is not much to go on if you attempt to establish that an urban legend really happened. These two validating formulas that urban legend narrators commonly use are just that, formulas: stereotyped verbal statements of traditional (i.e., nondocumentable) pseudoverification.

This is clearly the case, for example, with many of the stories involving a foaf at the wheel.

"The Hairy-Armed Hitchhiker"

One modern legend that English readers of *The Vanishing Hitchhiker* have repeatedly written me about sounds like a variation of "The Killer in the Backseat," or perhaps a drastic revision of "The Vanishing Hitchhiker" legend itself. Also, it reminds one somewhat of "Little Red Riding Hood": "Grandmother! What hairy arms you have."

In this legend a lone woman driver one way or another finds herself giving a lift to an elderly woman; but when the driver looks more closely at her passenger, she notes to her horror that the woman's arms or the backs of her hands are extraordinarily hairy. Realizing that she must have a disguised man and not a woman in the car with her, the driver coolly gets the passenger out of the car on some pretense, such as to check the tail lights of the car, or even to put air in the tires at a service station. Then she speeds away, leaving the passenger behind. Later she (or the police) finds a hatchet, knife, or meat cleaver lying on the seat or else hidden in the former passenger's handbag.

Rodney Dale does not mention "The Hairy-Armed Hitchhiker" in his book, and neither does Sanderson in his 1969 article on automobile folklore, but enough English people have told me variations of it to convince me that it is a well-known story there. Then in a lecture given in 1981 (see Bibliography for the published version), Sanderson mentioned the popularity of the story during 1977 when the so-called "Yorkshire ripper" was terrorizing the English and dominating the British news. He also called attention to a 1978 literary version developed as a radio drama, and to a prototype for the legend in an 1834 English newspaper report describing "a gentleman in his gig, who on opening the supposed female's reticule finds to his horror a brace of loaded pistols inside."* Further confirming the popularity of the story in England is another version from 1978 quoted by folklorist David Buchan in a paper published recently.

To my surprise, the 1982 American edition of *Heads You Lose and Other Apocryphal Tales,* by an anonymous English author calling himself "Francis Greig," gives "The Hairy-Armed Hitchhiker" a New York City setting. In this version, which I assumed was simply Americanized by the writer to fit the United States market, a woman takes a late train home from the city to Connecticut; there she meets a shabby old lady in the dark parking lot who asks for a ride, but she tricks the passenger into getting out when she sees her unusually hairy hands. The police find an axe with a shortened handle (why not simply a hatchet, I wonder) in her handbag that was left behind in the car. But even this did not prepare me for what happened next with the story.

In early spring 1983 "The Hairy-Armed Hitchhiker" began

---

*The legend and its nineteenth-century prototype are also mentioned by David A. Yallop in *Deliver Us From Evil* (London: Futura, 1981), p. 273. He calls the story "total myth, complete fantasy. . . ."

to show up as a local legend in the United States. Professor George Lewis, sociologist at the College of the Pacific, described the variations that were floating around there in a column he wrote for *The Stockton Record* (3 April 1983). This time the woman driver discovers the shadow of a person sitting in her car in a dark shopping-center parking lot. She gets two store security guards to come to the car with her, and they remove the person from her car and discover that they have a man dressed in women's clothing on their hands. In the backseat a little later on, the driver finds a heavy and very sharp axe. "Everyone in town, it seems," concluded Professor Lewis, "has 'a friend of a friend' to whom this terrible thing happened." By the end of the month "The Hairy-Armed Hitchhiker" was also reported as a rampant local rumor in *The Fresno Bee* (30 April)—"under her dress she is sitting on a sharp hatchet. . . ."

Simultaneously the same story was being heard in other regions. A school teacher in Racine, Wisconsin, wrote me that just after Easter vacation* her students reported that the same incident happened in the Regency Mall in Racine, and other local sources attributed it to Milwaukee and Chicago. On 4 May the *Seattle Times* published a piece headed "Retold tale of wigged accoster is just fiction" in which "The Hairy-Armed Hitchhiker" was said to be "sweeping Snohomish and King Counties." And on 1 June columnist Elaine Viets of the *St. Louis Post-Dispatch* published the results of her search for the roots of the new legend with this lead paragraph: "Warning: The following story is not true. I repeat: It is not true. Even if you know someone who works with the sister of the woman it happened to." In conclusion Viets quoted a revealing comment from a mother of a young single woman who had just learned from another daughter that the axe-man story was untrue: "Don't tell your sister. Maybe if she is scared she'll be

---

*Easter fell on 3 April in 1983.

more careful." Good advice—good lesson—but untrue story.

It's all very horrifying, very plausible, and very much impossible as an actual happening anywhere. So, remember, you read it here first.

"The Baby on the Roof"

You know how these things happen. A woman has finished her week's food shopping; she's in the supermarket parking lot, and she has just got the grocery bags stowed in the back of the station wagon. With either a baby in her arms or a toddler in tow, she walks up to the front door on the driver's side and fumbles in her purse for the car keys. In order to free a hand to select the proper key, she momentarily sets her purse on the car roof while she unlocks the door. She leaves her purse there when she drives off.

Usually this experience has a happy ending—either 1) the purse stays on the roof during the drive home and is discovered later, or 2) an honest passer-by finds it lying in the parking lot and returns it to her, or 3) another motorist points to it on the roof and she stops to retrieve it. This sort of thing could occur—probably has—and it makes an amusing anecdote to tell later, although it was not so laughable at the time. But at least it was better that the woman put her purse on the roof rather than the baby, and thereby hangs another tale.

In variations of the event, a skier sets his gloves on the car roof while fastening the skis into the rack, and then forgets them there. (Roads to ski areas are paved with lost gloves.) Or it may be a package to be mailed, a school book, or a lunch pail that is forgotten on the car roof. And, yes, it may even be the baby.

It is only a small step beyond these misplaced-object stories to the "really scary, but *true* story" that several people have told me happened to a friend of a friend of theirs. This couple with their baby were driving a long haul through the deserts of Utah or New Mexico; they stopped briefly at a rest area to switch drivers so that each one could take a turn at it and neither would get overtired. The husband, who was driving, stayed in his seat while the wife got out on the right, placed the baby (who was asleep in her car seat) on the roof, and walked around the car to slip behind the wheel. The husband, then, just slid over and pulled the right-hand door shut, and away they went again. The baby stayed on the roof. But the story has a happy ending: a state police cruiser or another driver soon flagged them down, and the baby was rescued, still snoozing peacefully in her little plastic seat.

"Of course it's true! It really happened to a good friend of my friend so-and-so," my informants say. Well, it could have happened, I'll admit that. I just have not yet met the parents who did this. Nor have I met anyone who knows them personally or who heard the story told in the first person.

When you think about it (and thinking about urban legends often casts doubt on them), the story of "The Baby on the Roof" is a little too tidy. First, it would take just the right driver-switching routine to assure that the vehicle operator would not get out, walk around the car, and see the baby perched up there on the roof. Second, car seats for children are not so easily lifted out. It's a clumsy business at best, usually involving undoing a safety belt, then tipping the seat up-and-out of the door. A sleeping tot taken on a long trip would more likely be on a mattress or in a car bed in the back of the auto anyway. Third, if it was such a long haul through the desert, other drivers would probably have been too few or going too fast to recognize a baby's seat on the roof for what it was in time for a successful rescue.

But if the event *did* occur, wouldn't it have made the news in a big way? This is especially likely, since the foafs to whom it happened seem to have been driving with their sometimes forgotten baby all over the Western American deserts for the past four or five years.

Babies, you might recall from *The Vanishing Hitchhiker,* have had a rather bad time of it in several urban legends. Most commonly—according to folklore—they are either stranded in their highchairs when the parents leave a few minutes early to begin an extended vacation and the sitter they have hired fails to come; or the babies are cooked in an oven (even microwaved) by a sitter who is high on drink or dope. And, of course, in this book we earlier encountered unfortunate babies either chewed on by watchdogs or else threatened by invading wolves or serpents and then rescued by watchdogs. There is yet another cycle of doomed-baby legends surrounding the bears in Yellowstone Park: supposedly a parent either places the baby in a bear's arms or on a bear's back for a photograph, and the bear disappears into the forest with the infant. (In another variant the tourists invite the bear to sit in the car with the children for the picture.)

Somehow the realistic and prosaic everyday threats to babies, such as falling, swallowing things, or catching cold, do not find their way into urban legends. My point here is not that babies are not subject to dangers, even rather odd ones, in real life, but that threatened or harmed babies have become a staple theme in modern folklore, reflecting parents' live concerns about the health and welfare of their offspring in an accident-plagued world.

A final element present in "The Baby on the Roof" that inclines me to regard it as legend is that so many other odd things end up precisely on car roofs in various other widely told tales. Thus, this detail too appears to be more a motif of folklore than a fact of life. I showed in *The Vanishing Hitchhiker* how the story of "The Runaway Grandmother" (body left on car roof-rack) is definitely folklore; now we have a baby in a similar situation, and there is yet another curious car-roof-sitting story that can clearly be identified as a piece of modern folklore.

"The Elephant That Sat on a VW"

Many journalists, but few folklorists, have been aware for years of a story that Herb Caen once labeled "The Elephant in the Parking Lot." In his *San Francisco Chronicle* column of 7 February 1971, Caen summarized it this way:

> That's a silly one that appears in columns whenever circus time draws near. This baby elephant, you see, escaped from its keeper and is found in a parking lot, resting on the front end of a Volkswagen and denting it. Later, the VW's driver, a woman, is stopped for speeding and when the cop says "What happened to your front end?" she replies, "You'll never believe this, officer, but—."

Depending on the size of the car in relation to the size of the elephant, either the car roof or the front end gets dented in.

Tom Buckley of the *New York Times* wrote a long report on "The Elephant That Sat on a VW" on 5 May 1975 that was widely reprinted in other newspapers. As he heard it, a woman from New Jersey drove her new red Volkswagen to Madison Square Garden in New York City to buy circus tickets. While she was parked there, a circus elephant taken out for an airing mistook her VW for the stool that was part of its act, and it sat on the car, pushing in the whole top. Circus officials provided her with documents attesting to what happened, and they agreed to pay her repair costs. Stopped by police as she was driving home, the woman avoided a drunkometer test and proved herself innocent of leaving an accident scene by showing the papers.

You might think that a *Times* reporter would doubt the veracity of someone saying she had a friend who drove a car into Manhattan on the relatively trivial errand of buying tick-

REPRINTED WITH THE PERMISSION
OF THE CENTER FOR THE
ENGLISH CULTURAL TRADITION
AND LANGUAGE AT THE
UNIVERSITY OF SHEFFIELD.
DRAWING BY DOC ROWE

ets. Add to that the unlikelihood of finding a parking place there, and of elephants being exercised on the city streets, and you have a highly suspicious car story if I've ever heard one.

But Buckley, a persistent reporter, went in search of his sources' source; all he found, alas, was foaf after foaf. First it was "a friend of my sister-in-law" who had told it; then "a cousin of a friend"; next, other assorted New Jersey cousins and neighbors, and finally a high-school student who heard it from one of her teachers. By then Buckley began to doubt that "one of the big prizes for investigative journalism was finally within [my] grasp," but he telephoned the circus officials anyway. It was the end of the trail, for the circus spokesman said, "It's a story that has been circulating for at least fifteen years. It never happened."

The same basic story involving this cute but dangerous behavior by an elephant is well known in Europe; it may even have started there. I've been told, for example, that the elephant sit-in happened during a circus parade many years ago in Munich, Germany. The elephant had mistaken the small red car for a stool used in the circus act. In September 1975 the Stockholm, Sweden, evening paper *Expressen* published a posed photo of a circus elephant seated against the front fender of a VW while the driver looked out his window in amazement. (Obviously, the Swedish editor expected readers to recognize an allusion to the legend.) In 1977 Rodney Dale heard several variants in England that he quoted in *The Tumor in the Whale*.

The English tradition of the story sometimes begins with a supposed auto-accident claim report submitted to an insurance company. Either the driver says he was following a circus parade when a train whistle startled an elephant into sitting down on his car, or a driver going through an English safari park has his car door bashed in by a pushy pachyderm. In one version of the safari story the elephant has poked its trunk inside a half-open window of the car to beg for peanuts. A passenger rolls up the window, trapping the trunk, and the elephant puts its front feet against the side of the car and pulls vigorously. In either instance, the English driver needs to stop off for a drink on the way home to calm his nerves, but then he fails the drunkometer test when the police stop him to ask about the damage to his car, so he is jailed. (Perhaps the drinking motif also relates to the usual stereotype of heavy boozers seeing "pink elephants.")

This is pretty much the way the story continues to circulate in the United States, with appropriate localizations. In St. Louis, Missouri, for instance, it is said that a young family has driven in with the children from sixty miles away in their VW to visit the popular St. Louis Zoo. Luckily, they find a parking place next to a steel cabinet that is used to store workmen's tools; unluckily, one of the zoo elephants taken for its daily walk has gotten into the habit of resting against the case. That day it rested on their car instead, caving in the front end and smashing the headlights. When the police stop the car on the way home for an explanation of the heavy damage, it takes a long-distance telephone call back to the zoo to straighten things out.

My favorite recent version of the story was sent to me by Elizabeth West of Boxborough, Massachusetts, who heard it twice during the past decade. Here's the way she got it:

THE NUN IN THE VOLKSWAGEN

A nun had been to visit Benson's Animal Farm (a local attraction) and had parked her Volkswagen bug in the parking lot. While she was there, an elephant escaped. While it was being chased, it backed into the nun's car, doing quite a bit of damage. However, the car was still able to be driven.

Later that day, the nun was driving through the Callahan Tunnel (in Boston, and known for its traffic snarls). There was bumper-to-bumper traffic, and another car lightly hit the nun's Volkswagen.

A nearby policeman stopped, and everyone got out of the cars. The man driving the car at fault said he could not have done so much damage, since he only barely touched the nun's car. She agreed, saying the damage had been done by an elephant earlier in the day. The upshot was that the nun got hauled into the police station on suspicion of drunken driving.

When Ms. West sent me this version she mentioned that when she was told it a second time she said to herself, "Hey, wait a minute, I heard this once before in a different context." We should all be so perceptive; or would that spoil the fun of the story?

"The Rattle in the Cadillac"

Even when an urban legend is attributed to the authority of a friend of a friend, there may be some further element of "proof" mentioned that is more concrete and specific. For example, in those versions of "The Elephant That Sat on a VW" that speak of documents from the circus, or of papers filed in an insurance claim, there is the presumption that these particular papers exist and that they could be produced in order to support the story. (The same is true about the note from Reggie Jackson left in the hotel mailbox in some versions of "The Elevator Incident.") Journalists or folklorists trying to verify their sources may be so stuffy as to ask to see such papers for themselves, but the typical person just hearing an urban legend will assume that the documents are for real and let it go at that.

A more solid piece of evidence is sometimes referred to in an urban legend about a new luxury car with a rattle. To begin with, supposedly someone—a foaf, of course—sees something that looks like a piece of abstract art framed and hanging on the wall in the den or plush office of a successful doctor, lawyer, or businessman. This peculiar artistic composition is made out of what appears to be merely ordinary nuts and bolts, broken pop bottles, and miscellaneous metal scraps. There's a story behind the work, as the owner explains.

It seems that he is a wealthy professional man (or sometimes a person who recently came into a large inheritance), and he had ordered a new Cadillac loaded with extras. The car was everything he expected, except for one flaw: it had a persistent annoying rattle, especially when being driven over railroad tracks or on bumpy streets. Taking the car back to the dealer, the man had every single part checked and tightened, but the rattle continued. Finally, after several more trips to the dealership, the car was dismantled piece by piece. Inside the door panel on the left side they found all the assorted junk that the owner then had made into the souvenir abstract arrangement. Sometimes the pieces are found inside a pop bottle or a tin can; and sometimes this container is suspended on a length of rope or wire so it swings around as the car moves. Practically always there is a note tucked into the can or bottle from the disgruntled factory worker who planted the junk in the door, saying something like "You rich SOB—so you finally found the rattle!"

The whole thing, of course, *must* have happened, since why else would a man decorate his tasteful home or office with a junk collage and tell such a tale? But have you ever seen the picture, or have you read the note for yourself? I have heard the story many times with varying details, but I have yet to see any proof that it happened. "The Rattle in the Cadillac" demonstrates how auto workers might feel about those who can afford to buy their most expensive products, but only the elusive foaf has ever really seen proof of assembly-line frustration being acted out in this particular creative way. If it really happened, someone somewhere has the car, the note, the junk, and the piece of junk sculpture. I'm waiting . . .

"Cruise Control" Stories

The ways of drivers with their cars seem to furnish endless themes for believable legends to modern American folklore. Furthermore, as new automobile models and features become available, tellers of urban legends will often begin to explore the possibilities for humor or horror. A good example of this is the recent spate of RV (recreational vehicle) lore, such as the widespread traditional story of "The Nude in the RV" wherein a man napping in the nude, or nearly so, steps out the back of his RV when the driver (his wife) stops momentarily, and he is left behind on the roadside (see *The Vanishing Hitchhiker*). Another RV story cycle deals with a camper van that has been outfitted with "cruise control."

In the late 1970s manufacturers began to sell private vehicles of various kinds equipped with a device to maintain a set highway speed (until the brake was touched); this was often termed "cruise control." Once this had become a well-known option, it was probably inevitable that some drivers—certainly some foafs at the wheel—would confuse this feature with something like the automatic pilot on airplanes.

The story is told of a man who has the cruise control feature on his new camper van carefully explained to him by the salesman. He buys the RV and then promptly drives out on the highway, sets the cruise control at sixty miles per hour, and steps in back to fix himself a drink. The driver survives the crash that comes about thirty seconds later, but his RV is a total loss.

Did you read that one in the paper? I've been told several times that it has been published, but (according to my informants' memories of the story) always with different details. Sometimes it was a retired couple that made the dangerous (but never fatal) error with cruise control; otherwise it was a young and naïve driver. The trip to the back of the van may be to make coffee or another drink, or to use the camper toilet. Occasionally the storyteller will describe the accident as it was seen (by a foaf, of course); then the explanation of what happened is given by the injured driver, who still can't figure out what went wrong.

Most recently the driver of the van with cruise control is said to have been a wealthy student from the Middle East. Naturally, he orders his camper with every option and convenience—from cruise control in front to a fully stocked bar in back. That combination of features leads to the predictable accident. The implication here, of course, is that rich Arabs don't understand technology, and as a result they may be "getting what they deserve" when they spend their wealth so lavishly in the United States.

This story of a 1970s car option has a counterpart in a car story of the 1950s, when automatic transmission was the latest gadget. In this one, which I call "Push-Starting the Car," a man has a new car with automatic shift, but the motor stalls with a dead battery, so he asks a woman (his wife, sister, neighbor, etc.) to give him a push-start with her car. He says, "I have automatic transmission, so you will have to go about twenty-five [or thirty-five, or forty] miles an hour to get it started." She says that she understands, but when he gets behind the wheel and looks in the rear-view mirror, he sees her backed off about half a block away and coming at him at twenty-five (etc.) miles an hour. Herb Caen published that one a few years ago (on 14 February 1971), calling it a classic, and I remember it well from the early days of Oldsmobile's "Hydromatic Drive" when I was in college in Michigan in the early 1950s.

A persistent feature in car legends of this kind is the denigration of a minority person (senior citizen, foreigner, woman, etc.) who allegedly misunderstands the nature of some new but fairly uncomplicated technological device. A slur against a racial group is involved in the similar legend about a black trying to learn to water ski behind a powerful tow boat. He gets into the skis in the water, sits back (or else stands on the dock) holding the end of the tow rope firmly with the slack coiled up before him, and he shouts something like, "Go, Ski Cat, go!" urging the driver of the boat to accelerate rapidly at full power. The force of the pull either pops his arms from their sockets or else whips him into the air and over the front of the boat, where he is run over and injured. Some narrators call this one "Ski King," and most people who know it seem to regard it as probably just a rumor, albeit one that shows a black (like the Arab in "Cruise Control") getting a deserved beating for presuming to take on a white man's sport. As we observe many times in folklore, the prejudices and stereotypes that people are reluctant to voice in direct terms will often surface in very obvious ways in their oral-narrative traditions of joke or legend.

Occasionally a product-misuse story of this kind—whether involving a car or other machinery—will conclude with the information that the sufferer sued the company and won a large settlement. This motif not only reinforces the supposed validity of the legend but adds the theme that the big company responsible for the product is blameworthy for creating something that can be dangerously misused. In Chapter 6 I discuss several other product-misuse legends.

"The Wife's RV Revenge"

Since the RV is a little house on wheels, people tend to be pictured in RV urban legends as being subject to the same kinds of mishaps and adventures that are possible in their homes. For example, "The Nude in the RV" story has its counterpart in an older and more widely known legend about a man, fresh from a shower, who steps outside his apartment door, wrapped in only a towel, to pick up the newspaper; he is accidentally locked out when the door blows shut. Another instance of a domestic slip-up—being caught in an infidelity— is usually an at-home story (as in "The Nude Surprise Party"), but it can also be a camper story.

In this one a woman has found out that her husband and his girlfriend are using the camper for their meetings. Waiting until they are inside and oblivious to anything going on outside, she locks the back door of the camper and takes them for a long, fast drive over twisty, bumpy roads. Finally, when she figures that they are completely sick of the ride—and of each other—she backs the camper up against a brick wall (sometimes at the police station) so they cannot force their way out, leaving them there to be discovered the next morning. In a variant, the jealous wife drives the camper home and backs it into the garage to trap the couple; then she releases them the next morning with her lawyer standing by as a witness.

People who have told me that story claim to have seen it published as a news story in the Midwest, but no one has yet given me a clipping or a reliable reference. But, even if it was published, oral tradition is the most likely explanation for the varying versions coming from both Midwestern and Eastern American locations. It couldn't have happened everywhere that it is told, and even if it happened somewhere, it has now entered folklore and has a new life of its own.

"The Coyote's Revenge"

We may conclude this survey of recent vehicular legends with this version of a popular tale sent to me by Dave Hug of Fort Collins, Colorado; I like to think that it represents abused nature getting back at thoughtless mankind:

> A man was camping out in the wilds with his pickup camper. At the edge of the clearing where he was camped, he ran across a wounded coyote. Hating coyotes anyway, he decided he'd create a little excitement. He had some dynamite in his truck, left over from blowing stumps on his farm. So he tied a stick of dynamite to the coyote, lit the fuse, and ran over behind some trees to watch the results. To his horror, the man watched the coyote summon his last bit of strength and drag himself over to the camper. There was nothing he could do as the coyote pulled himself under the camper and blew himself and much of the camper to bits.
>
> (This supposedly happened here in Colorado. Naturally, the truck was new and the insurance company refused to pay.)

Since the mythical coyote is such a notorious trickster in Western American Indian folklore, I am surprised that the man's lawyer did not sue the insurance company for failing to pay off for damage suffered from a predictable hazard. But it "served the man right," to cite the typical lesson of the urban legends involving cars or campers.

How do I know this one isn't really true? First, I have the evidence of other tortured-animal stories with similar switcheroo endings: an ignited cat or dog burns down the house or barn, a battered rattler strikes its tormentor, and so forth. Second, I have the older rural counterpart to this specific legend, as included by Rogers Whitener in his newspaper column (written out of Boone, NC), "Folk-Ways and Folk-Speech," for 23 June 1973.* In that one, a farmer traps a chicken hawk and decides to take revenge on it for all the poultry it has killed by tying a stick of dynamite to the bird and releasing it. You guessed it—the hawk perches on the man's roof, and the blast knocks the top off his house.

---

*As printed in *North Carolina Folklore Journal* 29 (1981): 5–7.

3

More Horrors

Grown Up—Still Scared

Gruesome horror stories that take place in familiar surroundings are a staple of urban legendry. Some of the most popular narratives in modern folklore—like "The Choking Doberman" and "The Severed Fingers"—are vivid accounts of threats, assaults, injuries, and sometimes violent deaths that supposedly occurred in everyday life to ordinary people. Since these legends are told as recitals of local events, they give the impression of having some basis in fact, even if their fantastic plots, calmly considered, are reminiscent of the most sensational thrillers by Edgar Allan Poe or Alfred Hitchcock. The storytellers assume that what they are describing actually happened, because they have heard (or read) that the stories are true. But the lack of authentication, the many variant versions, the traditional themes and motifs in the stories, and the formularized style in which they are told all indicate that most of these shocking narratives belong to folk tradition rather than history.

Among the most blood curdling urban horror legends are those that American teen-agers tell at slumber parties, on camping trips, or in dormitory bull sessions and the like. An inventory of the ghastly plot details in adolescent scare stories shows skinned and decapitated corpses, axes buried in victims' heads, fingers scratched down to bloody stumps in frantic escape attempts, and human hair turning white overnight from fear. In legends like "The Hook" and "The Boyfriend's Death" the setting is a couple's parked car, and the horrible threat is from a maniac lurking in the shadows of Lovers' Lane. In other popular legends the threatening figure is either inside the car itself ("The Killer in the Backseat"), in the same house with the preyed-upon adolescent character ("The Baby-sitter and the Man Upstairs"), or in a college dormitory ("The Roommate's Death").

Such gory legends, it must be realized, are not told primarily by deviants or delinquents; in fact, a good part of their credibility lies in the fact that numerous teen-agers of all social classes and educational levels have common knowledge of them. *Everybody* knows these stories! Their scare appeal is universal, even if they are sometimes told with an air of only half-belief, more for their power to generate a good shiver than for their truth quotient. Actually, urban legends are often transmitted, by teen-agers in particular, not as complete stories told by one speaker to a passive audience but, rather, as a group effort, with each person who is present adding to the general account of the supposed events the variations and details that he or she has heard.

Eventually, most people outgrow their youthful fascination with legends the likes of "The Hook" or "The Roommate's Death." They either forget the stories entirely in later years, or they come to regard them with a sophistication gained from age and experience as mere foolish whims of their school days. (Still, many adults, when reminded of an adolescent horror legend, exclaim that they assumed that the event happened in their hometown, but they never tried to verify it when they got beyond slumber parties.)

Adults, however, have their own urban horror legends that may overlap with the adolescent repertoire ("The Killer in the Backseat" is popular with all ages). Or adults may borrow typical teen-age themes (like the baby-sitter) but then follow a plot from the parents' viewpoint (the baby-sitter herself becomes the threat to the children).

The key to the development of a credible modern legend of suspense and terror seems to be the embroidery of a plausible basic element with imaginary horrific details. Each storyteller—or each participant in a group legend-sharing session—tells what he or she *thinks* was heard. But the "facts" slip and slide around, always being influenced by other legends that people have heard and by everyone's notion of what a well-told story should sound like. People do not memorize their folklore and repeat it verbatim; instead they reconstruct folk narratives each time they tell them, starting from some central motif and incorporating the bits and pieces of language and detail that were developed in many earlier recitations. Thus, every time a legend is retold it is both the same as before and different.

A good example of an everyday experience becoming a local horror legend was given by Tim Woodward of the Boise *Idaho Statesman* (14 October 1982). Reminded of "The Choking Doberman" kind of story by a lurid account he had heard of a man "trapped like a rat in a refrigerator" in Ketchum, Idaho, journalist Woodward went in search of the story that, he said, "[had] been riding the raconteur circuit for some time now." He found that the man involved was Louis Mallane, owner of Louie's Pizza and Italian Restaurant, "more commonly known just as Louie's in Ketchum." Here is the story that was circulating, as Woodward retold it in his column, "with perhaps one or two small embellishments of my own" (after all, he's a modern folk too):

> Mallane had just finished jogging when the disaster struck. On the spur of the moment, he decided to use the restaurant's new walk-in refrigerator to change his clothes. The door locked behind him.
>
> It's no joke being locked in a refrigerator. You imagine all sorts of unpleasantries—freezing, for example, or suffocating, or beating yourself to oblivion against the door.

As the story had it, Mallane spent hours trapped in his icy cell. He kicked the door and pounded on it, but no one heard him. He hurled himself against it, to no avail. He shouted until he was hoarse, with the same result. The door was too thick and heavily insulated for anyone to hear his desperate cries.

Fearing the worst, he exercised to keep warm. Exercising, of course, used the air up more quickly. The situation was grim. Something had to be done immediately. He had to find a way out.

Fighting panic and arctic temperatures, Mallane racked his brain for a way to remove the door's hinges. Nothing in the refrigerator could be used for a tool, so he searched his pockets and found a coin. He used it to try to loosen the screws, but his pitiful, frostbitten fingers had lost their grip.

Just as the Reaper was raising his scythe, Mallane heard someone coming. A waitress opened the door—and was shocked to see the half-frozen figure of her employer tumble from the icy abyss. He was rushed to a hospital, where he was placed in a special oven and given piping hot blood transfusions.

The situation certainly contains the stuff of a classic urban legend: it begins with a commonplace act (jogging), adds a very human miscalculation (using the walk-in refrigerator as a changing room), then incorporates Poe-like horror (trapped in a cold, dark place) and a last-minute rescue. Also, the descriptions of the man's desperate attempts to escape and the hospital's revival efforts are packed with graphic details like the lucky coin, the numb fingers, the depleted air supply, the "special oven," and the transfusions of heated blood.

The acceptance of the narrative as a true story in southern Idaho no doubt was encouraged by the fact that Louie's is a well-known establishment in the Ketchum/Sun Valley area, and that warnings to keep children away from abandoned refrigerators lest they suffocate inside are common among parents, teachers, and law-enforcement officers. Certainly the event *could* have happened just that way, but *did* it? Actually, something like it indeed happened; then oral tradition, plus some journalistic license, took over. Here is the story of "The Jogger in the Freezer" as Louis Mallane himself told it to Tim Woodward:

> "Well, it isn't anything I'm real proud of," he said. "The door is fixed so it could never happen again now, but that day it just closed behind me and wouldn't open. I remember sitting down and thinking, 'Hey, this isn't funny.'"
>
> "Did you really try to take the hinges off with a coin?" I asked.
>
> "No," he replied. "I just pounded on the door and they heard me outside. At first they thought I was in there working, but then my sister thought it sounded odd and opened the door."
>
> "Were you nearly frozen by that time?"
>
> "Frozen? No, the freezer wasn't even turned on."
>
> "It still must have been awfully frightening being trapped in there for so long! How long *were* you trapped anyway?"
>
> "Gosh, it must have been all of three minutes."

"The Licked Hand"

The story of "The Jogger in the Freezer" is a personal-experience horror narrative that became folklorized in the process of passing through the community in oral and written versions. The legend stage of the incident contained folkloric elements, but it did not really embody a folk plot, except in the general sense of a "fortunate escape" (like Brer Rabbit getting away from the bear, or a maiden being rescued from the dragon). Most urban horror legends, however, combine fully fictional plots with a credible setting and realistic characters to anchor themselves to supposed real-life events. One such story that circulates widely at different age levels is "The Licked Hand."

First, here is a children's version of this legend given in Mary and Herbert Knapp's book *One Potato, Two Potato* (1976). This text has a stylized opening formula, suspenseful repetitions, and a surprise ending to qualify it as what the Knapps call "a modern fairy tale":

> Once there was this little girl who lived on a farm that was way, way, away from anything. And her parents had to go to town. So they left the little girl with this big collie dog to protect her. The mother said, "Now be sure to lock all the windows and doors." So when the mother and father were gone, the little girl and the collie went around to all the windows and locked them. Down in the basement there was this one little window that wouldn't shut tight, but the little girl thought, "Oh well, I've got the collie dog to protect me." So she went to bed. In the middle of the night, she heard this drip-drip sound and it woke her up and she was really scared, but she put her hand down beside her bed and the collie licked her hand so she felt better and went back to sleep. Then she heard this drip-drip-drip again, but she put her hand down and the dog licked it and she went to sleep. It happened again! Then in the morning she went into the bathroom and there was the collie dog hung up on the shower with its throat cut and all the blood had run out of it. The little girl screamed and screamed. When her parents came home, they found a note under the bed, and do you know what it said? It said, "Humans can lick, too, you know."

The focus in this version of "The Licked Hand" is on the little girl, warned by her parents and thought to be protected by her dog. But leaving just "one little window" unlocked makes her vulnerable to threats from outside the home. This kind of setting is typical of a youngster's narration of the legend, as is such simple language as "way, way, away from anything," "drip-drip-drip," and "The little girl screamed and screamed."

Projecting a somewhat older viewpoint and vocabulary, while particularizing the rural setting, is this version published in Ronald L. Baker's *Hoosier Folk Legends* (1982) as it was told by a twenty-one year old male college student in 1967. The shift in time between the main event and the aftermath—quite uncharacteristic of folk narration—probably reveals the influence of TV or film plots:

In a little town south of here—ever hear of Farmersburg?—there was supposed to be a murderer, a psycho. Well, anyway, there were these two girls, real good friends. The parents of the one were gone for the night, so the other girl was to stay with her at her house. Just the two girls and the dog of the girl who lived there. For some reason, there were two beds in the room, and the girls slept in separate beds. Well, they'd heard about the man breaking out, and they were scared, so the girl who lived there sent her dog over to sleep with her friend so that she'd feel better.

Sometime in the middle of the night, the girl who lived there got scared and reached down to the side of her bed to pet her dog. When she did, the dog licked her, and she felt better about it all and went on back to sleep.

In the morning, she got up and saw that sometime during the night her friend had been killed. Her throat was slit and so was the dog's. She thought about it, trying to figure out when it could have happened, since she remembered petting the dog. Well, her folks came home, and there was a great big mess and all that stuff, and then it was all about forgotten. Then about twenty years later, when this chick had grown up and all, she got a note from this guy, the murderer. They'd never caught him somehow. The note said, "I'm coming to see you. I had my chance once before, but I didn't take it. Not only dogs can lick."

The curiously calm handling of the climax of the story—no screaming, no terror, only wonderment about the licking—indicates the narrator's detachment from the whole thing. Probably this is because the storyteller is an older male, repeating a story that is more typically known to younger females. The rather elaborate description in the story of who slept where, with the dog apparently moving from bed to bed in the dark, seems to reveal some puzzlement about how the plot events can be made to hang together logically.

Other versions told by adolescent girls (or remembered from that period by older women) present this same material differently. For instance, in a Texas version a spoiled rich girl who owns a German shepherd has a slumber party; but the girl refuses to sleep in the den with her guests, and instead she stays in the top bunk of her own bedroom with her dog taking its customary place on the lower bunk. When an assailant chops to bits all the guests in the other room, the rich girl comes half-awake, reaches down and feels what she thinks is the dog licking her hand, and then falls back asleep. In the morning she discovers the carnage, plus her pet hanging dead in the bathroom, with the words "Humans Lick Too" scrawled on the wall in the dog's own blood. In some versions told in the Midwest, the young women are college friends sharing a small house near campus and keeping a dog for security that always sleeps between their beds. One morning one of the students finds her roommate *and* the dog lying dead in the kitchen with their throats slashed, and with the words "People can lick hands, too." written in blood on a note laid on the table.

We seem to have in "The Licked Hand" a rough progression in plot development from a young child left alone in an isolated rural setting to a later urban variant with teen-age girls at a slumber party, or college students sharing a bedroom. In the most recent and updated versions—told by older narrators—the protagonist is once again a lone female with her guard dog. (As in "The Choking Doberman," there is the suggestion here that a woman living alone needs a dog for protection.) When a dripping sound is heard in these versions, it is thought to be a leaky faucet in the woman's apartment. The dog sleeps under the bed; sometimes the woman's feet are licked rather than her hand. In the morning she often finds her dog slain in the kitchen—sometimes stuffed inside the refrigerator—as she sleepily begins to make breakfast. The note usually reads "People can lick too."

"The Clever Baby-sitter"

Most of the basic fears revealed in urban horror legends remain consistent through time, while the specific plots and details of the stories vary. The endangered-baby theme, for example, has its latest manifestation in the legend of the baby-sitter roasting a child in the oven or zapping it in the microwave. But, as we have already noted, older stories based on the same anxiety involved babies trapped in highchairs, left on car roofs, or threatened by guard dogs or by wild animals invading the nursery.

One story of this kind, recognized as a rumor or legend, was sent to me by Charles A. Brown of Vero Beach, Florida, in 1980:

> When our children were young, twenty to twenty-five years ago, a friend was riding on a bus. She was sitting in front of two teen-age girls who were discussing the problems of baby-sitting. When the subject turned to crying babies and how to stop their crying, one girl was overheard to say to the other, "That's no problem. I just turn on the gas in the oven, put the baby's head in until it falls asleep, and then take it out."

Mr. Brown added, "This story was accepted as gospel by young parents of the time." That it was indeed an urban legend of the 1950s is verified by a text from Professor Baughman's files (collected in 1953):

> In New York City you have to be awfully careful about getting baby-sitters. You just don't know what might happen. My sister's girlfriend was sitting in the subway one day

when she heard two women discussing the kids they stay with and how they handled them. She heard one of them say, "I just take them into the kitchen and give them just a l-i-t-t-le bit of gas." (You know, that could be very dangerous. No, you can't trust everybody with your children.)

Jerome Beatty, Jr., told the same story as he had heard it* in New Rochelle, New York, in an article in *Esquire* (November 1970). His original source was a friend who claimed that she had been the lady in the bus who overheard the teen-agers talking, but later Beatty read and heard the same story attributed to both Denver and "down South."

Besides the consistent warning function of "The Clever Baby-sitter" story, the alert student of urban legends should recognize two other standard features of the genre: first, the source is a friend, or a friend of a friend; and second, the culprit is a distrusted class of person (here a youngster) who is misusing a modern appliance.

Restroom Legends:
"The Attempted Abduction"
"The Mutilated Boy"

The two pervasive modern horror legends with the best documented early histories are about either an attempted abduction or a cruel assault directed against a youth in a department store or shopping center restroom. Even though American journalists have repeatedly debunked the stories, and there is a well-known English literary version of one, these restroom legends continue to appear year after year as true accounts in local tradition, usually attributed to specific busi-

---

*In "about 1950" (personal correspondence to the author, 26 October 1983).

nesses of the region. The latest active phase of the restroom legends was in late 1980, and they seem to peak in roughly five-year cycles.

A news item from the *Capital Times* of Madison, Wisconsin, headlined "Abduction rumors have police puzzled" (10 November 1980) offered this summary of one typical form of the story:

> Madison police and shopping center officials are becoming increasingly disturbed over a plague of rumors circulating that young girls are being drugged and abducted from shopping centers.
>
> The rumors began circulating about five weeks ago when a story made the rounds that a teen-age girl was shot full of heroin in a restroom at West Towne [shopping center], and was being carried away by two women when she was rescued by relatives and taken to a hospital for treatment. . . .
>
> That story has been repeated increasingly in the past two weeks, except the location has shifted to East Towne. . . .

The article revealed that numerous calls to police about the alleged incident cited only "third- and fourth-hand information" and had produced "nothing solid to act on." Neither the shopping mall officials, the police, nor the newspaper in Madison could unearth any reliable information about an attempt to kidnap a girl, who would allegedly have been forced into prostitution if her abductors had succeeded. The *Times* article concluded by referring to another restroom story told in the Madison area some ten years earlier: " . . . a gang of 'hippies' allegedly assaulted and mutilated young boys at area discount stores. Those unfounded rumors circulated for several months before being put to rest."

In a follow-up story three days later (13 November 1980), the *Capital Times* amplified its report of the rumors—the assailants were also said to be injecting the girls with cocaine or LSD, and the home base of their nefarious operation was believed to be Chicago. Sometimes the victims were thought to have been actually abducted, but usually they were rescued by relatives. The *Times* also reported that similar rumors were circulating in Milwaukee, centering there on four separate shopping centers.

"The Attempted Abduction" has been a recurrent American urban legend for many years. Throughout the Midwestern states the focus of the sinful sex scheme is often reported as Chicago, Detroit, or St. Louis. Major flare-ups of the story in the past decade have occurred in Minneapolis, Sioux City, and Council Bluffs (Iowa), but hardly an urban center in the United States that is large enough to have suburbs and shopping centers has been free of it. In Eastern states the young victims, usually blondes, are said to have been nabbed for a New York City prostitution racket. In Salt Lake City some travelers from California are suspected of being the criminals who try to abduct young children from a local amusement park for transport to the West Coast (see "Kidnappings" in *The Vanishing Hitchhiker*).

Frequently—in any location—it is mentioned that the abductors try to explain their behavior as helping a sick friend or relative, but the drugged (or chloroformed) youngster is recognized and rescued even though her hair may have been cut short and hastily darkened with shoe polish. The drug injection sometimes is said to be administered to the buttocks of the victim through a crack in the folding seat of a movie theater, or else the child may be taken from the restroom of a theater or drive-in movie. Sometimes the motive for the attempted abduction is said to be using the victim in kiddy-porn films or selling them into black-market adoption.

The abduction legend tends to be fueled by news reports of actual crimes, of which there are, of course, many with full police documentation and media coverage. But the majority of the local scares rests mainly on hearsay and the oral repetition of older folk legends. A story from *The Miami Herald* under the byline of Sara Rimer (26 September 1980) shows the usual pattern of distribution and variation. The headline is "Truth is the victim in wild kidnap tale" with the subhead " 'White Slavery' rumor spreads in 2 counties":

> The manager of The Falls, a classy new shopping mall in Southwest Dade, first heard at his real estate class the rumor that wouldn't go away. One of his classmates had heard about it from his best friend's wife.
>
> But the real jolt came that night when Ron Kaminski introduced himself to someone at Stan's, a Fort Lauderdale bar. The reaction of his new acquaintance was startling, "Oh, you manage The Falls! That's where they're abducting all those girls!"
>
> It sounded too bizarre to be believed—girls being dragged out of the public restrooms and sent off to South America as slaves—but Kaminski, an earnest sort, got right on it. He talked to the managers of his 58 stores and five restaurants. He dispatched his Wackenhut guards. That was two weeks ago.
>
> "We ran into a blank wall," says Kaminski. . . .
>
> . . . the core rumor . . . goes like this: A mother and her teenage daughter were having lunch at a shopping-center restaurant. The daughter goes to the ladies' room and doesn't come back.
>
> The mother follows just in time, the story goes, to see her unconscious daughter being dragged off by two husky women. The women flee and the daughter is saved from life as a slave in South America.
>
> The story has many variations. Some say the abductors are women, some say men, some say men dressed as women. The victims are beautiful blonde teenage girls.

The Miami Herald story also reported, as we would expect, "Sources are questionable at best; most of the tale-tellers attribute it to the friend of a friend of a friend."

Folklorist Richard M. Dorson collected urban folk traditions in 1975 and 1976 in the congested and heavily industrialized Calumet region of northwestern Indiana (the area of Gary, Whiting, East Chicago, and Hammond). He found, among several other popular topics of inner-city folklore, a lively tradition of "crimelore." In his book *Land of the Millrats* (1981), Dorson accepted even first-person accounts of hold-ups and assaults as being modern folk narratives, on the basis of their oral circulation, their shock effect, and their stylized plots and characters. But the pair of stories from the region that Dorson awarded "unimpeachable folkloric credentials" were variants of the two restroom legends.

Dorson recognized that the more gruesome legend, the more deeply believed one, and (as research has shown) the older one of the two is not the lucky escape story but the "crime carried out" legend about the mutilated boy. Here is a text from Dorson's fieldwork:

> I heard a story, I believe about ten years ago, it would be about 1965—I was eighteen then—about a little white boy who had gone shopping with his mother in K mart, and he had to urinate. So, for the first time the mother decided to let him go in by himself to use the men's washroom, rather than going into the womens with her. He was in there an exceptionally long amount of time, and she got worried and asked some gentlemen to step in and see what the problem was, if there was a problem.
>
> And they found the little boy laying in a pool of blood with his penis cut off. Subsequently they found three little black boys walking through the store with a bloody penis in their pocket. As it turned out, they had cut the little white boy's penis off as an orientation, a method of getting into a gang that they wanted to belong to. . . .

Dorson felt that "The Mutilated Boy" legend reflected "two of the most anxiety-laden issues of modern times: racial fears and the decline of downtown businesses." He found the legend to be common especially whenever a new suburban shopping center had opened and people began deserting the older urban stores for the suburban mall.

Somewhat modifying the second of the themes Dorson mentioned, revealing instead a small-towner's suspicion of metropolitan crime, is this version from Baker's *Hoosier Folk Legends*, as it was told in the central part of the state by a resident of Brazil, Indiana, in 1970:

> One day the mother of my friend came home from Terre Haute shopping and was not only upset but very sick. She told us about while shopping at Meadows Center there was a clerk or someone who told her about how somebody had hidden in the rest room, and when a little boy went in this person had taken a knife and cut him up. This little kid about four had gone in by himself while his mother was shopping. Anyway, when the mother went to find him she found blood all over the floor and parts of him all over. This person told my friend's mother she had seen the blood. This was about four years ago. Also I heard a bunch of colored boys or white boys chopped up a little colored boy there, too. I know I was afraid to go in the rest rooms in the basement of Meadows for a long time.

The depth of people's concern about the restroom legends —"The Mutilated Boy" in particular—has been vividly conveyed to me by the versions I have repeatedly heard from worried parents, and by my mail on the subject. Having only touched on this theme near the end of *The Vanishing Hitchhiker*, I got numerous letters from readers asking about the legends. Typical of many people, a mother in Hinsdale, Illinois, relaying a castrated-boy story she heard in Milwaukee, wrote, "I don't know if this is legend or fact—but I haven't let my 5 year old son go in [to a shopping center restroom] alone yet!"

I have received batches of newspaper clippings from readers about abduction and mutilation rumors, as well as versions sent in missives ranging in style from scrawled postcards to carefully written, detailed letters. A woman in Dallas used her engraved personal-letterhead stationery to report hearing the story told first in Boston and later in Texas. In the latter instance, she said, the legend was used "as an example of rampant deviant homosexual behavior." And in both of her versions the storytellers claimed that the crime had not been reported in the newspapers because it was overly bloody. (Sometimes people say the police or the store involved are suppressing the story in order to avoid hurting business.)

Perhaps the strongest level of concern about the legend was expressed to me in a note from Wharton, New Jersey, neatly hand-written on tinted floral-design stationery. In this standard version—which clashed dramatically with the charming format in which it was sent—a five-or six-year-old boy bleeds to death in a department store restroom after someone has cut off his penis. The writer commented:

> When [my friend] told the story she was so distraught she could hardly get the words out. The co-worker who had told her had cried all day at work. I thanked God a million times I had only one daughter. I repeated the story to everyone I knew, especially those with young sons. But a few months later I repeated it to a friend in Scranton, Pa., who insisted the story was true, but it happened up there by her.
>
> I have believed this bizarre story to be gospel up until now, but I would be grateful if you know it as legend.

I wrote back to her pointing out that, unfortunately, daughters, too, suffer numerous threats in urban legends. But I assured her that the restroom story she had heard was a classic example of an unverifiable, widely told traditional legend. The journalists who have tried to find the sources of these reports of restroom abductions and mutilations have invariably reached dead ends; the folklorists who have studied them have readily located many traditional variants and have identified much earlier prototypes. So, however you look at the stories, they are mostly folklore.

A typical journalistic probe of the 1980 outbreak of "The Mutilated Boy" legend was published by Carol Pogash in the *San Francisco Sunday Examiner & Chronicle* (14 December 1980). In her current example of what she called this "ugly rumor," a five-year-old black boy was castrated by a white man and left to die in an Oakland, California, department store restroom. Pogash recalled that much the same story had also circulated in 1964, but now it had resurfaced "with a switch of races and location." (Sixteen years earlier, she reported, it was a white boy said to have been castrated by blacks in Central Park in New York City.)

What Pogash missed, however, besides the midwestern rash of rumors in the same year, was a 1965 news story about earlier California versions by Paul Coates in the *Los Angeles Times* (20 April). Coates's headline sums up how his research seemed to document the story's spread at that time: "An ugly lie, once nailed here, spreads eastward to Maryland." Let's see now—according to these writers, the story went from California to Maryland, and from New York to California, sometimes switching racial groups along the way. Is that an adequate explanation of how folklore travels and changes? Not if you are going to account for all other versions told in all other years, and in practically every other state of the Union.

These California journalists assumed that whatever specific *earlier* rumor or legend they had uncovered was necessarily the sole source of the *later* version of the same rumor or legend they had heard. But oral tradition (helped along by print and broadcasting) is much more complicated and diverse than this simple linear model suggests. Furthermore, the basic prejudices underlying the restroom legends are much older than these particular modernized plots.

The problem with most news media searches for the sources of legend is that investigative reporters are interested in the truth or falsity of recent accounts of events, rather than the history or meaning of long-enduring traditions. As a result, the news writer's usual technique is to interview knowledgeable (or even not so knowledgeable) people, seeking to elicit quotable quotations, and trying to get back to what may be called the "authentic source" of the story. Folklorists, on the other hand, know from the start that the ultimate sources of legends are long lost, so they proceed by collecting all possible variants, conducting bibliographic searches of the relevant scholarly literature, and trying to compare themes, motifs, and functions of folklore in a larger context than today's news. In other words, journalists naturally tend to seek the immediate story and its "source," while folklorists seek an understanding of the process by which the story developed and spread, hoping thereby to better understand the reasons for its popularity.

But even when a journalist takes a longer view in following up such a legend, the nature of "folklore" is often misunderstood, as indeed it usually is by most people. This is evident in an article titled "Anatomy of a Rumor" by Oliver Pilat in the April, 1965, number of *The Realist*. Pilat began with a version of the familiar story circulating that election-year autumn: *supposedly* a nine-year-old white boy was castrated and left to die, *presumably* by two black youths *said to have been* seen leaving the restroom in which the boy was *allegedly* found in October 1964 at the New York World's Fair (qualifiers and emphasis supplied).

This story was completely false, Pilat asserted: "It was, in fact, propaganda, skillfully devised and artfully disseminated." After diligently trying to trace the story, he found that although journalists, the police, the World's Fair officials, and many ordinary citizens had heard the story, the only detail that had any truth whatever to it was that the World's Fair was indeed going on at the time. Everything else was purely fictional hearsay, despite the fact that, as a Manhattan bus driver told him, "Everybody knows about it. Even the dogs in the street are barking about it!" Recognizing that "Anybody with a real or latent anti-Negro prejudice was likely to respond to some degree," Pilat sought possible motives for circulating such a rumor, and he was determined that the lie should be tracked to its source and its perpetrators exposed.

When Pilat learned that the story was also being told in Washington, D.C., in 1964, he declared, "My mind was made up. . . . I concluded that the public had to deal not with an ordinary epidemic, but with germ warfare, and one quite probably connected with the national election." Eventually he heard the mutilated-boy story from several other parts of the nation, and he became indignant that the "real culprit" behind spreading it had still not been identified. To Pilat, at least, the purpose behind the "propaganda" seemed "transparently clear"—the story of the white boy who was mutilated by blacks had been concocted, he thought, "to stimulate the so-called white backlash in the cities and thereby elect Sen. Barry Goldwater President." In an indignant conclusion to his essay (or is this another of the infamous *Realist* parodies of news reporting?) Pilat demanded a national investigation of the legend "before the propaganda sinks unnoticed, in all its genocidal falsity, into national folklore."

But *folklore*—not just national folklore, but international—is exactly what "The Mutilated Boy" story already was long before then. In fact, another journalist, David J. Jacobson, had provided a well-documented summary of this and other atrocity rumors in history as well as in recent tradition in his 1948 book *The Affairs of Dame Rumor.*

Pilat was absolutely right in pinpointing the racial prejudice underlying the legend as the story's primary theme, but he was dead wrong in thinking that the story was a timely libel invented in 1964 to influence the presidential election. Although "The Mutilated Boy" might have helped to arouse the white-backlash element to some extent in the 1964 elections, it cannot have been originated then by fanatic pro-Goldwater anti-Johnson forces. Instead, the social and political issues being widely discussed at the time may possibly have stimulated the revival of an age-old folk legend.

Without a doubt, the central idea underlying all versions of the restroom legends is a racist or otherwise prejudiced one: certain "other" people—members of a feared minority—are out to get "our" children. In version after version of "The Mutilated Boy" the victims are white and often blonde, while the aggressors are said to be black, Mexican, Indian, homosexual, or "hippie"; and when the victim is black, the killers are white. The attack always comes from members of some outside group, often as part of an alleged ritual or initiation ceremony. In "The Attempted Abduction" legend the criminals are "outsiders" from a large, probably decadent, nearby city, and occasionally they too represent a racial minority. In both legends the intended victims are young and innocent; the nature of the intended attack is to pervert or to eliminate their sexuality. Thus the minority tries to assault uncorrupted representatives of "our" culture at the very point where the culture's future lies.

Barre Toelken in his book *The Dynamics of Folklore* (1979) dubbed this major theme in folk tradition "the international minority conspiracy," and he paraphrased its latent message of "cultural paranoia" like this: "Watch out for those people, they're out to get us and they'll be likely to attack us in the most vulnerable places and most objectionable ways." To which one might add, . . . and they'll also strike without warning in the settings of our simple pleasures (amusement parks and movie theaters) or in our 'safe' middle-class centers of commerce (department stores and shopping centers)."

For generations in Europe the villains in "The Mutilated Boy" legend had been the Jews, and false stories of their alleged ritual torture and murder of Christian children fueled the racial and religious prejudices that led to persecutions of the Jewish people. Florence H. Ridley showed in her article "A Tale Told Too Often" in *Western Folklore* (vol. 26, 1967) that in the fifth century A.D. an historian named Socrates (not the fourth-century B.C. philosopher) gave an account similar to later legends in which, " . . . at Inmestar, in Syria, a group of Jews tortured and murdered a Christian child in mockery of Christ." But folklorist Bill Ellis has shown (*Journal of American Folklore*, 1983) that anti-Christian versions of the story circulated even earlier. He cites extremely graphic accounts of the alleged murders as recorded by Tertullian and by Minucius Felix, Roman lawyers of the second and third centuries A.D., in which supposed Christian initiation rites require the ceremonial murder of a Jewish child.

The reverse treatment of this story, claiming that Jews required an innocent Christian child's blood for their paschal (Passover) ceremonies or for other ritual purposes, became rampant throughout the Middle Ages. The legend survived in oral and printed tradition well into the nineteenth century and was revived by Hitler at the beginning of World War II. Sometimes it was claimed that Jews needed to mix Christian blood into their Passover bread.

Medieval chronicles and books of saints' lives abounded with versions of "The Mutilated Boy" legend, giving lurid details of the Jews' supposed treatment of the child, followed by accounts of bloody revenge taken by Christians against the accused. The influence of folk tradition is strongly evident in these early written instances of the story, while the oral versions themselves emerge to our notice in the classic nineteenth-century collections of folklore. For example, in the Grimm brothers' 1816–18 compilation of German legends from oral tradition, item number 353 is an example of such a story, localized to a particular site. It begins:

The Rock of the Jews

In the year 1462 it came to pass in the village of Rinn in Tyrol that a number of Jews convinced a poor farmer to deliver his own small child over to them in exchange for a large sum of money.

They took the child out into the forest to a large boulder on which they martyred it, killing it in the most wretched fashion. The boulder has been known ever since as the Rock of the Jews. They then took the battered and stabbed body and hung it from a birch tree not far from the bridge.

Donald Ward, translator of the Grimm's legends, points out the irony in the anti-Semitic theme of the European legends, since Christians themselves were the earlier targets of the same legends' lies. Ward writes: "The Romans, probably because they misunderstood the Holy Eucharist, accused the

Christians of practicing blood sacrifice and cannibalism. After all, the Christians themselves claimed that they consumed the blood and flesh of Christ while taking the Holy Eucharist."

The anti-Semitic strain of the legend was particularly popular in medieval England, with the most famous versions attributed by writers then to the deaths of William of Norwich in 1144 and Hugh of Lincoln in 1255. In both cases a devout young boy was rumored to have been kidnapped, tortured, and murdered by Jews as part of their Passover celebration; the body was thrown into a cesspool or a well. This crime, however, according to legend was revealed to the lad's mother by miraculous means, and the accused Jews were punished. The story of Hugh of Lincoln, told in gruesome detail by the thirteenth-century writer Matthew Paris, was also the subject of a British folk ballad that is still sung, called "Sir Hugh, or, the Jew's Daughter." It is number 155 in Francis James Child's great compendium *The English and Scottish Popular Ballads* (1882–83).

In most versions of the ballad, Sir Hugh is said to be playing football with his friends when the ball is accidentally kicked through a window into a Jew's house. Hugh calls to the Jew's daughter, asking her to throw it back, but instead she lures him inside to recover it. There she murders him cruelly, rolls the corpse in a case of lead, and throws it down a deep well. His mother later walks by, calling for him, and Sir Hugh miraculously speaks to her from the bottom of the well, asking her to arrange his funeral. In many variants of the ballad the description of the murder has at least a suggestion of ritual to it, as this scene from an eighteenth-century Scottish text, which sounds somewhat like an altar sacrifice, shows:

> She's laid him on a dressin-board
> Whare she did often dine;
> She stack a penknife to his heart.
> And dressed him like a swine.

> —*Child 155, text D, stanza 8*

Further, many texts describe a basin held to catch the boy's blood as he dies, presumably to be used later in a ritual.

Geoffrey Chaucer's "Prioress's Tale" in *The Canterbury Tales* (composed from about 1387 until his death in 1400) relates "The Mutilated Boy" legend as a religious miracle. A schoolboy who sings a Christian hymn loudly on the streets offends the Jews who hear him, so much so that they hire an assassin to murder him. They throw his body into a privy, wherefrom his voice miraculously issues once again, leading his mother to discover the crime and to secure his corpse for a Christian burial. Although Chaucer had the prioress set her version of the tale in an unnamed Asian city, he clearly had the English tradition of folk legend and ballad in mind, since he has his narrator mention in the concluding stanza "yonge Hugh of Lyncoln, slayn also with cursed Jewes . . . but a litel while ago."

The British ballad of "Sir Hugh" migrated (as did many other folk ballads) to the United States, where it once had a fairly vigorous life in oral tradition. Here, however, the charges against the Jews are invariably replaced by descriptions of a "Jewler's daughter," a "duke's daughter," or a "Gypsy lady" as the culprit; occasionally there is a "fatal flower garden" into which the flowers themselves lure the child and destroy him. Although the child's blood is sometimes still said in the American versions to be caught in a basin, no ritual purpose for it is ever mentioned. With the weakening and loss of the original prejudices that underlay the ballad, the traditional singing of "Sir Hugh" in this country has gradually faded.

While the *ballad* version of "The Mutilated Boy" has mostly disappeared in American folklore, the *legend* treatment of the plot, as we have seen, has flourished. By having the Jews replaced as scapegoats in the modern story by blacks, Mexicans, or other feared urban minority groups, the vicious old story achieved a new life. Despite these changes in specific stereotypes and prejudices, however, it is remarkable how stable some of the plot elements remain: the mother still searches for her lost child; the crime is still bloody and cruel; there is still a suspicion of a ritual purpose (initiation) behind the crime, and the locale mentioned is now a restroom rather than a cesspool or a well.

It appears that "The Attempted Abduction" variation of the restroom legend is a later development than "The Mutilated Boy," although both preserve the theme of the innocent child assaulted by outsiders. A possible offshoot of these legends is another, heard less frequently, concerning a woman who encounters a robber in the dressing room of a department store. In order to steal her diamond ring or gold wedding band, the robber cuts off her finger. (Sometimes she bleeds to death in the dressing room or on the way to the hospital.)

I have recently noted four special developments of the legends discussed in this section. First, in a Middle Eastern counterpart of the American "Goldilocks on the Oregon Trail" legend (Indian chief tries to barter horses for a young blonde pioneer girl), a Scandinavian tourist's daughter is supposedly bid for by an Arab sheik who uses camels as his offer. Second, in a Turkish setting, the story is told of a beautiful Western female traveler who disappears from her tour party; later her clothes are found for sale in a large Istanbul bazaar. Third, two Western tourists camping out in Afghanistan are found the next morning by their companion to have had their heads cut off while they slept in sleeping bags and the heads switched with the bodies. And fourth, in a London setting, a wealthy Arab, according to legend, agrees to pay 60,000 pounds for an English beauty's favors for just one night. She accepts the offer, and he pays her with 30,000 pounds cash in small bills stowed in each of two shopping bags from Harrod's department store. Here, then, are four more instances of recent legendary abduction stories involving dark minorities who are said to be lusting after our fair women.

Unfortunate-Pet Legends:
"The Bump in the Rug"
"The Dog's Dinner"
"The Dog in the Highrise"

Sometimes, when the victim in an urban horror legend is a pet rather than a person, the telling of the story elicits grins instead of shocked outrage or pity. A tragic plot is converted to comedy in these instances both because of the subject matter—after all, it's only an animal—and because of the feeling that the plausible event that is described probably did not happen. Especially if one becomes aware of variants of the tale, then no matter how horrible the story may be it is told and accepted as a mere joke. The unfortunate-pet legends also remind us of the harmless acts of mock violence that animal characters in movie cartoons and comic books inflict on one another: when it's Tom vs. Jerry, Roadrunner vs. Coyote, or Woody Woodpecker vs. Everybody, then everybody thinks the pratfalls and explosions are hilarious. These plots are "funny" because they are about make-believe animals in pretended conflicts, and because we have seen the same stories in slightly different versions many times before. The difference is that the cartoon animals survive, but the pets in legends usually do not.

Here is such a legend, "The Bump in the Rug," from folk tradition, just as a student of mine was told it by his father, and as the father had heard it from a former co-worker in the carpet business:

It was about twenty-five years ago a guy I used to work with, Jimmy Turner, told a bunch of people who worked at the store about a funny thing that had happened to him a few years earlier when he was working for another store [laying carpet]. He had finished his job and was cleaning up when he noticed a large lump in the middle of the room. So he got his hammer and pounded it down. The next day the lady he did the job for called and said that her favorite pet canary was missing and she was wondering if he had seen it.

At first, the student said, there was no reason to disbelieve the story, since his father said he had heard it told in the first person. But later, not only his father but his brother-in-law, another carpet layer, mentioned having heard other versions of the same event. Then, sometime after that, the student said he saw a similar story published in *Reader's Digest.*

"The Bump in the Rug" may or may not have been in *Reader's Digest* (I haven't found it there), but it certainly has had both printed and oral circulation for some time. A reader in St. Louis, Missouri, sent me an unidentified clipping "found in somebody's house organ some fifteen years ago" recounting essentially the same story. This time the carpet layer thinks he has dropped his pack of cigarettes while working on the carpet, and he pounds down the lump with a two-by-four. Later, while he is putting his tools into his truck, the woman asks if he has seen her parakeet, and just then he spots his cigarettes lying on the dashboard. In other versions of the story, known in England as well as the United States, the lost pet may be a hamster or a mouse. Sometimes the pet's loss is explained when a blood stain shows up on the rug and it has to be taken up.

Another nonanimal rug-bump story is told about a honeymooning couple who fear that their friends may spring some terrible prank on them. The newlyweds are in their hotel room ready to retire. Searching the room carefully for any clue to a trick, they find a lump in the rug under their bed. Uncovering this, they find a large metal bolt, which they unscrew, with the notion that it may be a microphone placed there to record the sounds of their wedding night. They sleep peacefully then; but the next morning the desk clerk asks if they heard the commotion early last evening when a large chandelier fell from the ceiling in the room just below, landing on another couple's bed. In a variant of this story, United States government officials on assignment in Moscow unscrew from the floor of their hotel room what they think is the "bug" hidden in the room by the police; this sends the chandelier below crashing to the floor, and the accident nearly sets off an international incident.

Speaking of international incidents, and moving on to another unfortunate-pet legend, here is an authentic news story that was circulated by Reuters in August 1971, and not for the first or last time, either:

> Zurich—A Swiss couple fled home from Hong Kong after their pet poodle, Rosa, was cooked and served to them garnished with pepper sauce and bamboo shoots at a Chinese restaurant.
>
> Hans and Erna W., who asked the Zurich newspaper Blick not to publish their full names, said they took Rosa with them to the restaurant and asked a waiter to give her something to eat.
>
> The waiter had trouble understanding the couple but eventually picked up the dog and carried her to the kitchen where they thought she would be fed.
>
> Eventually the waiter returned carrying a dish. When the couple removed the silver lid they found Rosa.
>
> They told the paper they suffered nervous collapse and returned to Zurich immediately.

Herb Caen had some fun picking that story apart when it was printed on page one of his own newspaper, the *San Francisco Chronicle*. First he noted the suspicious fact that the couple didn't want their names published; then he quoted a spokesman for the Hong Kong Tourist Association who pointed out that pets are quarantined for six months before entering Hong Kong. Finally, Caen proposed such names for the legend as "The Chinese Poodle Story," "Chow Mein," or "The Swiss Charred Poodle."

Oddly enough, writer John Train, who is characterized in a Preface as "a stickler for the facts, with a horror of the inaccurate," fell for "The Dog's Dinner" story—bamboo shoots, silver dish, and all—and published it in his book titled *True Remarkable Ocurrences* (p. 60) with the sole documentation "Reuter." His apparent assumption that a story circulated by news services and published by daily papers must be true seems naïve to the extreme; but, since Train was president of the *Harvard Lampoon* in his university days, perhaps we may suspect that he is not quite as believing as all that.

"Roast Rosa," as some newspapers have headlined the story, is, of course, an outrageously silly urban legend. Usually the old couple is traveling in Asia, typically Hong Kong, and their dog may be a poodle or a Chihuahua. Their sign language to the waiter may include pointing to their mouths and then to the dog; the waiter smiles, nods, and takes the doggie off to the kitchen. (Sometimes it is said that the dog was air sick on the way over and thus is especially hungry.) The serving arrangements for the pet include being presented to the diners under glass, on a bed of rice, with its own jeweled collar in its mouth, and (my favorite recipe for Rosa) with an apple in its mouth and parsley sprigs stuck in its ears. The shock of the whole grisly experience may be said to have killed the old couple.

The idea behind "The Dog's Dinner," of course, is that Orientals in general, and Chinese in particular, relish dogs as food. This notion—based on a slender thread of fact—contributes in turn to various rumors and legends about Oriental restaurants serving dog (or cat) meat, and legends about Asian immigrants in the United States capturing and cooking people's pets (see Chapter 4).

One more unfortunate pet, "The Dog in the Highrise," and then I'll stop. The urban folk character Truman Capote is said to have told this one on "The Tonight Show" as a true story. (A spokesman for Carson Productions wrote me in February 1983, "we cannot verify" the legend, which presumably means that the telling of it never happened.) But except for allegedly being related by one celebrity to another with zillions of people watching on late-night television, the performance of the legend by Capote—had it ever occurred—would have been essentially no different from when many people pass the same story on simply as the experience of our old acquaintance, the friend of a friend. Here's my own version of the story as I have often heard it:

> A young man in New York City has a date with a woman he has recently met at a party; she lives in a plush highrise apartment forty or so floors above the street. He arrives a bit early, and she is not quite ready to go; so while he is waiting for her to come out of the bedroom, he begins to toss a ball for her friendly dog which is frolicking around. Each toss of the ball goes a little further, and each time the dog dashes after it and retrieves it for another toss. Then, unintentionally, the young man gives the ball an extra-hard toss, and it bounces out an open window (or onto the balcony and over the rail) to the street below. The dog leaps right out after it.

After telling it, someone wrote to me, Truman Capote "wanted to know how his friend could possibly break the news to his date." In this version (which I suspect Capote told on *some* talk show or other) the woman came out a few minutes later, called "Bye-bye" to her pet ("He's hiding around here somewhere"), and off the couple went. But the way *I* heard the end of it, later on in the evening the young man just mumbled something like, "I thought your dog seemed a little depressed tonight," and then he hoped for the best.

Medical Horror Legends:
Malpractice
"The Proctological Examination"
"The Relative's Cadaver"

Whatever advances in techniques and successes of operations that modern medical science can claim (including implantation of the first artificial heart in a human being at my own university in 1982), most people still seem to harbor a lurking fear of illnesses, doctors, and hospitals. A cycle of ghastly medical horror stories, told—as usual—as true, reflects these concerns. Murphy's Law usually operates (if you will pardon the expression): if anything can go wrong here, it will.

Medical horror legends often describe supposed authentic instances of malpractice in which a friend of a friend suffered some kind of sad reversal, often literally. The wrong limb was amputated, or the wrong baby was sent home from the hospital, or even the wrong patient was treated. A simple flopped X-ray (a nearly impossible occurrence), and the wrong lung or the wrong kidney was removed, so the patient dies. In a medical horror legend with a semi-happy ending, a beautiful young girl named Annie died for lack of anyone properly trained in CPR (cardio-pulmonary resuscitation) techniques to save her life. So her wealthy father financed the development of a life-like practice dummy for CPR training, stipulating that the face on the model should be that of his beloved daughter and that all the future dummies made on this design should be known as "Annies" in her honor.

References to fat farms and plastic surgery—two health and happiness luxuries of the wealthy—combine in a medical legend told to me recently backstage in a television studio in New York City. It seems that an overweight customer of a reducing retreat lost so much ugly fat while she was on their diet and exercise program that she had her plastic surgeon take some tucks here and there on her stretched-out body to firm things up again. Then, unfortunately, she slipped off her diet, regained all the flab, and burst through her new tighter skin and died.

A similar medical motif occurs in another gruesome tale I call "The Proctological Examination." (I heard this one first on a Houston, Texas, radio talk show.) The patient is undergoing an examination during which the specialist must insert a probe with a small electric light on it into the rectum. Supposedly a spark from a loose connection ignites the intestinal gasses, and the patient explodes (more about exploding people in Chapter 4).

Medical students, at least in folklore, are notorious for grisly jokes with sometimes tragic results. The classic story in this category concerns body parts removed from cadavers in the anatomy lab and then hidden in roommates' belongings or dangled from a shade pull or a light switch. The standard conclusion is that the shocked victim is later found gnawing on the hand or arm, with his or her hair turned snow-white overnight from the scare. I pass over these medical collegiate-gag tales lightly, since they are more a part of academic folklore than of the general run of urban legends. One medical school legend, however, does have wider distribution and deserves more discussion here; this is the one about a relative's cadaver that turns up for a student's dissection subject.

Probably many readers of the daily press were as amazed as I was in mid-April 1982 to find this unlikely event reported as a news item. I quote from the *Deseret News* (16 April 1982) of Salt Lake City, but many other papers picked it up as well:

CADAVER HAD FAMILIAR LOOK

A young medical student knew her great aunt planned to donate her body to science but was shocked to discover the woman among cadavers assigned to her anatomy class.

The great aunt's body—shipped to the laboratory at the University of Alabama School of Medicine in Birmingham from out of state—was removed from the class, the Journal of the American Medical Association reported Thursday.

"A student informed the director that the distinct possibility existed that one of the cadavers (not the one she was dissecting) was a great aunt," two medical school staff members wrote in a letter to the editor.

The student met with her instructor before the second day of laboratory work and it "was ascertained that the cadaver was indeed her great aunt," wrote Dr. Clarence E. McDanal Jr., and E. George Salter Jr.

The letter referred to in the news story, as it appeared in the *Journal of the American Medical Association* on 16 April 1982 (vol. 247, no. 15, p. 2096), expressed the doctors' own amazement at the coincidence: "What is the percentage," they wrote, "of a student's encountering a relative in the form of a cadaver in a gross anatomy laboratory? Such an event may occur in a science fiction novel or it may be the theme of a television production. . . ." Or, they might have added, it may be the subject of folk legends.

The Alabama medical school incident *did* occur; I have Dr. Salter's signed testimony, though he declined to comment further on the event after it attracted the attention of the media, so as not to jeopardize the cadaver donor program. (Among others, the science fiction magazine *Omni* publicized the story [in November 1982], adding a staged photograph of a gowned med student reacting with horror, and a slightly doctored quotation from Dr. McDanal.) And evidently similar coincidences have occasionally occurred before: for example, an English doctor wrote me that *World Medicine* had reported in 1973 that in a New Delhi, India, teaching hospital, student Jawahir Singh at his first dissecting class shouted out, "Stop! That's my mother" and fainted. It turned out that there had been a mix-up at the local mortuary. But we must assume that the many anonymous reports of such things in oral tradition supposedly happening are medical horror legends, not descriptions of personal experiences. The foaf in the anatomy lab, so to speak.

A folklore student's 1973 term paper written at the University of New Orleans on "The Oral Tradition of the Physician" contains two anonymous tellings of the folk version that are typically vague and varying:

1. A couple of years ago, a guy had gone to anatomy class on the first day of school. When he pulled open the box, there was his mother! She'd been missing for a couple of weeks.

2. This happened just a while ago. But the cadaver was the guy's father. His parents were divorced, and he hadn't seen his father in years.

While it might seem that the above 1973 tellings could have been inspired by news reports of the New Delhi incident, "The Relative's Cadaver" as a folk legend is a much older story. The most famous attachment of it to a known personage involves the English novelist Laurence Sterne (author of *Tristram Shandy*), who died in 1768. Sterne ended his life in somewhat reduced circumstances, and his body was interred in a poorly kept graveyard in an obscure part of London; he was attended, legend says, only by "two gentlemen." Executed criminals were sometimes also buried there, and grave robbers were known to have been active in the same cemetery during the previous year. These facts must have encouraged the wild story that soon raced around London that Sterne's friend John Hall-Stevenson published as the truth the year after the author's death; however, he later admitted that the story was unverifiable. Biographer Percy Fitzgerald repeated a suitably folksy version of it in his *Life of Laurence Sterne* in 1896:

> Now follows that strange and ghastly scene, at which the meagre figure of poor Yorick [a pen name Sterne sometimes used], upon which he and others were so often merry, was to make a last appearance.
> When the 'two gentlemen' were seeing the earth laid upon their friend's remains, there were other and more profane eyes watching from the road, and marking the spot. At that time the tribe of resurrection men pursued their calling as lawlessly as highwaymen did theirs upon the road. And this 'new Tyburn burying-ground' had already acquired a notoriety, as being the scene of constant outrages of this kind. . . .
> Two nights after, on the 24th, the men came, dug up the body, placed it in a case, and sent it away down to Cambridge.
> 'Mr. Collignon, B.M.,' of Trinity, was then Professor of

Anatomy, and it had been disposed of to him. These aids to medical science being costly, and procured with difficulty, Mr. Collignon invited some friends to see him illustrate anatomy on the body that had been sent down to him from London; and an old friend of Mr. Sterne, who was of the party, was inexpressibly shocked at recognising the familiar features, and fainted away on the spot.

Fitzgerald wrote that "the evidence on which the story is founded seems too convincing not to be accepted," and he cited several friends-of-friends who believed it to be true, all of them, of course, long dead by the century after Sterne's passing. Wilbur L. Cross, of Yale, in his standard work *The Life and Times of Laurence Sterne* (1909), pointed out the discrepancy even in Hall-Stevenson's early account of claiming that Oxford rather than Cambridge was where the dissection took place; but Cross still insisted that "The ghastly tale . . . may be accepted as essentially true." He cited a source who claimed to have received the story "directly from one of the gentlemen who was present at the dissection." Everywhere you look, more foafs!

A recent critic/historian, David Thomson, in *Wild Excursions: The Life and Fiction of Laurence Sterne* (1972) reexamined closely all of the evidence for the story of Sterne's body ending up on the dissecting table, plus the attendant legend that his skull was preserved by the doctors at Cambridge. Thomson concluded that these were nothing more than folk rumors of the time turned into academic anecdotes of the biographers. As another investigator had once put it (see *This is Lorence: A Narrative of the Reverend Laurence Sterne*, by Lodwick Hartley [1943], "The complete disappearance of everything but the tradition should naturally cause the story to be treated with the greatest skepticism." Just remember that statement if someone tells you "The Relative's Cadaver," unless, of course, the teller happens to be a doctor or a student who was *there*.

4

More Dreadful Contaminations

"The Death of Little Mikey"

This is a true story. When I was flying to New York City recently, I found myself seated next to a native New Yorker who was returning home from a western vacation, age about fourteen. The boy's father was napping, so my seatmate turned to me for conversation. "Why are you going to New York?" he asked. I explained that I had written a book about modern folklore, and I was going to be interviewed on a television news program the next morning. "What's modern folklore?" he wanted to know, so I put a copy of *The Vanishing Hitchhiker* in his hands, remarking that he probably knew lots of these stories himself.

He leafed through the pages, reading a title or a story here and there, but he never seemed to find an urban legend that he had heard of. Then in the chapter "Dreadful Contaminations"—amid the Kentucky Fried rats, spiders in hairdos, and other nasties, he spotted this reference to the effervescent candy called Pop Rocks: "A few Pop Rocks (sometimes an entire package), according to the typical story, were swallowed whole and the internal fizzing killed a child." The boy snapped the book shut (no reader, he), handed it back to me, and asked, "Do you know how little Mikey died?"

"No, how?" I responded, remembering Rule 1 of good

fieldwork: "Always let your informant tell his story, whether you know the punchline or not." And so I was told—somewhere over Nebraska, I believe it was—about how that cute little boy, Mikey, the one who eats a bowlful of an unfamiliar cereal without saying a word in the Life Cereal television commercials, had swallowed a handful of Pop Rocks, then taken a drink of soda pop, and his stomach had exploded.

"Now *that's* an urban legend, and a good example of modern folklore," I declared smugly, "so you did know one of my stories after all."

"You mean that little Mikey *didn't* die from eating Pop Rocks?" my new little New York buddy asked in disbelief. "Of course he didn't," I explained in my best professorial manner. "There's not a bit of truth to that silly story."

"OK, then [understood: 'smart guy'], how *did* he die?" the boy snorted, and I had to confess, he had me there.

"The Death of Little Mikey" is a perfect combination of a celebrity death rumor (e.g., Jerry Mathers, who played Beaver on the TV series "Leave it to Beaver," was supposed to have died in Vietnam), and a Dreadful Contamination story (e.g., something icky is *in* us, or *on* us). The beauty of it is that no one can prove a thing, since Mikey is an ad writer's invention acted out by a freckle-faced child actor whose name we don't know and who is seen (but not heard, since he has no lines in the ad) by television viewers. So who's to say he didn't die from eating Pop Rocks, smart guy?

The Little Mikey story has its variants that most kids seem to know: that Pop Rocks contained some illegal drug, that there were spider eggs in them (like in Bubble Yum, you know), that the same thing would happen if you swallowed an Alka-Seltzer tablet, that the candy was declared illegal by the government, that the company reformulated the candy so they would no longer "pop," and so forth. Despite the fact that Pop Rocks are no longer manufactured, the stories linger on.

Here's the real scoop on Pop Rocks. Invented in 1956 by General Foods research scientist William A. Mitchell, these "carbonated candy crystals that crackle on the tongue" (as *People* magazine described them) were first marketed in 1974. But despite being available only in California and a few other selected areas, Pop Rocks sold more than 500 million packages in the first five years. *Time* reported in 1978 that "Kids are like junkies—hungry for the stuff," and that truckloads of Pop Rocks were being conveyed to New York, where the street price could be double the store price of twenty to twenty-five cents a package. (By 1979, *People* reported, bootleg prices were up to $1.00.)

But the rumor that some child who had eaten a package or more and then drunk a carbonated soft drink had exploded seemed to spread as fast as the taste for Pop Rocks themselves. (Maybe the kids just like to live dangerously.) Despite General Foods running full-page advertising in some forty-five major newspapers, writing some 50,000 letters to school principals, and sending inventor Mitchell on the road to explain that Pop Rocks generate less gas than half a can of soda pop and could induce nothing worse in a person's body than a healthy burp, the story continued to spread.

For a single full-page ad in the Sunday [4 February 1979] *New York Times,* the company paid $18,240, according to a front-page story in the *Wall Street Journal* two days later. The ad itself was a masterpiece of corporate image-boosting. Addressed to "Dear Mom and Dad" and presented as an open letter to parents from the candy's inventor (father of seven children and grandfather of fourteen), the copy merely alluded to "wild rumors" without actually specifying any. William Mitchell was shown in a photo surrounded by five happy children, and the letter was concluded in a folksy manner: "You know, you hear a lot of people talk about how 'serious' business is, that people who work for big corporations don't have very much 'fun.' Well, 'Pop Rocks' is a proof that this isn't so. This is a fun product."

But the legend survived, now attached to a particular child, and Pop Rocks did not. Readers of the *Times* ad were invited to "drop [Mitchell] a line"; when I wrote to General Foods in 1983 asking about Pop Rocks, I got only a printed form in reply, saying, "We're sorry to tell you that the product you asked about is no longer being produced." And, just to complete the record, Quaker Oats Company, manufacturers of Life Cereal, confirm that "Little Mikey" is alive.*

As with adult legend-tellers, children who transmit the Pop Rocks story may cite a supposedly reliable source for it. For example, here is the experience that legend-sleuth Gary Alan Fine, a sociologist at the University of Minnesota, described in a paper on preadolescent legends published in 1979:

> . . . a player [on a boy's baseball team] informed me that he had read an article in a medical journal which his mother had brought home from the hospital where she worked about Pop Rocks causing death. He assured me that the report was about a boy who had died from eating too many Pop Rocks, and promised that the following day he would bring a copy.
> . . . I waited with anticipation. The following day he brought an article which his mother had picked up at the hospital. However, this story in the June 13, 1977, issue of *Newsweek* made no mention of any death or injury from Pop Rocks, but did mention that some parents were needlessly concerned about possible danger.

The references made by some narrators to Alka-Seltzer tablets seem to link the Mikey story to an earlier exploding-body legend (and we should also recall "The Proctological Examination" in Chapter 3). I am endebted to Robert I. Sutton, a research associate in psychology with the Institute for Social Research at the University of Michigan, for sending me

---

*In an article on corporate rumors and legends in *The Kansas City Star* (23 June 1983; section B, pages 1 and 3) staff writer Brian Burnes quotes Marcia Watts, manager of corporate communications for Quaker Oats, saying that the actor who played "Little Mikey" was three years old when the commercial was filmed in 1971. His name is John Gilchrist, and he is definitely alive.

this similar version—applied to an animal—that was told to him about 1972 by a sailor stationed at the Alameda (California) Naval Air Station:

Have you heard about those crazy sailors over at Alameda? Well, it seems that they get awful bored during the endless drilling that they are forced to do as part of their training. I hear that this one fellow has found a way to entertain himself and his buddies while they are drilling. Last week, he brought some Alka-Seltzer with him to marching drill and threw some tablets at a bunch of those seagulls that populate the base. It seems that one of the seagulls ate a tablet. After it ate the tablet, it took off—I bet it was feeling real weird. The damn bird started getting bigger and bigger until its guts exploded and the bird crashed on the ground. The sailors in formation thought it was the funniest thing they had ever seen—they started laughing so hard that they all started rolling on the ground. Boy, did they catch hell!"

"Bosom-Serpent" Legends

The idea of some dangerous, potentially fatal, foreign element getting inside a human body is a common one in urban legends. But the notion of Pop Rocks reacting with soda pop and then going "pop!" inside and killing the victim is only the latest commercial version of an old theme.

In traditional European folklore a frequent example of a similar idea is the story of the so-called bosom serpent in which a snake, frog, or lizard infests a human body. In old Irish legends, for example, where this motif (B784. *Animal lives in person's stomach*) was common, a farmer might get a snake inside him by drinking some milk and then lying on the ground to nap; the snake (with a supposed affinity for milk) would creep into his mouth and slither down his gullet. The best way to get it out again was thought to be by placing a bowl of milk nearby and having the sufferer lie still with his mouth open, waiting for the snake to smell the food and crawl forth.

In a counterpart legend in modern American folklore, a woman tourist falls asleep on a Mexican beach, and a spider bites into her arm and lays an egg there. (In English versions it is a vacationer on a Spanish or other southern beach.) This time, rather than luring the hatched creature out again, the resulting boil on her arm or leg eventually must be lanced, whereupon hundreds of tiny spiders come running out.

The "bosom-serpent" legend was known early in this country both to Nathaniel Hawthorne (who based a short story on it in 1843) and to Henry David Thoreau (who entered it into his journal in 1851); and it has frequently been relocalized and retold in American folklore. Here is a typical older oral version published in the *Hoosier Folklore Bulletin* in 1943, as it was remembered by an Indiana University student who heard it told at a summer camp in New York State:

> Two fellows went out on a hike one day, and they had their canteens full of water. It wasn't long until they ran out of water and began searching for some stream, for they got very thirsty. They came upon a stream finally, and one of the boys bent down to take a drink. Well, he took this drink and jumped up very suddenly, exclaiming that he had swallowed something solid. Looking down, the boys discovered that there was a bed of snake eggs there. They didn't think much of this and after the day's hiking was over they went home. About a year later the boy who had said he had swallowed something solid, developed an enormous appetite, but remained constantly weak. Finally his mother said that something ought to be done about this, so she took him to a doctor. Well, the doctor examined him, and then decided to pump his stomach. The boy was very much surprised when the doctor pumped a ten foot snake from his stomach.

Some kind of egg ingested from moving water was the form in which Thoreau knew the story. He had written, with a metaphorical application in mind, "How many ova have I swallowed? Who knows what will be hatched within me? . . . The man must not drink of the running streams, the living waters, who is not prepared to have all nature reborn in him,—to suckle monsters."

The fear of getting something alive inside you from drinking unsafe or moving water is still found in folklore, as in the current notion that drinking from a garden hose may give you worms. Another continuing taboo is sleeping on the ground: the insects called "earwigs," they say, will creep into your ears. What "they" do not know, however, is that the name "earwig" is probably directly derived from the ancient folk acceptance of this fallacious notion, and that this particular little insect is no more likely to enter ears than are any other small creatures. (Another suggested etymology for "earwig" is that since its wing is vaguely ear-shaped, the name is a corruption of "earwing.")

An ingenious variation of the earwig story has the doctor finally extracting the insect from the ear on the *opposite* side of the victim's head and then exclaiming in horror when he examines it, "Good God, this is a *female* earwig!" (Doctors commonly study entomology in college so as to be ready for just such an emergency.) On the rare occasion when an earwig does enter someone's ear, it may merit a news story: an item circulated by the Associated Press in late August 1982, when there was a real infestation of earwigs in the Boise, Idaho, area, described the case of Boisean Janet Ward, who had suffered great pain and distress from having an earwig creep into her ear in 1971. And they were still talking about it in Boise eleven years later!

The dreadful idea of something entering the body, contaminating it, perhaps multiplying there, and either having to be gotten out or else *bursting* out (as in the film *Alien*) is enough to give you nightmares; and perhaps some of these stories simply stem from bad dreams brought on by overindulging, and that awful "full feeling" that results.

On a psychological level, however, it is hard *not* to perceive these legends also as representing pregnancy fantasies, expressions of subconscious horror at the idea of impregnation and childbirth. A persistent form of the story even makes specific reference to pregnancy, as if to validate that interpretation of the larger general body of "bosom-serpent" traditions. Back in 1948 David J. Jacobson discussed both common forms of this variation in his book *The Affairs of Dame Rumor:* the woman who hatches an octopus egg inside her body, and the girl who becomes pregnant from swimming in the same pool with men.

No matter how you look at it, most of the legends of this kind seem to deal with sex and impregnation—if not literally, then through the symbolisms of the fluid medium, the body-within-a-body, and the obviously phallic image of the penetrating snake. In the following recent version from the California coast we have all of these themes, but with the tentacles of an octopus multiplying the snakey-symbol eightfold. (The traditional folk motif underlying the story is B784.1.4. *Girl swallows frog spawn; an octopus grows inside her with tentacles reaching to every part of her body,* but don't ask me how frog eggs hatch octopi):

> This teen age girl, growing up in a California coastal town, was obviously pregnant—stomach starting to swell, morning sickness, etc. She, however, tearfully insisted to her mother that she couldn't possibly be pregnant. She had never "done it" with a boy and it just wasn't possible.
>
> As time went on, however, the signs continued. Her stomach continued to grow, her appetite increased, and so forth. Her mother insisted she was pregnant. The family doctor insisted she was pregnant. The girl insisted it wasn't possible. She was still a "good" girl.
>
> Finally x-rays were taken and the girl was vindicated. She had a large tumor in her stomach and surgery was performed immediately. To everyone's amazement the sur-

geons removed, not a tumor, but a small, live octopus that had fastened itself to the lining of the girl's stomach.

What happened to this girl supposedly is really possible. Octopus eggs are microscopic in size and laid in clusters of tens of thousands. They are usually affixed to kelp at the ocean bottom by a sticky secretion. It is not beyond the realm of possibility that a few could escape and float to the surface where they could be swallowed by an unsuspecting swimmer. . . . Anyway, don't scoff, because the girl was a close friend of my older brother's girlfriend. (Text courtesy of Thomas M. Brown of Woodland Hills, California.)

Perhaps the ultimate merging of the old creature-in-body contamination legends with a modern theme of urban legends is represented in this text from Baker's *Hoosier Folk Legends* of a "bosom-serpent" story, complete with the luring-out motif but combined now with a business ripoff theme:

A few years ago there was a company who put out sure-fire diet pills, guaranteed to lose weight in no time. People began to take these pills, and in no time the people were losing weight. After a few weeks these people began to lose too much weight. So the government investigated. They opened the pills and found the head of a tapeworm. Tapeworms are hard to get rid of. They had the person starve himself for days. Then they set a bowl of hot milk in front of the person. He had to keep his mouth open. After a while the tapeworm began to come up his throat 'cause he smelled the milk. They kept moving the bowl further away until the tapeworm was completely out.

In a variation of this story, related by Elizabeth Tucker in her article on wonder-diet folklore, there seems to be a specifically sexual suggestion in the particular circumstance in which the infestation is discovered:

A young woman had tried all kinds of diets that didn't work, and finally she decided to try diet pills. They made her lose so much weight all at once that she was really happy. Then one night, when she was lying in bed with her husband, a tapeworm crawled right out of her nose. It had made her sick and caused her to lose so much weight all of a sudden.

"The Poison Dress"

A dreadful contamination of the body via unclean clothing rather than from the bites of insects or the swallowed eggs of reptiles—and always leading to a horrible death—was the subject of a gruesome legend popular in American folklore of the 1930s and 1940s and still heard occasionally today. Here is the earliest version of it that I have found published in a folklore journal (*Hoosier Folklore Bulletin* in 1945), but other sources mention hearing the story a decade or so before:

> Recently there was a certain story spreading over the entire Midwest which took everyone by storm. It seems there was a banquet at a prominent hotel in a certain city. One particular girl who was going decided it was important enough to have a new dress. She bought one at a local department store, a simple but exquisite gown. At the dance after the dinner, her escort noticed a peculiar odor while they were dancing. She had been feeling faint, and she believed it was the odor. She thought the dye in the dress had faded; so she went to the washroom and took off the dress. There was nothing wrong; so she went back to the dance again. However, she felt more faint, and the odor still remained. She thought she had better sit down, and on the way back to their table, she fainted. Her escort took her home, and called a doctor. She died before he got there. The boy explained about the odor, and the doctor investigated the dress and found that the dress had a familiar odor. He ordered an autopsy, and they discovered that the girl had formaldehyde in her veins. The drug had coaglated her blood, and had stopped the flow.
>
> They investigated the department store where she had

bought the dress and learned that the dress had been sold for a corpse and had been returned and sold to the girl. When she perspired and her pores opened, she took in the formaldehyde which killed her.

The midwestern cities in which this incident allegedly happened included Chicago, Cincinnati, and Indianapolis. Generally the "prominent hotel" as well as the "local department store" (also an elegant one) were named. Sometimes the formaldehyde was said to have closed the girl's pores, causing her death; other times the stories specified that embalmer's fluid permeating the dress had painfully killed her by embalming her alive. Almost always the girl became ill first at a dance at which she wore her new (usually white) dress. The mysterious odor emanating from the dress is a standard motif in these legends, and frequently the original user of the dress was said to have been a Negro, while the girl who is killed by it was white.

The guilty parties involved in the story were claimed to have been either the store officials, who had accepted the used garment back for resale, or an unscrupulous mortician who was switching dresses on corpses and selling the better garments while burying his clients in inferior ones. (Occasionally the mortician was blameless: he had simply put the wrong dress on a corpse first, corrected his error, and then returned the first-used one to the family.) Often it was claimed that the store, the hotel, or the mortician had paid off the victim's family in order to keep the terrible story from the press.

Baughman has assigned the modern "Poison Dress" legend motif number Z551., but the essential concept of the poisoned garment is found in Greek mythology. The classic instance of it there sounds remarkably like the modern legend. Hercules, the old story begins, was married to Deianira. When a centaur named Nessus tried to abduct his wife, Hercules slew him with an arrow. In his death throes, however, Nessus told Deianira to keep a vial of his blood as a love charm. Later, when

Deianira became jealous of a young woman whom Hercules had captured, she soaked a new robe of her husband's in the blood of Nessus. When Hercules put it on and the garment became warm, the robe burned his flesh, and the pain was excruciating. When he tried to rip the poisoned robe from his body, pieces of flesh came away with the material, and Hercules demanded to be placed upon a funeral pyre, where he died consumed by the flames (Motif D1402.5. *Nessus shirt. Magic shirt burns wearer up*).

We cannot know for certain that "The Poison Dress" legend descends directly from the Greek myth, but it certainly matches the horror of the ancient story in an updated form. Even the source of the poison from a dying creature of another race seems to match the modern legend. In the recent tellings, the legend continues to incorporate modern ideas. For example, note the modern cosmetic touch in this 1970 telling given in *Hoosier Folk Legends:*

> A local woman shaved her armpits and went shopping. She bought a dress, and when she wore it the first time got terribly sick and died. When the family checked into it and an autopsy was performed they found a colored family bought the dress and used it on a dead relative. Embalming fluid had seeped out onto the dress. After they had her laid out for showing, they returned the dress to the store and got their money back. When this woman who had recently shaved wore the dress the embalming fluid in the dress penetrated her skin and killed her.

"The Corpse in the Cask"

In *The Vanishing Hitchhiker,* while discussing "The Runaway Grandmother" legend, I touched on two grotesque variants of this missing-corpse story that involved an unwitting act of cannibalism. In the modern version, Grandmother's corpse was cremated when she died abroad, but her ashes were mistaken by her relatives, to whom they were shipped to be buried, for curry powder, or some other condiment, and they were eaten sprinkled over a casserole. In a much older treatment of the same theme (from the Renaissance), a Jew's body was pickled in spices and honey for illegal shipment home to Italy, and on the way there parts of the corpse were taken from the jar by gentile strangers—thinking them to be some food specialty—and eaten.

Still another variation of this particular dreadful-contamination legend fits in nicely here among the similar stomach-turning tales we are surveying.

Like the legend about Little Mikey and the Pop Rocks, as well as the "bosom-serpent" stories, this narrative involves getting something awful inside you—swallowing the unthinkable glop. Like "The Poison Dress," this narrative includes references to a fluid preservative and to a corpse. And I've already warned you that something close to unwitting cannibalism is involved; so it all adds up to a perfectly ghastly legend, which has *got* to be a legend, since it's too bad to be true.

The authentic historical background for "The Corpse in the Cask" legend is that in the days before refrigeration or other effective meat-preservation techniques, persons who died far away from home were either buried where they perished, or else they had to be preserved in the only way available—usually immersed in a barrel of alcohol—for shipment back home. This became standard procedure for Europeans who were trading, exploring, or waging war abroad, provided that the deceased was a prominent enough person to merit such special efforts. Inevitably, then, rumors arose that somewhere along the way some of the preserving fluid was inadvertently drunk. Hence, the legend of "The Corpse in the Cask."

Probably the most famous occurrence of this story is the one that became attached to *the* British naval hero of all British naval heroes, Admiral Horatio Nelson. After Lord Nelson fell at the Battle of Trafalgar in 1805, his body was placed in a barrel of brandy (not rum, as folklore sometimes has it) for shipment home. At Gibralter the fluid was replaced with wine. But, according to hearsay, when the barrel was opened in England, it was noted that it was considerably less than full; and thus the story arose that sailors aboard the ship *Victory* had sipped off some of the preserving medium.

From that incident, it is claimed, the phrase "tapping the admiral" arose, although this is not a phrase you are likely to hear very often nowadays. British sailors formerly said "tapping the admiral" for drinking rum, against regulations, out of a coconut from which the milk had been drained; later the phrase was used for drinking surreptitiously from a cask by means of a straw inserted through a small hole.

Many wandering Englishmen actually did end up being shipped home inside barrels of spirits after they died abroad, and in numerous instances the barrels were *supposedly* (who can say?) tapped, presumably always unwittingly. The specifics of the stories varied, as befits folklore. For example, the barrel of wine containing the remains of General Edward Pakenham, who fell in the Battle of New Orleans in 1815, was said to have been accidentally diverted to South Carolina, where it was served at a party.

Rodney Dale repeats a recent English version of "The Corpse in the Cask" that brings the aftermath of the old custom down to the present. A family has bought a huge old Georgian/Regency house, and in one of its many cellar rooms they discover a dozen large barrels. They begin to cut them in halves to use as planters, and one of them is found to contain Jamaica rum. After a year or so of enjoying various rum drinks and desserts, the family has finally emptied the barrel and starts again to cut it in half. Inside they find the well-preserved body of a late colonial from a century or so earlier who had been shipped home immersed in the spirits but had never been buried. (This is one of the urban legends rendered as a fully developed short story by "an English poet and critic, who

. . . wishes to remain anonymous"; see "Francis Greig," *Heads, You Lose* in the Bibliography.)

Surely there is a strain of poetic justice in almost all of these stories, since regularly the contaminated alcohol is either drunk by someone who more or less deserves his fate, or else the corpse is that of someone who outranked the drinkers. Thus, gentiles (according to the story) eat the hated Jew; common sailors drink the admiral's brandy; Americans party on the defeated English general's wine, and those who have merely bought into the lordly manor house drink up the rum left there by its past rightful owner. This same idea persists in a version of "The Corpse in the Cask" recently told in France. I am endebted to professor of psychology Jan Berkhout of the University of South Dakota for sending me a summary of this story as it was heard there:

> Cheap bulk wine is imported from Algeria in tank ships, either arriving in Marseilles or by barge direct to Paris. The story always involves the slow draining of the tank into a bottling line, the departure of the bottles, and then the discovery at the bottom of the tank, too late to recall the bottles, of the dead Algerian. In one version the Algerian has a knife in his back; in another he has been strangled or hanged and still has the rope around his neck.

As Professor Berkhout pointed out in commenting on this version, it reflects the French distrust of foreign wine, the prejudices against Algerians, typical modern attitudes toward current merchandising (supposedly, the bottling company is able to suppress the story), and the final irony of the Moslem, who is forbidden to drink alcohol, being submerged in a barrel of the stuff.

I must admit that it is never a "cask" in which the corpse is found—always the larger "barrel," or else a gigantic tank. But I allow myself a little poetic license in titling this legend, which (God knows) is horrible enough to need the touch of alliteration to cushion its effect. And things are only going to get worse as we continue looking at dreadful contaminations. Brace yourself for the food and restaurant rumors!

Food and Restaurant Rumors and Legends

"The Kentucky Fried Rat" and "The Mouse in the Coke" are the best-known American food-contamination legends. Both of these rodential gastronomic horrors were discussed at length in *The Vanishing Hitchhiker,* along with some shuddering side glances at rumors of rat salads, wormburgers, spider-egg bubble gum, and other such nasties. But there is more, *much* more (ugh!), if you only listen to what people say about various packaged, processed, and restaurant-prepared foods.

Exactly what portion of this kind of lore is genuinely folk may be debatable, since the news media regularly report contamination scares that are based on facts (remember Tylenol?). And people spread by word of mouth a complete mishmash of what they have read, what they have heard, and what they *think* they have read or heard.

In the past couple of years alone, for example, I have seen actual news stories quoting named individuals (usually the victims, their attorneys, or law-enforcement officers) describing a piece of human skin found in a can of Stokely-Van Camp tomato juice, and a live beetle found in a container of Dannon raspberry yogurt. I have been told stories about seeing a cockroach crawl out of a bowl of cream of tomato soup served in a restaurant, and of finding a chilled (but still living) snake in a package of frozen chittlings. And at the furthest extreme of incredibility, I have heard vague rumors about a cigarette butt found in a Hershey chocolate bar, a dead mouse discovered in a box of Cheerios, a thumb frozen into a commercially sold ice cube, and, in a gem of specificity (except that the people involved were *not* specified), a gloved finger found in a jar of Progresso marinating sauce.

But which similar details in such stories are coincidence, and which are the likely folklore "motifs"? Notice the preponderance of red-tinted foods (bloodlike?), the recurrence of human body parts (especially fingers), and the direct mention of brand names of a kind that tend to sound "safe" or homey. But just because certain features of food rumors and legends keep popping up and seem to fall into traditional patterns does not mean that the whole stories are always false, although it does make one skeptical until further proof than just "a friend of a friend told me" is offered.

Obviously, foreign matter of various kinds is bound to get into food now and then, and I truly do want to verify the stories of this kind that are authentic; but often—so very often—searching for the source (unless I have a reliable news account) leads me only to blind alleys. Again and again in Salt Lake City, for example, I have had earnest, honest people tell me that a human finger was found in a jar of pickles opened at a party in this very community. "It sounds like a folklore motif," I tell them, but they press on me the names of friends and relatives who were supposedly there, or of the lawyer who prosecuted the canning company, or of the newspapers that ran the whole story. But the hard facts—the finger, the pickle jar, the legal settlement, the news story, or any eyewitness description—where are they? Well, I'm still looking.

There are several clear folkloristic aspects to the food and restaurant stories concerning supposed contamination, whether based on actual happenings or not. First, the selection of certain incidents for retelling and oral elaboration becomes traditional in itself. (Many dreadful things might contaminate fried chicken or a soft drink, but it's the rodents that get into most of the stories.) Thus, the most popular stories seem to reflect the subjects of our particular horror; we loathe the thought of things like rats, cockroaches, spiders, snakes, or severed human body parts.

A second folk idea reflected in such stories is that packaged and processed foods cannot possibly be as pure and wholesome as home-cooked, and that restaurant food—especially from fast-food or ethnic restaurants—is of inferior quality and likely to be unclean. Then, following a typical folk-narrating pattern, some particular company or restaurant chain or ethnic group is named in the story, which seemingly *proves* the truth of the wild tale.

The very manner in which contamination stories are told orally helps qualify them as modern folklore. The validating formulas (like "I heard this on the radio . . ."), the dramatic oral style, the verbal reactions of disgust (from audience as well as teller), facial expressions, gestures, and even the groping for half-remembered facts and details all contribute to the appeal and effect of such narrations as "folk" performances.

Probably the best folklore credentials for such legends should be awarded to those few narratives (whether based on truth or not) that circulate in especially detailed oral variants, that are only very vaguely attributed to a source (i.e., a foaf), and that preserve a particularly bizarre or memorable version of a typical combination of motifs. What I have in mind is something like "The Rat in the Rye Bread."

Some forty years ago—in 1945—*Hoosier Folklore Bulletin* mentioned the story of a rat baked into a loaf of bread; the brand was always specified. David Jacobson described this tale again in 1948 in *The Affairs of Dame Rumor,* saying that the supposed event had been attributed to a bakery in Toronto. Through the years this same story has been repeated about numerous local bakeries, with the type of bread often identified as rye. (Is this because rye bread is thought of as being more folksy, peasanty, or "natural"?)

Allegedly "The Rat in the Rye Bread" has been reliably reported in the media, and many who tell the story claim that they are merely recalling a news story. But their words fall naturally into the patterns of oral tradition: we hear (with full dramatic effects) about the crunchy section bitten into in the bread slice, the checking of the remaining loaf, the discovery of the rat remains there, the law suit brought against the bakery, the health inspection that followed, the shocking violations that were uncovered, and the enormous monetary settlement. The victims (or winners, depending on how you look at it) were friends of friends, but the published news story itself is unavailable.

And how these food legends are updated! A rat gets batter-fried in a fast-chicken place, of course; but haven't you heard about the local donut franchise store, in the kitchen of which a male employee was supposedly caught masturbating into a batch of donut batter? Who says folk creativity is dying out— I mean in making up such a story, not in performing such an unspeakable act. It's really *not* true, folks.

One of the most venerable categories of food-contamination legends concerns the idea of human or pet remains said to have been served in an ethnic restaurant. Rats, cats, dogs, and fingers lead the list of awful additives, these occurring commonly in stories about Chinese, East Indian, or Italian restaurants that serve chop suey, curries, or some exotic stews and sauces. The fingers often are said to come from cooks who had leprosy, while the animal parts supposedly come from unscrupulous owners cooking captured pets. (And, readers will recall, once the whole body of a dog—poor little Rosa— supposedly came from the customers themselves.)

Just for variety, then, you sometimes hear about people-sausages (also available with cat or dog meat) made by ghoulish German butchers. Or canned dog food used on pizza is another biggy, especially in the Scandinavian countries, while tacos come under suspicion in other parts of the world. The incriminating evidence of such contamination may be found in the restaurants' freezers, in the garbage cans, or even from samples picked out of the food itself. (I especially like the stories in which a veterinarian or an archaeologist is dining at an ethnic restaurant and decides to take a bone from the delicious stew back to the lab for analysis. Better he had dined at home; a little knowledge is a dangerous thing. Cat bone, of course.) In another popular variation, a traveler in Greece

(Italy, Spain, etc.) gets a bone stuck in his or her throat while eating "chicken salad" at a restaurant; a doctor back home removes it safely, then identifies it immediately as a rat bone.

In January 1972 the English folklore journal *Lore and Language* published a request that its readers submit any versions they had heard of stories involving animals (rats and Alsatian dogs, usually) being cooked into meals at Chinese restaurants. By July the journal was able to report "substantially similar versions" of the legend from Edinburgh, Newcastle, Darlington, Whitby, York, Leeds, Doncaster, Sheffield, Manchester, Hathersage, Norwich, and London. In the following few years further British versions as well as some from Germany were submitted, while in 1978 an Australian counterpart from the 1880s was pointed out. (In this one a Chinese cook made puppy pie, which was thought to be rabbit.) Finally, in 1980, contributor Graham Shorrocks surveyed the wealth of material uncovered by the query. Given the number of versions from both Britain and abroad, all alleged to be true, involving standardized motifs like "Animals in fridge," "Rat-bone in throat," and "Empty pet-food cans in the dustbin," Shorrocks found it impossible to determine whether specific stories had moved across international borders, whether similar conditions had spawned similar stories, or whether some of the stories were indeed true.

The same dilemma would confront an American folklorist trying to compare and evaluate the numerous recent reports of Oriental refugees or immigrants capturing Americans' pet cats and dogs for food. Many people—and not a few newspapers—have taken such stories seriously enough to pass them on or investigate them, but never (to my knowledge) has an organized assault upon our pets in order to turn them into Oriental food delicacies been uncovered. Perhaps such rumors have been imported along with some of the displaced people they are told about; perhaps prejudices similar to those held in Europe have brought about the creation of similar lore; or, perhaps, a few of the stories are true.

Florence E. Baer of San Joaquin Delta College in Stockton, California, published her detailed study of the "Orientals Eating Dogs" legend as it developed in that community in 1980 and 1981. By 1980 more than 3,000 Southeast Asian refugees had settled in Stockton, a community of some 170,000 people; rumors and legends about the Vietnamese eating dogs and cats had begun to spread. (Although these refugees had come from Laos and Cambodia as well as Vietnam, they were referred to in most of the stories simply as "Vietnamese.") The predominant motifs were the same ones found wherever similar groups of refugees had settled: evidence for the pet-eating was supposedly found in the Asians' garbage, Americans were alleged to have been approached by Vietnamese people wanting to buy their pets for food, cat tails were said to have been seen hanging over the side of a cooking pot, the police were covering up the cases, and so forth. The sources for these stories were the familiar friends-of-friends and allegations that "It's all true. It was in the paper."

What *had* been in the paper repeatedly, Baer found, were official denials of the stories, statements from officials and from garbage-collection companies that no such thing had been documented, and reports of efforts to educate the refugees in American language and customs. But, since these news stories often repeated the oral-traditional stories in considerable detail, they also seem to have circulated the legendary lore as much as to have exposed them as fraudulent. Baer also described a considerable amount of verbal and physical abuse directed against "Vietnamese" refugees settled in Stockton stemming from people's belief that the pet-eating stories they had heard and read about were true. (A bumper sticker: "Save a Dog—Eat a Refugee.") She concluded that underlying the whole complex of anti-Vietnamese refugee lore seemed to be the folk idea of "limited good" that translates into a typical attitude, "That the refugees are consuming—using up—our share of this world's goods. If that world is a world of limited good, where there is only so much and there may be no more, who can afford to share?"

The same anti-Asian refugee lore with the pet-eating story as the centerpiece has been encountered all over the United States. As an example of a localized version of it, the following news story from the Fairfax, Virginia, *Journal* of 8 February 1982 represents a particularly full treatment, and it is shot through with evidence of a vigorous oral tradition:

ANIMAL GROUP HEAD SAYS ORIENTALS EAT PETS
By Mary Anne Shreve
Journal Staff Writer

The local president of a humanitarian organization has accused Oriental residents in Springfield of catching—and eating—neighborhood pets.

Though he acknowledges his "information" is "second and third hand," Jerry Southern, President of the Metropolitan Washington Branch of United Humanitarians Inc., has made his accusations public in a letter to Fairfax County Supervisor Marie B. Travesky and a press release to local media. . . .

Southern said he first heard the rumor from his wife, who in turn had heard it from a friend. His wife's friend "either lives in the area or has a friend who lives in the area," he said.

The Journal was aware of Southern's charges at the time but could find no support for them from police, trash companies, or other animal protection officials, all of whom denied any knowledge of the alleged incident.

Now Southern has repeated his charges in a press release, and *The Journal* still can find no support or direct evidence of pet eating.

Southern, a former Fairfax County Humane Department employee, wrote to Travesky last month:

"It is alleged that employees of a trash collection service operating in the North Springfield area (specifically in the vicinity of Heming Ave.) discovered what appeared to be the pelts of a number of dogs and cats in the trash containers at a particular residence known to be occupied by a family of Oriental extraction.

"This information was then reported to the Fairfax County Police Department. The police supposedly then obtained a search warrant, entered the house in question and found the bodies of a number of small animals in a freezer. . . . The family quickly vacated the premises and apparently no further action was taken by the FCPD."

Southern's letter concluded: "Why has this entire matter been hushed up?!!!"

His press release claimed that United Humanitarians Inc. conducted "an exhaustive investigation" that revealed that Fairfax police and the health department were "called into the matter by employees of a trash collection service that found animal pelts in a trash container."

. . . A spokesman for the Fairfax County Police Department denied such an incident ever occurred; he called Southern's account "a far-out story that someone has concocted and foisted on the world."

Police Public Relations Officer Warren Carmichael said: "None of our people has ever heard of anything remotely related to it, and we have had no increase in reports of missing animals. . . ."

"Something that big," he said, "I'm sure would have been heard by at least a few people. And no one in any of our stations had heard about it. In fact, they asked me what I'd been smoking."

Carmichael said the police had not searched a house for pet meat and that there was no "cover up." . . .

Officials at both the main and Springfield branch offices of the health department said they had heard about the rumor, but their departments had not been involved in any cases of pet snatching.

Spokeswomen for the two major trash companies that serve North Springfield—Woodbridge Trash Co. and BFI Industries—said they had not even heard the rumor. . . .

Southern said his "investigation" consisted of conversations with dozens of Springfield residents who "had heard the rumor about the theft of pets and believed that an 'Oriental family' had been stealing, killing and consuming animals for food."

However, he said: "Only two people professed to absolutely verify that the incident occurred."

Asked if the two had actually witnessed the incident, Southern said they had heard about it from others.

Bettijane Mackall, president of the Animal Protective Association of America, said there was "no doubt" in her mind that incidences of pet eating were happening in Northern Virginia "because there is a big Oriental population in this area now."

She received a telephone call last fall from a woman in Great Falls who had placed an ad to give away her collie, she said. The ad was answered by a Korean family who seemed to like the dog and wanted to take it away, according to Mackall. The woman was agreeable and said the dog would make a good pet. The family then told her the dog was not going to be a pet, but a meal, said Mackall.

However, My Hien Hoang, a Vietnamese refugee who came to this country seven years ago, says it's unusual for Orientals to eat dogs and cats, and she doubts Southern's allegations.

Asian peoples, like Americans, keep dogs and cats as pets, and, like the Americans, become attached to the animals. Using them as food happens rarely, and usually only among country peasants, she said.

If this whole notion of Oriental-Americans eating our pets were not so seriously held by such well-meaning people, it would seem like nothing but a joke. As a matter of fact, there *is* a joke based on the idea, showing, at least, how folklore may contradict itself. (Legends take the idea seriously, while jokes make fun of the same notions.) Joke: "Have you heard of the new Vietnamese cookbook? It's called '100 Ways to Wok Your Dog.'" (I didn't claim that it was a *good* joke.)

One last thought about food rumors and legends. Allow me to remain skeptical, at least for the present, about the recurring reports in these trying economic times of elderly citizens who are forced by circumstances to live on canned dog food. There's something just believable enough, but also bizarre enough, in that story to make me think that "The Starving

Senior Citizens" is another "new" urban legend. And ditto for the one about people using government food stamps to buy steaks to feed their dog.

"The Stolen Specimen"

Illustrating once again how the themes of urban legends may recombine to form "new" stories is a dreadful contamination legend that draws its punch not only from the implication of someone drinking the wrong bad thing but also from the notion, familiar in other cycles of legends, of a stolen package containing an unwanted item (like a dead cat or grandmother's corpse). I received a recent version of this hoary story from Victor Kassel, M.D., of Salt Lake City, a specialist in geriatric medicine. By way of thanks for a minor service I had rendered (looking up a folk reference for him), the good doctor sent me this account. (That's the kind of nontaxable return I enjoy getting!):

> One of the interesting myths associated with medical care is the "urine in the whiskey bottle." This story is recounted by many doctors and many patients. Essentially, it is told that a patient has been asked to save the urine specimen for twenty-four hours and bring it to the office for examination. The largest container available for the specimen is an empty whiskey bottle. The patient accumulates the specimen in the bottle and brings it to the office. The bottle is usually in a brown paper bag and is placed on the back seat of the car. On the way to the office, the patient makes a stop at a store, and upon returning to the car finds the full whiskey bottle stolen. The rest is left to the listener's imagination.

I have also heard that the patient was a pregnant lady bringing her sample to the doctor in a mini-bottle, or that she was found doubled up with laughter by someone to whom she then told the story (Herb Caen's version, "The Howling Lady," printed on 14 February 1971), or that she had left the car windows open on a hot day, allowing the thief to grab the bag or bottle (the way Ronald Baker's 1972 version in his *Hoosier Folk Legends* is told). Rodney Dale gives two British versions in *The Tumor in the Whale,* one having the bottle lifted when the lady is riding a bus to her doctor appointment and the other saying she had left the sample in her bicycle basket. Haig whiskey is mentioned in these texts, while Old Granddad or Jack Daniels are the favored brands in the United States. But since the stories themselves are far more interesting than mere summaries, here is a very well-detailed version told as a true story by his source, and sent to me by John B. Dashney of Salem, Oregon, who also suggested the legend title "The Stolen Specimen":

> A new group of students [in an orientation program for diabetics] were being shown how to test their urine. The hospital did not have enough specimen bottles to pass around, so the group was told that any clean glass container would do. One of the patients forgot about the container until just before time to leave for class early the next morning. A quick search disclosed an almost-empty Gallo wine bottle in the refrigerator, so she quickly poured out the wine, rinsed out the bottle and urinated into it.
>
> Upon arriving at the hospital, she discovered that she did not have change for the parking meter. She went into a nearby pharmacy to get it, leaving the specimen bottle on the front seat of her car. When she returned, the bottle was gone, but she saw a wino sneaking off across the lot toward Pringle Park. She let him go and had a good laugh thinking over his reaction to the first swallow.

Mr. Dashney added, "When I told this story to a new group of clients some six months or so later, I was told, no, it had happened in Portland a couple of years before, or somewhere else . . ."

The connection of this legend with diabetes testing reminds one of the old med-school prank in which an instructor demonstrates for the class how he can detect a trace of sugar in a urine sample simply by sticking his finger into the fluid and then licking it. What the class does not notice as he does this is that he sneakily switches fingers between the sample and his tongue. Sometimes the doctor is supposed to have entrapped a student into imitating him, and then he shows him again— slowly this time—how it is really done.

There is a solid-food variant of the dreadful-drink story in which a package that appears to be some kind of food but that actually contains a stool sample or animal excrement is stolen. (Of course, this may also be considered a variation of the old "Dead Cat in the Package" legend discussed in *The Vanishing Hitchhiker.*) I quote from a first-person account given to me by a colleague early in 1982:

> What is amazing is that the following story is true (it happened to my father). My father takes his dog for a walk twice a day, and, like a responsible dog owner, he cleans up the feces and puts them into a bag which he carries to a litter barrel. One day, he used a small white bag, the kind used by bakeries. He continued walking, and was passing through a small business district, when three young boys ran up behind him, grabbed the bag, and ran off. Naturally, he didn't give chase. He still laughs when he imagines the boys as they open the bag, expecting a baked goodie . . .

My inclination was to disbelieve the story since A) I had been told a similar "true" version by a radio interviewer some weeks earlier, and B) Herb Caen also published *that* one (on 1 November 1978), saying that someone's Aunt Catharine actually had it happen to her. Confirming my suspicions was a letter from Kay Haugaard of Pasadena, California, in March 1983; she had just heard essentially the same story retold from a "true" report that was broadcast on a radio program. What seems especially doubtful about all of these dog-dropping tales is not so much that street thieves would grab a bag, but that they would choose a person who was walking a dog to rob.

Then there's this version, which truly echoes the dead cat and dead grandmother theft stories. It was sent to me by Ann Thompson of College Station, Texas, in July 1983, and is " . . . supposed to really have happened":

> A housepainter, working in Fairbanks, Alaska, lived out in the Bush. He did not have indoor plumbing to make living easier, so he saved all his empty one-gallon paint cans for use in the winter time when the temperature was −30°F. and lower. As each can was filled he put the lid on and hammered it down firmly, then stored the can out in the shed for the contents to freeze solid. Each spring he would load all the cans into his truck and take them to the public dump, there to dispose of the lot. One spring the painter went out to his shed to collect his cans, only to find that someone had stolen the lot. He laughed and wondered what the thief would think upon opening the cans.

5

Sex Scandals

Miscellaneous Sex Legends

Folklore, ancient as well as modern, is full of references to sex; conversely, people's serious ideas about sex are also full of folklore. The result is that we have dozens of miscellaneous legends about sex, as well as scores of legends about what might be termed "miscellaneous sex." (My subtitle is deliberately ambiguous.)

In *The Vanishing Hitchhiker* I surveyed some of our sexy modern folk narratives under the heading "Dalliance, Nudity, and Nightmares," but few of the most shocking of the sex legends were mentioned there. This time, the fig leaf is off. Since legends, however, tend to be considerably more demure than jokes are, nothing that could not be repeated in the locker rooms of the best country clubs in the land finds its way into this chapter. In fact, that is just the kind of setting in which these stories circulate.

A classic urban legend that I earlier discussed in print (see "The Nude Surprise Party") often involves adults who accidentally catch an adolescent couple in the act of . . . well, of coupling. In the conclusion to that story the boy gets out of town and the girl loses her mind. Another legend based on the same situation often brings up the topic of contraception, either an old-fashioned mechanical means of avoiding pregnancy or else a modern chemical/hormonal method. In this story a married couple return home unexpectedly early from an evening out; they find the baby-sitter (sometimes said to be their own older daughter) in the bedroom engaging in sex with her boyfriend. Shocked as they are, the adults refrain from lecturing the embarrassed young people on the evils of premarital sex; they only ask worriedly if the kids have taken any precautions. "Of course we have," the girl replies smugly, "we're using plastic wrap." (In England, where the same legend is known, the product is called "cling foil," and it doesn't work any better there than here, except for its intended purpose, that is.)

The popular variation on the plastic-wrap-contraceptive story is the one (also known in England) in which the girl who has been caught in the act shamefacedly admits that she has been stealing her mother's birth-control pills for some time. "But," the woman protests, "I haven't missed any of my pills lately." Ah, but her daughter had substituted baby aspirin or saccharin tablets in the pill container, and so the next month her forty-year-old mother finds herself to be pregnant again. Not a nice situation, but the good news is that in most versions Mom at least had not been suffering any headaches recently.

Sex education classes in school are, of course, where the kids of today are supposed to have been getting all this boldness while losing their innocence about sex at the same time. (Just ask any legend teller with children in junior high school about this.) The horror stories concerning such classes are numerous, and they include accounts of filthy-dirty films shown to the kids, coed touchy-feely sessions in darkened rooms, supervised practice in masturbation, clay-modeling of realistic genitals, a school teacher who allegedly stripped naked as part of a sex class, and a young boy who supposedly went home and raped his little sister in order to practice what he had learned in class.

The fantasies of unlimited sex and of sexual favors granted with no strings attached—familiar in some dreams, in most pornography, and in much jokelore—are found in modern legends as well. These stories typically include some twist of fate or of poetic justice. In one version of this theme the lovely young widow who runs a country inn sleeps with one of two men who have checked in together for separate rooms. But the lucky man prudently gives her his partner's name instead of his own. A year later the woman dies, and in her will she grants the deed to the inn plus a sizable sum of money to the wrong man, who had never even been aware of his buddy's night of pleasure. Another such story is about a sailor in a foreign port who is asked by a very old and rich man to spend the night with a nubile young beauty who turns out to be the man's own wife. In the morning the sailor is given a bag of gold coins and the explanation that the man wanted an heir to leave his wealth to, so that his relatives will not acquire it.

Sex obtained by an unscrupulous man from a woman he has drugged and seduced is another staple of modern sex legends. A familiar college-campus version of this one describes an innocent young coed given a drug in her drink by a fraternity man at a party; he then has sex with her while her inhibitions are relaxed. But whereas many female students know this story, believe it to be true, and tell it in localized forms, very few of them have had the experience personally, or have even met a first-person source. Similarly, the story of the dentist who has sex with female patients while they are under the influence of anesthesia strains our will to believe. Newspapers, allegedly, have headlined the story "Dentist arrested for filling wrong cavity."

Perhaps the ultimate modern sex-fantasy stories are the ones that revolve about the supposed aphrodisiacal effects of the substance popularly known as "Spanish Fly"—actually cantharis, or a preparation made of dried Spanish, or blister, beetles *(Lytta vesicatoria)*. This nasty-sounding concoction, which every American boy seems to have heard of but not one in a hundred has seen or possessed, is the subject of an equally nasty legend. Supposedly a lad slips his date some Spanish Fly in a drink or an item of food, but he overestimates the amount needed for a good result. He takes the girl out parking or to a drive-in movie, tries his best to satisfy her enormous cravings for sex, and after leaving her briefly alone in the car returns to find that in her frenzy she has impaled herself on the gearshift lever.

Plain ignorance about sex combined with racism is another area furnishing material for miscellaneous legends. A recurrent story, for example, concerns a white woman said to have borne a black child, usually because her husband had recently visited a prostitute who shortly beforehand had been with a black man. This legend, I am told, is frequently "reported," with the usual lack of documentation, in European newspapers. (Similarly, David Jacobson's *The Affairs of Dame Rumor* mentions the apocryphal claim that Marie Thérèse, wife of Louis XIV, was said to have borne a black baby.) In the same category there's also the legend mentioned in a letter to the London *Tribune* published on 17 May 1968 concerning a white woman delivered of her baby by a black doctor; on the infant's navel, it was said, appeared two birthmarks resembling black fingerprints.

Closer to home, one of the wildest allegedly-true sex stories I have seen was published in hundreds of American newspapers in "Dear Abby"—Abigail Van Buren's syndicated advice column—on 6 November 1982. To "prove" that a woman could actually become pregnant while remaining a virgin, a reader sent in this summary of an article found in "a reputable magazine":

> It seems that during the Civil War (May 12, 1863, to be exact), a young Virginia farm girl was standing on her front porch while a battle was raging nearby. A stray bullet first passed through the scrotum of a young Union cavalryman, then lodged in the reproductive tract of the young woman, who thus became pregnant by a man she had not been within 100 feet of! And nine months later she gave birth to a healthy baby!

The exactness of the date mentioned in this letter, plus the supposed reliability of the source quoted (*American Heritage* for December 1971), gave this "Bullet through the Balls" story an air of credibility. However, a look at the trail of published accounts that lie behind the recent telling conveys another impression entirely.

The several printed versions of the story that I have noted all seem to go back to a lengthy footnote in a fascinating book called *Anomalies and Curiosities of Medicine* by George M. Gould and Walter L. Pyle, first published in 1896. (Most medical libraries, as well as many university and public libraries, own well-thumbed copies of the 1956 reprinting of this weird tome, which is loaded with grotesque and sometimes titillating illustrations.) Gould and Pyle were sticklers for truth, as represented by the hundreds of plausible and well-documented cases of medical wonders that they gathered information about. But this particular remarkable-impregnation account they included only in passing, as they explain, "not because it bears any semblance of possibility, but as a curious example from the realms of imagination in medicine." They report the story "in brief" (though still in considerable detail) as they claim to have found it told in the British medical journal *The Lancet* in 1875, being quoted there, they say, from *The American Medical Weekly* of 7 November 1874. (Doubtless both of these references do exist, but I have not been able to find the story in either of the sources indicated.) Here is Gould and Pyle's version of the story (pp. 44–45):

> L. G. Capers of Vicksburg, Miss., relates an incident during the late Civil War, as follows: A matron and her two daughters, aged fifteen and seventeen years, filled with the enthusiasm of patriotism, stood ready to minister to the wounds of their countrymen in their fine residence near the scene of the battle of R——, May 12, 1863, between a portion of Grant's army and some Confederates. During the fray a gallant and noble young friend of the narrator staggered and fell to the earth; at the same time a piercing

cry was heard in the house near by. Examination of the
wounded soldier showed that a bullet had passed through
the scrotum and carried away the left testicle. The same
bullet had apparently penetrated the left side of the abdomen of the elder young lady, midway between the umbilicus
and the anterior superior spinous process of the ilium, and
had become lost in the abdomen. This daughter suffered an
attack of peritonitis, but recovered in two months under the
treatment administered.

Marvelous to relate, just two hundred and seventy-eight
days after the reception of the minie-ball, she was delivered
of a fine boy, weighing 8 pounds, to the surprise of herself
and the mortification of her parents and friends. The
hymen was intact, and the young mother strenuously insisted on her virginity and innocence. About three weeks
after this remarkable birth Dr. Capers was called to see the
infant, and the grandmother insisted that there was something wrong with the child's genitals. Examination showed
a rough, swollen, and sensitive scrotum, containing some
hard substance. He operated, and extracted a smashed and
battered minie-ball. The doctor, after some meditation,
theorized in this manner: He concluded that this was the
same ball that had carried away the testicle of his young
friend, that had penetrated the ovary of the young lady, and
with some spermatozoa upon it, had impregnated her. With
this conviction he approached the young man and told him
the circumstances; the soldier appeared skeptical at first but
consented to visit the young mother; a friendship ensued
which soon ripened into a happy marriage, and the pair had
three children, none resembling, in the same degree as the
first, the heroic *pater familias.*

Gould and Pyle's own skepticism about the story seems
justified, considering the attribution of the incident to a
"friend of the narrator," the borrowing of the tale from one
printed source to another a full decade or more after the
alleged event, and the coincidence (bordering on sympathetic
magic) of the bullet going from one man's to another's scro-

tum. However, when Dr. F. Donald Napolitani of New York City reported the story in the *New York State Journal of Medicine* in 1959, he identified it as an "authenticated" case that he had found "reported November 7, 1874, in the medical annals." While I have been unable to track down Dr. Napolitani's citation ("*Med.Ann.* 1:62"), his language confirms that he probably used one of the elusive accounts paraphrased by Gould and Pyle. Not only are the essential facts and figures the same, but phrases like "a gallant young lad" and "a piercing scream" betray a common source. The exact path of the bullet is more closely described here, and Captain Capers, the attending physician, according to Dr. Napolitani's version "stated that he gave no credence to the young girl's assertion of her innocence and purity" until he later operated and extracted the presumed bullet remains from her baby.

In the summary of this report that *American Heritage* published in 1971 under the headline "The Case of the Miraculous Bullet," none of Gould and Pyle's doubts are conveyed; nor is any hint of the identification of Napolitani's published source. Instead, the case of the bullet through the balls is simply said to have been "carefully recorded for the annals of medicine [implying a source that is neither specified nor verified] by a Union doctor." A footnote states that Dr. Napolitani "insists that it actually could have happened," which is not exactly a description of what he wrote, although the intent seems similar.

It also happens that John Train—he who accepted "Roast Rosa" (aka "The Dog's Dinner," see Chapter 3) as a "true remarkable occurrence"—is another modern believer in the "Bullet through the Balls" story. Train quoted, in 1978, directly from Gould and Pyle, but with silent excision of such terms as "realms of imagination," "gallant and noble young friend of the narrator," and "marvelous to relate." (He also misprinted the title of the source journal as *The American Weekly*, which may be a third version of the title of the same publication that still eludes my search.)

With all these published versions adrift, it seems likely that the case of the miraculous bullet will continue to crop up now and then as a supposedly authenticated instance of virgin birth, despite mine and Dear Abby's skepticism. For the advice columnist replied to her 1982 correspondent that when she ran the same story some years before, a ninety-year-old South Dakota Indian wrote in to tell her that he had heard that it was an Indian maiden who was impregnated by a bow and arrow. Well, Dear Abby, I'm with *you* on this one; the whole thing sounds to me like an old wartime legend or perhaps a nine-teenth-century doctor's or editor's hoax.

Then there are the miscellaneous sex legends that are al-most more joke than belief tale, because they hinge on an improbable punchline rather than a credible, or semicredible, series of events. Ordinary words that are misunderstood to have a double (sexual) meaning provide a couple of examples. A woman is checking out her purchases at a cash register in a discount store, but a box of tampons in her shopping basket lacks the price tag. So the clerk announces over the store public-address system, "I need a price check on a package of Tampax on aisle three." Everyone in line turns to stare at her, and the poor woman is terribly embarrassed. When the am-plified query comes back over the system—"Do you want the ones that push in, or the ones you use a hammer on?"—she flees the store without her goods. Shortly afterward a second query is heard: "Whatever happened to that price check you wanted on thumbtacks?" Also reflecting women's possible shame and anxiety about menstruation is the "Stuck Tampax" legend in which a young woman must actually go to a hospital emergency room in order to have a tampon removed when it has become lodged too tightly in her body. That evening she is horribly embarrassed to find that the young man she has a blind date with is the same hospital intern who had removed the tampon for her. In some versions of the story there is a happy ending: they fall in love and get married. (Is there an implication here that no one else would have her after that experience?)

A second sex-word-error story must be extremely well known across the country, judging from the many people who have sent it to me as a true tale. A bright and beautiful young lady zipping home for the weekend from college in her nifty sports car is stopped by a highway patrolman for speeding. Taking a chance, she says to the cop as he starts to write the ticket, "Couldn't I just buy a couple of tickets to the policemen's ball instead?" And the patrolman is supposed to have replied, "Miss, state policemen don't have balls!" (In one version *she* melts with embarrassment, but in others *he* is so flustered that he lets her go free.)

More or less in this same category (at least it can be said to be "miscellaneous") is the legend about the woman on her way to her gynecologist for an examination who uses the ladies' room just beforehand and finds that the toilet paper supply is gone. But she has a facial tissue in her purse and uses that instead. Unfortunately, there are also some trading stamps in the purse, and a strip of them becomes stuck to her body, without her realizing it. When the doctor begins the examination, he spots the Green Stamps at once, of course, and cannot resist remarking, "Gosh, Mrs. So-and-so . . . I didn't know they gave Green Stamps nowadays." Variant versions have her laughing her head off, changing doctors, or suing the doctor for . . . what *would* it be for? Unprofessional levity, I suppose.

And then we have the stories of sexy films and sexy stage performances. Both do exist, to be sure—but did certain alleged ironic events involving them actually happen? Number one, from a reader's letter: "A couple goes to the Poconos for an anniversary weekend to one of those fancy places with heart-shaped bathtubs and mirrored ceilings. They return to the same place the following year, and the place now has X-rated movies on TV, so the couple turns it on. And there they find themselves as the "actors" in the movie, and they are now suing the hotel." My spicy file of variants from other parts of the country includes stories about a sex orgy for free with a gorgeous hooker because "the movie man paid for that one," and various tales about a man paying to view a live peep show that turns out to feature the same woman he had been with the night before, and in the same bed. (What I always wonder about these stories is why the kind of man who would do it with these partners in these places would object so strongly to being observed by others of the same ilk.) But who am I to question, being only a detached student of this racy material?

A curiously similar news story, though not really about sex, was published in the *New York Jewish Week* for 9 May 1982; I am endebted to both Nancy C. Starr of Cherry Hill, New Jersey, and S. B. Shear of Sharon, Massachusetts, for sending me copies of the piece. Both suggest that it may be a legend, and I am inclined to agree. Supposedly at a recent wedding in a Jewish catering hall the father of the bride was embarrassed and inconvenienced when the large amount of cash he had brought with him to pay the caterer disappeared from his wallet while it was left in his coat hanging over a chair during the dancing. The father was able to write a check; but later, in viewing the videotapes of the party it was discovered that a man—and not just any man, but the groom's own father—had lifted the money. The thief was confronted, he confessed, and the wedding was annulled. "It happened," the news story concludes, "in the New York area, in the year 1982." Or did it?

In May 1983 the *Chicago Sun-Times* summarized another variation of the videotaped-theft story, mentioning the magazine *North Shore* as its source. This time there is no reference to a specific religious affiliation of the wedding party, the missing sum is said to have been $20,000, and the father of the bride sends the groom's father a copy of the videotape and shortly after his money is returned. Writer Art Shay of *North Shore,* according to this report, "takes an oath it's the gospel truth, though no names are mentioned."

Which brings us, finally, to the letters-and-certificates category of miscellaneous sex legends. The first we might call "The Missent Letter." It describes a serviceman stationed at a foreign post who writes an extremely sexy letter to his girlfriend but accidentally sends it to his mother. Later he hears from his father that Mom nearly had a heart attack when she read all that stuff. (Talk about an Oedipus complex!) A second version of the theme is "The Misunderstood Note": during a rape trial a young woman cannot bring herself to repeat what her assailant had done to her or said to her, so the judge asks her to write it out, telling her he will pass the slip among the members of the jury. The note eventually reaches an attractive woman on the jury who nudges the napping male juror sitting next to her and passes him the slip of paper. The man reads it, looks around in confusion, and sticks it into his pocket. When the judge asks him to take it back out and pass it along, the man replies, "Your Honor, this note is a private matter between this lady and myself."

The sex-certificate story is a little like "The Rattle in the Cadillac" legend in that, supposedly, the people involved have the document framed in their home as a souvenir of their vacation in Mexico (or France). Some time before, according to the story, they had vacationed in the foreign country, and while the man was off somewhere on his own, the wife paced back and forth on the sidewalk in front of their hotel in some impatience waiting for his return. A policeman apprehended her as a prostitute and had just written out a ticket when her husband arrived and explained the situation. But the policeman insists that the ticket has already been written and that a fine must be paid or the woman will go to jail. The only other solution that is possible, he says, is for the man to buy her a license to practice prostitution in Mexico City (or Paris). The husband does so, and there you see it hanging on the living-room wall back home in Minneapolis, an unusual conversation piece, unusual except that scores of other couples are supposed to own similar certificates, though I have yet to see one.

"The Stuck Couple"

A sex-scandal urban legend that has been heard by most American males at one time or another (and probably reflects their unconscious fear of women) concerns the couple who become so tightly stuck together during sexual intercourse that they can be separated only with medical aid. Usually their sex act was an illicit one, and often the couple are hopelessly stuck inside a car, as well as tightly to each other. Sometimes the story is told as a joke, and the unfortunate woman gets the punchline, "But how am I going to explain this [the destruction of the car] to my husband?" Yet even with this snappy too-good-to-be-true conclusion and the utter unlikelihood of the incident ever having happened, "The Stuck Couple" is also internationally known as an "authentic" story, and it is often said to have been published in the newspaper with full particulars.

An alleged case of this incident having taken place in England is given in John Train's 1978 book *True Remarkable Occurrences,* complete with several tidbits of inconclusive verification, and even a footnote. Unfortunately, there is neither a date for the publication nor a specific reference to a published source. As Train presents the story (p. 20):

LOVERS CUT FREE FROM EMBRACE

LONDON—A tiny sports car leaves a lot to be desired as a midnight trysting spot, two secret lovers have learned.

Wedged into a two-seater, a near-naked man was suddenly immobilized by a slipped disc, trapping his woman companion beneath him, according to a doctor writing in a medical journal here.

The desperate woman tried to summon help by honking the horn with her foot. A doctor, ambulance driver, fire-

men, and a group of interested passersby* quickly surrounded the car in Regent's Park.

"The lady found herself trapped beneath 200 pounds of
pain-racked, immobile man," said Dr. Brian Richards of
Kent.

"To free the couple, firemen had to cut away the car
frame," he said.

The distraught woman, helped out of the car and into a
coat, sobbed: "How am I going to explain to my husband
what has happened to his car?"—*Reuters*

Rodney Dale published a different English version of "The
Stuck Couple" in 1978. He had heard from a friend of a friend
that the couple became trapped during sex in their car while
it was parked across the end of someone else's driveway—
certainly an unlikely place to carry on an affair. The top of the
car had to be cut off in order to rescue them, Dale reported,
and the woman, being apologized to by the rescuers for the
destruction of her husband's car, replied, "That's all right. It's
not my husband." Variations in the story told in the United
States include the pseudoscientific notion that if lovers are
frightened "in the act" the woman's muscles may cramp up
and thus trap the man, or the idea that prominent persons in
the community were involved in the scandal. Sometimes, too,
alcoholic drinks, freezing weather, carbon monoxide from the
car exhaust, and extremely compact sports cars are involved
in the particulars of the story.

The best-known "authoritative case history" of *penis captivus*
as a result of *vaginismus* in medical literature turns out to be
a hoax that may itself have been suggested by an early form
of the modern legend. In 1971 doctors Sidney W. Bondurant
and Stephen C. Cappanari of the Vanderbilt University Hospital took a hard look at a letter signed by a doctor "Egerton Y.
Davis" in an 1884 issue of the *Philadelphia Medical News* that

---

*Including women volunteer workers who arrived to serve tea, the
London *Sunday Mirror* reported.

described a celebrated observation, supposedly firsthand, of a case of *captivus.* Allegedly, Davis, said to be a former U. S. Army doctor, had answered a call for help while he was in England from a man who had accidentally surprised his coachman in bed with a maid—a large man and a small woman—as a result of which the two became stuck together in the act of intercourse. (However, they were not in the coach at the time.) The doctor wrote that he finally had to administer chloroform to the woman in order to induce sleep and cause her to relax enough for the man to get loose.

Bondurant and Cappanari identified the writer of this letter as the famous Canadian doctor and medical educator Sir William Osler, whose "fanciful half," Egerton Y. Davis, was invented on this occasion in order to embarrass a pompous colleague of his who held an editorial position with the *Medical News.* The letter was mailed for Osler from Montreal while he himself was not in Canada, and rumors were then circulated that Dr. Davis had moved to Canada. Out of curiosity about the possible acceptance of this "case" among modern doctors, the authors of the exposé submitted an anonymous copy of the letter to several Vanderbilt Hospital faculty and house staff for comments. Most of these subjects had heard of *penis captivus,* it turned out, and about half of them were willing to believe the particulars of this case or at least thought it was possible; but only one had ever seen such a case, and it involved not human beings but "a Scottie bitch in his frontyard." No doubt Sir William Osler would have been gratified by these results.

A psychologist at the University of Haifa, Professor Benjamin Beit-Hallahmi, has made questionnaire surveys of sex knowledge and sexual folklore among subjects in both Israel and the United States for a number of years. He kindly shared some of his findings with me, including an unpublished paper titled "Dangers of the Vagina." Since 1976, he writes, he has compared data from the two countries and has found stuck-couple stories to be well known in both, though they are somewhat better known in Israel. "Despite the fact that all authoritative sources on human sexual physiology deny the possibility of the *penis captivus* phenomenon," Beit-Hallahmi concluded, "such stories are still prevalent." The two elements common to most versions of the legend that he has collected are *surprise* (which brings about the sticking) and *punishment* (which the couple must suffer for their illicit intercourse).

A further variation on the stuck-couple theme merges with a distinctly separate urban sex legend which we might call—

"The Sheriff's Daughter"

This time the couple get stuck together in the backseat of their car while at a drive-in movie. Unable to get separated on their own, they finally gain the attention of another patron, who notifies the manager of the theater, who stops the film and turns on the lights, then summons the sheriff. The lawman not only arranges for the couple's rescue but recognizes the girl as his own teen-age daughter.

Here's the concluding motif of that version developed into a separate legend as recalled from collegiate tradition of the early 1960s and sent to me by Professor Paul Heller of Norwich University, Northfield, Vermont, in 1980:

THE COP ON THE BEACH

During summer vacation an upperclassman meets a beautiful teen-ager in a coastal, summer-resort community. Before the summer ends they attend a beach party and she decides to spend the night with the fellow in his tent on a secluded area of the public beach. The cops discover the illegally pitched tent, and one of them enters to investigate. He proceeds to arrest the couple for trespassing and further charge the student for his statutory rape of an underage girl. The couple are frightened and bribe the cops in exchange for sexual favors offered by the girl. The first policeman withdraws from the tent and relays the offer to the second one, who accepts and prepares to enter the tent. As he pulls the young lady to him he discovers that she is his daughter.

And having arrived now at the subject of family relations, let us look at a final recent sex legend that is in that category but that also brings in modern technology. This one is—

"Superglue Revenge"

In *The Vanishing Hitchhiker* I merely alluded to recent stories about misuse of "superglue." (People superglued to toilet seats, baby playing with superglue gets stuck to highchair, woman's finger attached to eyelid when she tries to superglue false eyelashes on, etc.) I have also mentioned such superglue legends in passing on radio talk shows, and as a result I have been flooded with letters and other inquiries asking whether the following story (a typical text) is true:

> A woman went home on her lunch hour to pick up some items she needed for work, though she normally ate lunch at work. Upon her arrival home, she noticed her husband's car in the driveway. When she entered the house she heard voices coming from the bedroom and she realized what she had walked in on. So she immediately left the house, returned to work, and plotted her revenge. When she went home that evening, she cooked her husband's favorite dinner, changed to a sexy negligee, lit the candles, chilled the wine, and enjoyed a romantic evening with her husband. After dinner she enticed him into the bedroom, undressed him, and sexually aroused him; and, when he was fully erect, she superglued his penis to his abdomen. He required surgery for its removal.

Unfortunately, I cannot tell my eager readers positively whether the "Superglue Revenge" tradition is true or false;

certainly it is true-to-life in terms of psychology, and I do believe the stuff could be dangerous if used improperly (though I have never managed to glue mighty loads of heavy broken things with but a single drop). What I can report is that the story has come out of hospital emergency rooms all over the country, and that it has been passed on from innumerable friends of friends to other storytellers. Sometimes it is even told—as true—by teachers of health, psychology, or nursing. Then too, when you think about it, "Superglue Revenge" is very much like "The Solid Cement Cadillac" story discussed in my earlier book: there the husband symbolically tied up his wife's illicit sexual activity (as he imagined it) by filling up the car of her supposed lover. But here it is the woman (who also has a car in the driveway as her clue) who immobilizes her husband, this time doing it literally rather than figuratively.

May we draw any larger conclusions about our culture or our hang-ups from this group of modern legends about sex? Such conclusions would be somewhat tenuous, since we have considered here only the "true" stories (not the rich variety of fictional sex jokes or superstitious lore), and most of the legends from my earlier book have gone unmentioned. But, even so, a few general points are obvious. First, the urban legends about sex seem most typically to be told from a male heterosexual point of view. The fantasies alluded to are mainly concerned with having sex freely and guiltlessly with a variety of women. The goal seems to be to avoid pregnancy or permanent attachments of any kind. The female in the stories is usually depicted as a prostitute, a victim, or a pawn in a man's game (like the old man's young wife or the sheriff's teen-age daughter). Even when a wife or mother is involved, she may become simply the accidental target of a man's fantasies (as in the missent letter story); or, she "earns" her license to become a whore.

Another side of this male dominance in the sex legends is shown by the insulting way that certain male characters in the stories treat women. Thus, the gynecologist (assumed here to be male) makes a tasteless wisecrack about the woman's mistake, with negative implications about her character. The store clerks laugh at the woman's menstrual period, and the state patrolman (in some versions, at least) snickers at the young woman's accidental sexual pun. And just as the fraternity man drugs and seduces young women at college, the dentist (perhaps the frat brother after graduation) takes advantage of his patients. Realizing that women probably tell all of these stories just as commonly as men do, we must assume that the images and attitudes contained in the plots reflect women's fears about males' viewpoints toward them just as surely as they reflect the males' own prejudicial notions.

Whatever fantasies, looseness, or boldness regarding sex these legends might seem to display on the surface, at their root most of them are essentially conservative as well as being indicative of some crucial areas of ignorance about sex. The whole unscientific notion of there being effective aphrodisiacs, for example, is seemingly accepted as true, as is the folk idea that a good girl will go completely wild and reveal her true inner lusty nature under the influence of alcohol or other drugs. The "right" attitude for a woman to have is suggested in the stories to be a state of innocent disregard for sex, except within marriage, so that giving her a license to play the whore or giving her the wrong man's name and address is regarded as "a good joke." Males, as I have suggested before, are shown in the urban sex legends as being both distrustful of and afraid of "their" women, so that those men who step outside of society's boundaries for what is allowable in sexual behavior are punished by being caught in the act (stuck in the act, really) or found with the wrong woman or, in the extreme case, shot through the scrotum so that a woman can be a virgin mother. (Even though this last story is more than a century old, it is still being told today.)

Perhaps only "Superglue Revenge" slightly breaks away from some of these commonplace ideas, though it too involves the desire of a man to have all the women he wants, and the related male fear of a woman tying him up and injuring him sexually. But, at least, here for once the woman has taken charge of events and somehow gets even with her erring mate. So it takes superglue to break down that "Superman" complex. Where can the legends go from there? We'll just have to wait and see.

6

Media Sources
and Business Legends

"I read it in the paper."

There is a passage in the opening chapter of Nathaniel Hawthorne's 1851 novel *The House of the Seven Gables* that sounds very familiar to a modern student of urban legends. Referring to the interplay of oral and written accounts of old family legends, Hawthorne wrote, "Tradition . . . sometimes brings down truth that history has let slip, but is oftener the wild babble of the time, such as was formerly spoken of at the fireside and now congeals in newspapers. . . ." He recognized then what is still true, that the press may publish fanciful folklore alongside solid news; as Hawthorne imagined it, the stories traveled from the fireside to the news columns. Thus, it seems likely that people then might have validated some unlikely story that they repeated as a true incident, just as people do nowadays, by saying, "I read it in the paper."

Journalists seek the truth, of course, but they also love a good story, and in the natural course of their work they frequently have thrust upon them all manner of nearly irresistible odd tales and news tips. Most of what eventually gets into the news columns is verified and documented with reasonable care (considering the speed with which modern newspapers are written, edited, and printed). But the signed columns of humor, opinion, and even editorials are another matter; here the currently favorite rumors and legends may be mentioned, discussed, weighed, and perhaps even supported or debunked. But whatever the contexts in which such stories appear in print, the reading public tends to remember only the *story*, to forget about the journalistic commentary, and to declare quite seriously when repeating the juicy parts later, "I read it in the paper."

That even the international news bureaus sometimes circulate modern folk narratives by teletype has already been amply demonstrated in this book. I sometimes wonder if some waggish writers and editors for AP, UPI, or Reuters deliberately send out an apocryphal story on the wire now and then just to see how many newspapers will pick it up this time. And when you stir into this folk-journalistic stew the letters to the editor, the advice and "action line" columns, and all the broadcast talk shows and news programs (especially those on radio), the chances of a doubtful story that is circulating orally coming to many people's attention in the mass media as well are very good indeed. Who is going to disbelieve a story if it was heard told on good authority and someone also allegedly "read it in the paper"?

A rare firsthand report of a discussion of urban legends by a group of modern writers and editors was published in the magazine *New Jersey Monthly* in August 1982 by a writer for that periodical who tape-recorded an editorial meeting. Among the staff members talking over the tales they had heard, the one person who was regarded as "the group skeptic" (Editor #2) turned out to be the best storyteller of them all. Observe:

> Editor #1: Didn't anybody ever hear the one about kids who took LSD and put a baby in the oven?
>
> Others: No.
>
> Editor #3: They probably didn't mean to . . .
>
> Editor #2: It supposedly happened in New Jersey?
>
> #3: How about the dog in the microwave, or is that a true story?
>
> #2: A *dog* in the microwave?

#3: Yeah, the lady bathed the dog, and to dry it off she put the little dog in the microwave and blew up the dog.

Editor #4: I heard that it was a woman and the cat was out in the rain and she dried it off in the microwave.

#2: *(Sarcastically)* Oh, was that here or in California?

#4: That was here . . .

#3: Someone told me about the guy who was a short-order cook, who got his insides cooked out . . .

#2: Oh yes—but that was also something I read in the *Times*—as if I believe everything I read in the *Times*. It was a woman, actually, who worked in a fast-food restaurant— this was about ten years ago—and she suffered a variety of peculiar symptoms and went from doctor to doctor. And she just got worse and worse. And she eventually died, and when they performed an autopsy on her, they found that her internal organs were completely cooked from the microwaves that were leaking from this—from the old microwave ovens that *were* found to have a great deal of the microwaves, and the woman's—all her internal organs were cooked. And that's why she died. But that was different— I read it in the *Times*.

Sure, "That was different"; but please see pages 63 and 64 of *The Vanishing Hitchhiker* for a discussion of "scientific" versions of the cooked-insides microwave horror legends. And then think about this: how many doctors would that woman have been able to consult with her internal organs already zapped to medium rare?

A similar reminiscence about some urban legends known to members of the British press was published in a 1982 letter to the editor of *Folklore* by Brian McConnell, who was a writer for the London *Daily Mirror* between 1957 and 1966. While cautioning folklore scholars that a modern urban legend tends to be edited down by journalists into merely "an anecdote for social amusement," and that no record is kept by newspapers of the unsubstantiated stories they hear about, McConnell nonetheless offers an interesting account of the kinds of apocryphal stories that were most commonly reported to his office.

The phoned-in tips, he recalls, "are told with surprisingly detailed facts, names, locations, etc. . . . they are also told by educated, middle class people, almost certainly professional or white collar workers, and when they give their addresses (as they frequently do because they expect to receive some reward for the story) the addresses are most frequently good suburban households. The stories relate to people who also have equally good residences or better." Among the specific stories he was often told, McConnell lists "The Stolen Corpse," "The Elephant That Sat on the Mini," and three distinctly English legends that he calls "The Flying Cow," "The Wrongful Arrest," and "The Hatchet in the Handbag (i.e., "The "Hairy-Armed Hitchhiker")." Unfortunately, what McConnell did not keep track of was how many of these urban legends of Fleet Street eventually found their way into print, one way or another. But probably the statement "I read it in the *Times*" is as common among legend tellers in London as it is in New York.

Product Defect and Liability Legends

The mass media sometimes mention negative rumors and legends concerning specific companies and products, even when these claims are obviously false, because—true or not—the slanderous material that is passing rapidly from person to person is *news* in any case. Besides, the businesses in question then often provide the press with statements of rebuttal or denial that are also newsworthy.

Many more such stories of defective or dangerous products circulate only in oral tradition, getting no closer to publication than being phoned in occasionally to newspapers or radio stations by people who want to know "When are you going to do a story on the such-and-such scandal?" But don't expect to see a news story soon verifying, for example, that the dangerous Atomic Golfball with a radioactive center killed a child who cut one open (which is, of course, what every child wants to do with a golfball); or that Marlboro Lights have an ingredient absorbed into the filter that makes you become addicted to that brand alone, but that also eventually causes cancer; or that someone was awarded a gigantic cash settlement from the manufacturers of Levi's because a teen-ager sat in a filled bathtub wearing a new pair of jeans in order to shrink them to a snug fit and then he or she (usually she) was squeezed to death by the contracting denim. No way—for these tales are just folklore.

Another recurring business legend to watch out for is the one about the "Five-Year Parts Law." When your know-it-all neighbor gets a tremendous deal on a car or lawn mower or household appliance because that model is going out of production, and when that same neighbor brags to you that he's safe for at least five years because the government requires manufacturers to produce spare parts for that length of time after they stop making a product, well—you can have the last laugh. More folklore; there's no such law. And, incidentally, there wasn't a "Popcorn Experiment" in the 1930s (or any other time either) embedded into feature movies so that you were subconsciously seduced into buying more popcorn at the theater because images of hot buttered popcorn were flashed quickly by during the screenings. It didn't happen, and it wouldn't work, according to psychologists.

One strange modern folk notion about a manufactured product that made the news lately concerns a home system for predicting the sex of an unborn child using the well-known commercial drain cleaning product Drāno. According to the traditional method, which is sometimes tried at baby showers, a bit of urine (sometimes saliva) donated by the mother-to-be is added to a few Drāno crystals on a saucer; if the bubbling mixture then turns green, the woman will have a boy, if it turns yellow or amber, a girl.

Inevitably, a doctor who heard about this folk sex-test was

inspired to run an experiment on it. Dr. Robert M. Fowler, pediatrician at the University of Wyoming, made the scientific breakthrough on this one. He tried the Drāno test on 100 pregnant women and reported his findings in a letter to the *Journal of the American Medical Association* (20 August 1982). The results, he found, were just about as reliable as flipping a coin or as random guessing. In fact, about one-fifth of his subjects even failed to produce the same color-reading consistently, and the babies born from these particular women were evenly divided between boys and girls (11 to 10), which, depending on how you read statistics, might seem either to prove or disprove the Drāno test.

Dr. Fowler's test conclusions were reported in many newspapers shortly after his *JAMA* letter appeared, and the magazine *Family Circle,* appropriately enough, ran a capsule summary of it in January of 1983, all of which should have been gratifying to The Drackett Company of Cincinnati, Ohio, the manufacturers of Drāno. I had written to the Drāno people inquiring about the baby test in November of 1981 and received a prompt and concerned reply to the effect that Drāno is "a powerful product" that could be highly dangerous when used in the way some folks were doing. The company director of public relations urged me to join the fight against allowing such product misuse "to become part of the respected body of folklore," which, of course, I would be glad to do if I knew how. (Sorry, Drāno, it's *already* folklore.) Furthermore, when I have tried to convince some true believers that there is absolutely no scientific basis for the Drāno test, I have sometimes been assured gravely, "Well, you know, the company has changed the formula of Drāno so that it no longer works—but it *used to* work every time; why a friend of my neighbor's tried it during all three of her pregnancies, and. . . ."

A product-defect rumor that has developed some of the narrative qualities of true legend in the past few years and has received considerable media attention is the one about a disposable butane cigarette lighter supposedly blowing up and killing someone. A typical version of this story published in a local newsletter was sent to me by James W. Day, an attorney in Carrollton, Illinois, who wrote, "I have made some inquiries and found that the story of the deaths is absolutely unfounded." Here is his printed version as it appeared in *Forestry News* (vol. 1, no. 17, January 1980), published by the Two Rivers Resource Conservation and Development Project of Pittsfield, Illinois:

DISPOSABLE BUTANE LIGHTERS—DEADLY HAZARD

In recent months, the Union-Pacific Railroad has had two fatal accidents caused by butane lighters. These accidents occurred in welding areas when an employee was welding with a butane lighter in his pocket. A spark from the welding landed on the lighter, burned through, exposing the fluid, which exploded. One lighter was in a shirt pocket and killed the individual instantly. The other lighter was in the pants pocket and caused an amputation. The man later died.

It is estimated that there is the same amount of force in a butane lighter when it explodes as there is in three sticks of dynamite. Please warn anyone using these lighters of the potential hazard. Most folks don't realize that they are walking around with the equivalent of three sticks of dynamite in their pocket.

As it happens, however, many folks know about that story, though the details vary somewhat. Some say it was a construction worker rather than a railroader who died while welding, and that it was a soldier with the lighter in his pants pocket who suffered the amputation of a leg. The descriptions of the accident can be remarkably vivid, especially considering that no eyewitnesses to it are ever the ones telling the story; still, these people seem to know all about the huge hole that was blown in the man's chest, or the explosion as massive as that of three (or up to six) sticks of dynamite. Herb Caen wrote in the *San Francisco Chronicle* in December 1979 that the butane lighter story arrived in his mail on "official-looking US Dept. of Transportation stationery," complete with the specific references to the Union Pacific railroad and the usual comparison to three sticks of dynamite. He quoted a UP PR man: "That story swept the country the past month but we have no record of such an accident. It keeps popping up everywhere. Some myths die hard."

The butane lighter fatal-accident story may reflect both disapproval of cigarette smoking and people's suspicion of throwaway products, as well as some uncertainty that butane is a safe fuel. The mention of a particular railroad line is harder to explain, although it is interesting that there is also an airliner analogue to the story: disposable lighters with a "visible fuel supply" are sometimes said to have caused violent midair explosions and fatal crashes.

Early in 1980 the story took another turn, as reported by (among others) columnist Joan Beck of the *Chicago Tribune.* On 17 June, under the headline "The butane lighter joins our folklore of fears," Ms. Beck discussed the then-current folk idea that an exploding butane lighter had caused the critical burns suffered by actor/comedian Richard Pryor. She mentioned the earlier attachment of the story to railroad workers, and quoted Consumer Product Safety Commission statistics that showed only 198 complaints nationwide about butane lighters in the previous three years, of which just 56 were lighters allegedly "exploding." But a spokesperson called this "a soft term," telling Beck, "As far as we can tell, the lighter must have been put down while still burning and then flared up." With some 250 million-plus disposable butane lighters sold in the United States annually, things sound pretty safe, so I agree with Joan Beck's conclusion that "maybe we have enough that's real to worry about already without scaring ourselves about our cigarette lighters."

We could worry instead about our contact lenses, for example. In late March and early April of 1983 safety directors of industrial plants and companies across the country began circulating memoes to their employees warning them against a possible danger to the eyesight of certain workers wearing contact lenses. Here is the opening section of a typical example of this warning notice as it went out to the vocational education branch of the Detroit, Michigan, public school system (it was sent to me by Dolores Jocque of Hamtramck, Michigan):

TO: ALL EMPLOYEES

RE: CONTACT LENSES

We have been advised of the following hazard that occurred within two other companies.

TWO RECENT INCIDENTS HAVE UNCOVERED A PREVIOUSLY UNKNOWN PHENOMENON OF SERIOUS GRAVITY.

(1) A workman threw an electrical switch into the closed position which produced a short-lived sparking.

(2) An employee flipped open the colored lens of his welding goggles to better position the welding rod. He inadvertantly struck the metal to be welded, producing an arc.

BOTH MEN WERE WEARING CONTACT LENSES. On returning home from work, they removed the contacts AND THE CORNEA OF THE EYE WAS REMOVED along with the lenses.

Result: PERMANENT BLINDNESS!

A copy of a local variation of the same safety memo was brought to me by a student who had found it posted on a school bulletin board. He believed a definite place named in the document was the town of Duchesne, Utah, but a closer reading revealed that it was "Duquesne Electric," not even the name of a Utah company. This memo was typed on the letterhead of the Granite [Utah] School District, dated March 29, 1983, and stamped at a diagonal across the top "IMMEDIATE

ACTION REQUESTED." Further, the first line of the document read "NOTICE******NOTICE******NOTICE****** NOTICE", and someone had added for good measure in a margin the handwritten comment "Important!" After roughly the same text as the Michigan example, this one concluded with the advice that supervisors should "prohibit all contact-wearing personnel . . . from wearing this mode of corrective lenses, or mandate that dark green protective eyewear be consistently used."

Such memoes, with their telltale capitals and exclamation points, usually offered the quasi-scientific explanation that electric arcs would generate microwaves that instantly dry up the fluid between the eye and the contact lenses, thus bonding the two together. (Other versions of the story simply say that the victim had looked into a microwave oven, and perhaps there's a connection with the old legends about a child grabbing at an electrified mannequin from a water-borne carnival fun ride and getting electrocuted, or a boy urinating on an electrical outlet for a prank and being killed by the resulting short curcuit.) Supposedly, at any rate, the horrendous contact-lens accident was absolutely painless to the victim.

The Associated Press, getting reports of this warning from far and wide, looked into the matter of contact-cornea bondings and blindings and issued its debunking story, which was widely reprinted, on 4 April 1983. The AP reported that the National Society to Prevent Blindness had heard this story in various forms since about 1967. The Food and Drug Administration said it had no report of occurrences of this kind, and spokespersons for two companies that were often named in the safety memoes—Duquesne Light Co. of Pittsburgh and United Parcel Service—said they had heard of the stories but never tracked them down. The AP story concluded that evidently the 1983 spate of warning stories could be traced to a bulletin describing this "unknown phenomenon" posted in February at Genstar Stone Products Co. in Hunt Valley, Maryland; the safety director of Genstar learned the story by letter from another firm, and doubtless the trail would lead back to a friend of a friend if one tried to go further than that. By mid-March the Genstar officials realized that no such hazard existed, and they dropped the warning, but by then it was too late to arrest the spread of the story.

A *Chicago Tribune* story on the same day expanded on the Associated Press information by mentioning that the International Brotherhood of Electrical Workers had received calls about the cornea accidents from about 200 of its local branches in the United States and Canada; the union sent a letter to each one of these denying the reports. Also, the L. E. Myers company of Chicago, the *Tribune* reported, had notified its 2,000 employees about the alleged accidents and promised to investigate further.

At least one insurance company—Liberty Mutual of Boston —has distributed a memo to companies for which it has issued workers' compensation coverage to discredit the cornea-fusion legend. In a "Loss Prevention" bulletin dated 31 March 1983, a company executive carefully reviewed the elements of the story and found them entirely lacking in credibility. This detailed three-page document is a virtual summary of folk ideas contained in the legend—the named companies where the supposed incidents occurred, the possibility of microwave radiation from such an incident, professional medical opinions on possible dangers to wearers of contacts, the results of journalistic investigations, and so forth. But even Liberty Mutual cautions, "Please bear in mind that our attempts to stop this rumor do not in any way endorse the use of contact lenses in the industrial environment," and the memo concludes with a brief summary of certain work-related hazards of wearing contacts.

The idea of the victims of product failure or misuse cases either receiving generous settlements from the offending companies or else recovering huge damages in the courts looms large in many of these legends, just as the same idea does in legends about contaminated food or drink. Perhaps the most impressive treatment of this particular theme—because it is believed by some lawyers as well as lay folk—involves a supposed accident with a power lawn mower. The story is that a man working with his mower that has a horizontally rotating blade decides to pick up the mower while it is running and trim his hedge. The blade neatly severs the tips of all his fingers. (In a variant I have heard, two men join in lifting the mower and their sixteen individual fingertips are cut off, the thumbs in either story being out of harm's way on top of the mower.)

Professor of Law James P. Murphy of the University of Bridgeport (Connecticut) School of Law sent me a learned gloss on this particular kind of product-liability case, summarizing the legal theory involved. It seems a manufacturer may be held liable in such cases for any reasonably forseeable misuse of a product, provided the manufacturer has not issued a warning against such misuse. The lawn mower story, however, he regards as being too farfetched and unpredictable to be covered by such a principle. Yet, Professor Murphy writes, "responsible, otherwise clear-headed businessmen and executives would be ready to believe that a court held the manufacturer liable" for such incidents. In an article in the law review *Forum* (vol. 14, 1978) that Professor Murphy included, the following reference is made to this particular severed-finger legend:

> Horror stories about unfair judgments circulated among insurers can drive rates up, even if these stories are unrepresentative or false. The [company name] advertising campaign told of a judgment against a lawn mower manufacturer for injuries suffered when the plaintiff lifted the lawnmower to cut hedges. No one can verify that this case actually occurred. Nevertheless, it is often repeated and doubtless confirms the impression of ratesetters that insurance rates must anticipate the wildest judgments.

The *folk* contexts in which the lawn mower story is circulated, then, include lawyers, insurers, and weekend home yardworkers. I have also heard of the story being told by lawn mower salesmen and repairmen when asked by a customer, "What's the worst accident you know of with one of these machines?" And when these people tell the story, it *is* true to say that this case is the worst they have "heard of!" Just because it never happened doesn't really matter, because it's darn good advice not to pick up a running power mower.

"Mickey Mouse Acid"

The illegal drug "business," like many of the legitimate commercial endeavors, has attracted its share of modern folklore, including product-defect legends, though of course there are not stories describing the drug manufacturers' legal liability either for misuse of their products or for injuries to users. Within subcultures where drug use is accepted or tolerated there exists a rich esoteric oral tradition describing ingenious drug production and smuggling, narcotics busts, and legendary suppliers and users. But among people with little or no direct experience with unlawful drugs, the folk stories that circulate are more likely to be about the horrendous (exaggerated) effects of taking drugs, both on users and nonusers. In these legends—"exoteric," we may call them, since they are from the outside looking in—the person who is zonked-out by a heavy drug dose may be said to have microwaved a baby, stared at the sun until blind, or (in the worst horror story I have encountered) cut the heart out of an infant with a broken soft-drink bottle. As with most urban rumors and legends, the supposed verification for such grotesque claims consists of vague and undocumented references to friends of friends or to supposed media reports.

The media may actually transmit apocryphal drug stories, of course, but usually they include a disclaimer of some sort if the incident cannot be validated, as with this 1971 example

from Herb Caen's column, which is so beloved of urban folklorists:

> There was the one about the police officer giving an
> anti-narcotics talk to a high school class. At the end, he put
> a marijuana cigarette on a dish and told the class to "pass
> it around, sniff it, look at it carefully, so you'll know it when
> you see it." By the time the plate gets back to him, there are
> three marijuana cigarettes on it. Or five, or seven."

So—there is the story in the paper, just like people said
then (and are still saying) that it was. But—besides the variations mentioned for the specific number of cigarettes on the
plate—Caen also remarked, "I ran the story a couple of years
ago with a lot of hedging, having found it impossible to
confirm. Since then it has been printed with variations, all over
the world." This pot-in-the-schoolroom story, then, is surely
just as true as the sex-education horror stories mentioned in
Chapter 5, which is to say, not true at all.

A favorite theme of drug legends is that of illegal narcotics
use in some very wholesome and familiar setting; this is the
counterpart of the kidnaping legends that are set in suburban
shopping centers, or of the food contamination stories centering on the favorite fast-food restaurants. In fact, long-suffering
McDonald's comes in for yet another round of undeserved
slander in this category, for there are traditional claims that
Ronald McDonald, the company-image representative in the
clown suit, was fired for taking drugs (or for being gay), and
that a certain kind of McDonald's coffee stirrer had to be
changed because it was coveted as an ideal cocaine spoon. A
similar legend has it that the people who play the Disney
characters at Disneyworld are all drug addicts.

The most insidious urban drug legend, as well as the one
with the greatest narrative development, describes how LSD
dealers try to make addicts of our young children by polluting
the image of Mickey Mouse himself. (Is nothing sacred?)
Surely it is a dreadful thought, but just as surely it is a folk

WE HAVE been informed that a very dangerous drug is being circulated illegally in some parts of New England. You should be aware of its presence in the area and its severe danger to all who might come in contact with the substance. Please caution your children to be on the alert for any materials that fall into the category described and to make note of the individual who might want to pass it on to them.

Blue

Yellow

MICKEY MOUSE ACID (L.S.D.) has been circulated widely throughout some parts of New England as a part of or in the form of a "sticker" or label. It may be available to school age children (See picture).

DO NOT HANDLE !!! CONTACT WITH MOISTURE AND SKIN COULD CAUSE THE SAME EFFECT AS TAKING A DOSE OF ACID ORALLY ! ! ! The picture is Mickey Mouse in the Walt Disney Movie -- "The Sorcerer's Apprentice" from "Fantasia". The actual size is ½" square. Mickey Mouse is wearing a red gown, blue hat, yellow shoes and has the appearance of a "lick and stick tatoo". All Disney Cartoon characters have been used in the distribution of this L.S.D.

If you have seen the substance, know the whereabouts of its, or have any information regarding it, please call your local Police Department at once.

fantasy, for there would obviously be too little profit to be earned from selling drugs to small children to make the risk and the investment worthwhile.

The legend of "Mickey Mouse Acid" received wide circulation all across the United States in anonymous printed or typewritten one-page handouts bearing a rough sketch of Mickey garbed more or less as for his role as the sorcerer's apprentice in the film *Fantasia*, and with an explanation like this, which was copied verbatim in all its typographical extravagance from a typical example that showed up in Atlanta but evidently stemmed from New England:

WARNING!

WE HAVE been informed that a very dangerous drug is being circulated illegally in some parts of New England. You should be aware of its presence in the area and its severe danger to all who might come in contact with the substance. Please caution your children to be on the alert for any materials that fall into the category described and to make note of the individual who might want to pass it on to them. MICKEY MOUSE ACID (L.S.D.) has been circulated widely throughout some parts of New England as a part of or in the form of a "sticker" or label. It may be available to school age children. (See picture.) DO NOT HANDLE!!! CONTACT WITH MOISTURE AND SKIN COULD CAUSE THE SAME EFFECT AS TAKING A DOSE OF ACID ORALLY!!! The picture is Mickey Mouse in the Walt Disney Movie—"The Sorcerer's Apprentice" from "Fantasia". The actual size is ½" square. Mickey Mouse is wearing a red gown, blue hat, yellow shoes and has the appearance of a "lick and stick tatoo" [*sic*]. All Disney Cartoon characters have been used in the distribution of this LSD. If you have seen the substance, know the whereabouts of it, or have any information regarding it, please call your local Police Department at once.

"We have been informed" is a nice touch here, since the phrase merely suggests verification without specifying any. (Who has informed whom? These warning leaflets are seldom signed, and they usually look like blotchy third-generation photocopies of the kind that folklorists call "Xerox-lore.") The police are mentioned in the handout in a perfectly reasonable way: any concerned citizen would surely want to notify authorities about drug soliciting among children, but this is not to say that the local police actually have found instances of "Mickey Mouse Acid." To the contrary, I am not aware of any documented instance of LSD being absorbed into a cartoon-character sticker or transfer, although the drug transmitted on the medium of a thicker paper—as so-called blotter acid —is a common practice, and sometimes blotter acid "tabs" are imprinted with pictures or designs. But even if a drug supplier wanted to catch small children's attention, why would he select a characterization of Mickey Mouse from an old, relatively uncommon, and distinctly adult-oriented film instead of employing the image of some current kid-craze figure?

The Mickey Mouse Acid handouts, despite their unreliability, have been the source of many news stories, sometimes quoted almost literally and usually presented without an explanation of the source. For instance, Professor M. Thomas Inge of Clemson University sent me a 20 January 1982 clipping from the Clemson, South Carolina, *Messenger* that attributes the legend to the nearby city of Pendleton and contains these revealing paragraphs of unattributed material:

> PENDLETON—Pendleton Police and other law enforcement agencies in the country are warning parents and young students of a children's "tatoo" [*sic*] which may contain LSD.
>
> Mickey Mouse Acid (LSD) has been circulated widely throughout some parts of the country as a part or in the form of a sticker or label. It may be available to school age children.
>
> The sticker is a picture of Mickey Mouse in a Walt Disney Movie "The Sorcerer's Apprentice" from "Fantasia."
>
> . . . Police warn that the sticker should not be touched . . . etc.

A journalist who took a hard look at the Mickey Mouse Acid story and identified a source of its proliferation in the Midwest was Jim Quinn of the Fort Wayne, Indiana, *News-Sentinel.* Quinn's report, published on 10 December 1981 in Fort Wayne and widely circulated by news services, names Jack McCormick, superintendent of the Ohio Bureau of Criminal

Investigation, as the person who was the "unwilling father" of the story in his own and nearby states. One slow news day in Columbus during the summer of 1981, McCormick explained, every reporter in town wanted to break the monotony of covering the legislative debate on the state budget by pressing him for confirmation of the Mickey Mouse Acid rumor that was beginning to be passed around. McCormick told them that as far as he knew there was no such thing as LSD-laced lick-and-stick transfers, at least not in his jurisdiction, although rumors of such a product were known throughout the East and Midwest. All he knew about in this regard was the familiar blotter acid.

When a drug pusher was arrested shortly thereafter near Columbus with 5,000 tabs of blotter acid in his car—all of them marked with little blue stars—McCormick patiently explained again to the press that stars alone did not prove the Mickey Mouse connection, and that, besides, none of the stars that were chemically tested contained any LSD. When reporters demanded to know whether the police chemists had tested all 5,000 pieces of paper, McCormick grew impatient and began to give them what he called "some technical stuff," making some of it up as he went along. His statements, further embroidered by the media, gave the legend a new lease on life, since, as Quinn concluded, "It appeals to people who think there are evil forces loose corrupting America's youth." But the fact is, as one headline to a reprint of Quinn's story so nicely put it, "Stories of LSD in Walt Disney tattoos was a goofy tale at best."

A likely source for the anonymous handouts on Mickey Mouse Acid are actual police department bulletins describing the appearance of blotter acid sheets when they show up in local markets. For example, a 1980 bulletin issued by the New Jersey State Police Narcotic Bureau contains illustrations of tabs imprinted with "Sorcerer's Apprentice" figures, and it cautions, "Children may be susceptible to this type of cartoon stamp believing it a tattoo transfer." There is also a warning statement in the bulletin against handling the blotter acid with bare hands. Probably well-meaning citizens, seeing such official warnings, generated their own versions of the bulletin containing the claim that actual transfers or lick-and-stick tattoos were found to contain LSD.

Even if Ohio law enforcement officer Jack McCormick unwillingly gave the legend a regional boost, he did not really originate it. Indeed, the root idea of contaminated small attractive bits of paper that are in common use seems to have been around at least one hundred years earlier. The English folklorists Iona and Peter Opie show this in a fascinating article titled "Certain Laws of Folklore" published in 1980. To illustrate the principle that "Today's Extraordinariness was probably also Yesterday's," the Opies cite the rumors that attended the introduction of "penny blacks" or "Queen's heads" gummed postage stamps in 1840. "The story soon circulated," they relate, "that the glue was poisonous, that the most vile ingredients were employed in its manufacture, that human material was not excluded, and that those so rash as to lick the Queen's head were in danger of contracting cholera." The survival of this belief in England was proven to the Opies in October of 1966, shortly after an "underworld character" named Ginger Marks mysteriously disappeared. Here is their report:

> One of us had just finished writing a postcard in a Soho post office when the man next to us, filling in his football coupon, warned: "Never lick a stamp."
> "Why not?" we asked.
> "Never lick a stamp," he repeated. "You may be licking Ginger Marks."
> "How d'you mean, licking Ginger Marks?"
> "Ah," the man replied, "He went into a glue factory, dinnen'e? Everyone in south-east London knows that."

A final ambiguous instance: on 13 March 1982 the Salt Lake City newspapers reported that local narcotics officers had arrested several drug dealers and confiscated "a large quantity of so-called 'Snoopy Acid.' " The news stories continued by explaining only that this is what the material was *called,* and that the acid was supposedly "soaked into cartoon decals"; but the articles did not claim that the cartoon character was actually pictured on any of the captured evidence, nor did they explain how you can soak anything into a decal. (Even the "lick-and-stick tattoo" paper is not porous enough to absorb drops of LSD, besides which the "right" way to apply the tattoos is to lick the skin, not the paper.) So I'm just waiting for rumors about Garfield Acid, or Smurf Acid, or maybe Mary Worth Acid. That'll be the day.

There is something about the amateur drawing of Mickey Mouse on the handouts I have seen that strikes me as odd. The illustration really doesn't look much like the Disney character, either in general or as he was costumed for the "Fantasia" role, but then we must assume that it was drawn from memory, either by the alleged drug pushers or by the issuers of the WARNING! notice. What I find interesting is not so much Mickey's appearance but his action in the sketch, for he seems to be juggling a stream of stars and little circles (balls? moons?); and there are exactly fourteen stars and a dozen circles dancing in the air over his pointed cap, for a total of TWENTY-SIX items, conspiracy fans!! Now—once again—that's a SORCERER'S apprentice, in a pointed cap I remind you, surrounded by twice-THIRTEEN (!!!) suspicious symbols. Something very fishy is going on here, just as sure as Ivory Soap is 99 and $44/100$ percent pure, which it isn't, of course. See next legend.

The Procter & Gamble Trademark

You have probably seen it hundreds of times—that cute old-fashioned trademark on all of the Procter & Gamble personal and household products, like Crest toothpaste, Crisco shortening, Pampers diapers, Tide laundry detergent, and dozens of other familiar brands, but above all on the flagship P&G item, Ivory Soap, "99 and $44/100\%$ PURE®IT FLOATS." The trademark may sometimes be very tiny (just about ¼-inch across on the toothpaste tube), but it's nearly always there somewhere on P&G products and advertising: it shows the profile of an old man's face in the crescent moon, facing left at a scattering of thirteen stars, all enclosed in a circle. A king-sized relief of the design adorns the facade of the Procter & Gamble headquarters in Cincinnati, and it identifies at a glance most of the company's memoes, press releases, and correspondence.

If you ever got curious about this trademark and called or wrote the company asking about it, you would have received a P&G handout explaining that the design evolved from a crude sketch of a cross in a circle that was first used around 1851 to identify shipping cartons of Star Candles, an early company product. Gradually this simple symbol evolved to a recognizable star, then to thirteen stars (representing the thirteen original colonies), and last it incorporated the "man-in-the-moon" figure that was as popular around the turn of the century as the "happy face" drawing became three-quarters of a century later. "Finally, in 1930," the company release explains, "a sculptor was commissioned by P&G to design today's authorized version of the famous 'Moon and Stars.'"

But if you have read the newspapers at all, or listened to rumors and legends for the past three or four years, you very likely have encountered other explanations of the origin or meaning of the P&G Moon-and-Stars trademark, accounts that brand it as infamous rather than famous. The moon-man and the thirteen stars, so the story goes, are really Satanic symbols, and the appearance of the drawing on so many everyday products is alleged to be P&G's way of referring obliquely to its support of a demonic cult (usually "by contributing 10% of their annual earnings"). Seemingly, everything about the trademark that can possibly be fit into this fantastic rumor has been "explained": the moon-man's (or "sorcerer's") hair forms a devil-like horn at the top, and the curlicues of his beard when viewed backwards in a mirror can be read as the "mark of the beast"—the number 666. The stars too, if connected properly by drawing in three curving lines, form another 666. And the whole thing, some people claim, represents the antichrist that is prophesied in the Bible, though other people may repeat an earlier folk explanation for the trademark that related it to the "Moonies" cult rather than to Satan.

This patchwork of rumored "meanings" for the symbol is often given a true legendary-narrative framework by adding the further explanation that the founder (or president) of P&G long ago made a pact with the devil guaranteeing that his company would prosper if the devil's sign were placed on every product. Also it is claimed that a company representative recently admitted the whole terrible truth (depending upon which version of the "truth" you happen to have heard) on a nationwide television talk show, like "Donahue" (or "Merv Griffin," or "60 Minutes," or . . . you name it). A bar of soap so pure it floats, indeed! Star Candles, ha! *This* is the ugly reality that lurks behind the familiar design, or so some folk will tell you that they heard from a friend of a friend who saw the TV show, or who heard it in church from someone else who saw it, or at least who heard it from someone who knows someone else who saw it. And as often as not these earnest, pious folk will show you a poorly printed, mimeographed, or photocopied handout sprinkled with capital letters and exclamation points and signed "A Good Christian" that conveys the story in full detail.

Of course, nothing—absolutely nothing—about this whacky wonder tale rings true. Procter & Gamble is a thoroughly modern manufacturing and marketing giant, not a creepy crew of devil worshippers with a Faust-like leader either at the helm of the present company or lurking in its dark past.

Ten percent of earnings, or even a smaller amount, donated to any suspicious or special cause whatever could never be buried in the annual report or hidden from the stockholders. There is no evidence of a moon-and-stars symbol like this one ever having been used by witches, sorcerers, or Satanists, and certainly not by "Moonies." The company's own explanation for the design is not only reasonable but can easily be documented in the corporation records or by reviewing the older P&G packages or advertising. The clearest indications of all that this is the stuff of urban legend and not of a dark hidden vein of reality are that none of the "sources" for the story ever turns out to be reliable, and most of the themes in the story are well known in other folklore.

The basic idea of a pact made with the devil in order to gain some earthly wealth, usually at the expense of one's own soul and in return for some concession to the devil's desires, is a very old and enduring one. (We allude to this theme in the common saying "The devil made me do it.") The specific notion that a huge modern company has hidden ties to a Satanic cult is not unprecedented either. In 1977, for instance, the McDonald's restaurant chain was widely alleged to be donating a portion of its profits to the Church of Satan; people claimed that they had heard Ray Kroc, the company founder and president, admit this on the "Phil Donahue Show." Around the same time the rock group Kiss was also said to be involved in Satanism, with the group name being interpreted as meaning "Kings [or "Knights"] in Satanic [or "Satan's"] Service." As a matter of fact, Kroc had appeared on "Donahue" in May 1977 (according to a story in the *Philadelphia Inquirer* on 10 October 1978) during which he talked about introducing the McDonald's fish sandwich in Cincinnati, which has a substantial Roman Catholic population. Kroc is said to have commented, "Watch, now the Pope will change the rules about not eating meat on Fridays." And, as a further fact that proves nothing, Kiss at the time was a very grotesque group in its dress, makeup, and performance style. So there was just enough "truth" behind such stories of the late 1970s to keep the doubtful rumors going for a while.

But there was nothing in either the McDonald's or the Kiss rumors quite as perfect as P&G's cryptic trademark upon which to build a more detailed and enduring urban legend. The McDonald's Golden Arches were never taken to be the Gates of Hell, nor was Kiss ever a pervasive enough influence in American popular culture to be feared by citizens as a general menace. But the Moon and Stars emblem was a pattern that virtually every American had seen, as well as one lacking a self-evident explanation. With a little imagination, every element of the trademark could be fit into a demonic pattern. As a result, the P&G trademark positively cried out for a folk explanation. The thing had to mean something, didn't it?

McDonald's lived down its Satanism rumor in 1977 and survived the equally silly wormburger rumors of 1978. The company then faded back into its innocuous but hugely successful nice-guy image (at least until the next rumor comes along). But the Procter & Gamble company, to its horror, found that the Satanism rumor that became attached to its hallowed trademark suddenly achieved massive recognition, and it was actually being taken seriously by thousands of people, often very religious and upright ones who would not hesitate to boycott a company that they distrusted.

In the fall of 1981 the Procter & Gamble trademark rumor (or legend, depending on the narrative content involved) had proliferated to such a degree that the company's headquarters was being flooded with inquiries. Within six months that year the number of calls and letters coming in on this matter had increased about sixfold, and by early summer of 1982 P&G grew so alarmed about it that they launched a counterattack on several fronts. Subsequently, within a year's time (whether as a direct result of the company efforts or not is debatable) the rumors and legends began to fade, providing a classic instance of the speed with which such anonymous traditional unverifiable reports may wax and wane in modern culture.

POLICE INFORMATION

CAUTION: Children may be susceptible to this type of cartoon stamp believing it a tattoo transfer.

Four thousand (4,000) "Mickey Mouse" stamps laced with an hallucinogenic drug "LSD" on the reverse side have surfaced in Essex County, NJ. Fifty (50) of these stamps have been bought in Bergen County, NJ for $2.00 per stamp. Regular "blotter" type acid sells for $3.00 to $7.00 per dose. Union and Middlesex Counties are only finding "blotter" type acid on plain paper. The age group selling acid is between 15 and 20 years old. "Superman" stamps are also said to be in circulation.

Below are photos of the "Mickey Mouse" stamps and packaging:

Red cardboard top w/picture of Mickey Mouse

Sheets, 5" x 5" w/picture of "Mickey Mouse"

Foil and clear ziplock plastic bag

Enlargement of stamps

Exactly where, when, and why the idea of a connection between P&G and Satanism arose is a mystery, but the first glimmers of negative rumors about the trademark had been noted in 1980 when persistent queries began to arrive, primarily from southern Minnesota, asking if the moon in the company symbol indicated that P&G had been acquired by the Rev. Sun Myung Moon's Unification Church, or if the company was supporting the "Moonies" financially. A few hundred such calls or letters per month from consumers in 1980 zoomed to thousands per month by late 1981; then inquiries coming from the Northwest and California began to shift to the Satanism theme and to include the claim that a national TV talk show had been the source of the information (possibly borrowing these ideas from the earlier McDonald's rumors).

In January 1982, after months of answering individual questions individually, Procter & Gamble went public on the issue. The company sent out news releases that explained the history of their trademark, asserted the total lack of any company contact with Satanism or with Rev. Moon's group, and stressed the complete fabrication of the story that any company executive had discussed Satanism or anything like it on a national talk show.

Newspapers, of course, loved this story and gave it good coverage, often depicting the trademark itself, and using headlines like "P&G trying to exorcise devil rumor" or "P&G washing out Satan rumors." However, the reader-service and action-line columns of many daily papers continued to get questions about the stories, and by spring 1982 the P&G phones were still ringing, now at the rate of some 12,000 calls a month, with people still asking for the truth behind the symbol. Many callers indicated that they had heard of the story either in church, from others who were churchgoers, or on a religious broadcast of some kind. The antichrist, 666, the "Mark of the Beast," and Satan all continued to figure prominently in typical versions of the story. Regions where it was spreading (besides California, the Northwest, and the Midwest) soon included several southern states, especially Tennessee, Alabama, Mississippi, Oklahoma, and Texas.

A typical letter to the *Action* column of the *Seattle Post-Intelligencer* (25 January 1982) demonstrates how seriously many people had taken the P&G rumor:

> Dear Action: This is very strange.
> I work for a doctor. Three of the doctor's patients—all

unknown to one another—are blaming bouts of depression on Procter & Gamble products in their homes. They claim P&G's trademark—depicting a moon, 13 stars and a man's head—is the symbol of Satan.

Two of them said they "heard" that TV personality Phil Donahue had interviewed "an important Procter & Gamble executive" who said he was "into Satanism."

The third patient said she "heard" the P&G executive had said the same thing on the Merv Griffin talk show.

When asked where they heard this rumor, all three told the doctor that the story had been told by somebody at church. . . .

But if anyone had to suffer depression from this story, it should have been the Procter & Gamble public relations officials. The calls reached a peak of 15,000 during June of 1982, and they completely occupied fifteen telephone operators who were assigned full time to respond to them. By then the rumors had spread to all fifty states, and news stories had carried them abroad. There were some hints from the company (which is usually secretive about such matters) that P&G sales were beginning to suffer, and there were reported instances of harrassment and vandalism directed against company officials or against personalities (like singer Loretta Lynn) who had appeared in P&G advertising.

In a press release from the Cincinnati headquarters dated June 24, 1982, Procter & Gamble stepped up its attack on the rumors by quoting five prominent American religious leaders saying that they had reviewed the evidence and were convinced that P&G was still pure. Reverend Jerry Falwell, founder of the Moral Majority, for example, said, "It is unfortunate that such false accusations are made in the first place, but even more concerning that they can be spread as rumor by people who call themselves Christians. I have discussed these rumors with the Chairman of the Board of Procter & Gamble, who happens to be from my home town in Virginia, and I am certain neither he nor his company is associated in any way with satanism or devil worship." Other churchmen made similar statements, and these disclaimers were well publicized in American newspapers. Two spokesmen for religious groups stressed their personal acquaintances in, or ties to, Cincinnati, Ohio, possibly in an attempt to defuse the McDonald's/Cincinnati connection that might have been suggested by association with the earlier corporation/Satanism rumor.

Also in June of 1982 Procter & Gamble circulated to the press copies of letters from the producers of the "Donahue," "60 Minutes," and "Merv Griffin" television programs attesting that no P&G official had appeared on their broadcasts at any time to discuss any subject; but still the calls and claims about Satanism continued unabated. On 1 July 1982 Procter & Gamble took the unusual step for a corporate rumor-fighting campaign of bringing lawsuits against individuals in two states (Georgia and Florida) for libeling the company by circulating "false and malicious" statements. The people named in the suits had either stated publicly or distributed literature claiming that P&G supported Satan or that its trademark was a Satanic symbol; claims were also made that the individuals had tried to encourage others not to buy P&G products. Griffin Bell, former United States attorney general, represented Proctor & Gamble in the Atlanta, Georgia, suit. On 20 July P&G issued a notice that four further lawsuits were being brought against individuals in Georgia, New Mexico, and Tennessee.

Attacking in yet another direction during the same month, Procter & Gamble invited writers from two major newspapers —the *New York Times* and the *Chicago Tribune*—to Cincinnati in order to view its rumor-fighting operation firsthand and to speak with top company executives.

In a long story written by Charles Madigan, the *Chicago Tribune* gave Procter & Gamble's problems top placement on page one of the Midwest Edition of Sunday, 18 July 1982. The headline read, "A story of Satan that is rated P&G," and the news story described "calls so bizarre they could well be coming from space." The rumor was described as having "gradually slithered its way around the country," often appearing on anonymous mimeographed sheets, of which P&G had so far collected "42 different variations." Besides quoting Bill Dobson, the P&G spokesman who was usually mentioned in all of the rumor-putdown stories, and various of the fifteen employees in the consumer services division who handled rumor calls and mail, the *Tribune* article introduced J. D. Jesse, chief of security for the company, and the "steely-eyed investigator" who hoped to "nail the person who started all of this." But, as Dobson indicated to the *Tribune* writer, trying to chase a rumor was like trying to grab a handful of smoke or to squeeze warm jello. The abiding concern that summer in Cincinnati was whether the lawsuits would at last succeed in suppressing the rumors where all other attempts had failed.

The *New York Times* version of the P&G story, written by Sandra Salmans, appeared on the first page of the business section on 22 July. It featured a sample of one anonymous handout that is titled "THE SIGN OF SATANISM." A Procter & Gamble spokeswoman is quoted as answering patiently to the ever-recurring calls, "No, sir, that's a false rumor. That's our trademark, we've had it about 100 years." The *Times* story also gave details of the company's databank on the rumor:

> A three-inch-thick file documents the company's strategy: a map of the United States, showing the geographical sweep of the rumors; tallies, state by state, of the queries to the consumer services department; tallies, day by day, of the nature of the complaint ("Satanic"; "Mentions lawsuits"; "Has heard/seen media reports"; Check more than one if appropriate").

Mentioned explicitly in the *New York Times* story was a suggestion that had often been made casually by other interviewers and commentators—that firms selling competing products might have started these negative stories concerning Procter & Gamble in order to promote their own sales. But although

Bill Dobson admitted that all but one of the defendants of the suits brought by P&G did work for other companies selling household products (Amway, Shaklee, and a grocery broker-age firm), no evidence existed to link the companies them-selves with starting or encouraging the trademark story. In fact, P&G was not even suggesting that the people it was suing had any economic motives; "We just want to stop them," a company executive declared.

On the bad news side in mid-summer 1982, the *Kansas City Star* reported on 26 July that a version of the P&G trademark story had been sent out there illegally and anonymously on the Union Pacific railroad computer system and it "clattered out of printers at stops along the way." On the good news side, both Dear Abby (3 August) and Ann Landers (6 September) answered questions in their popular advice columns about Procter & Gamble's trademark with a solid mixture of hard facts and sensible advice.

Further evidence that the rumors might at last be dying down came in Procter & Gamble's fourth-quarter 1982 fiscal report of a net income gain of 14.6 percent and of sales ad-vancing by 6.4 percent. The company financial report made no mention of the trademark rumors, but some newspapers that commented on the financial picture wrote headlines like "P&G beats the Devil" (*San Francisco Chronicle*) and "Procter & Gam-ble gets Satan rumors behind it" (*Chicago Sun-Times*). The lat-ter paper suggested punningly what seemed likely, that "the tide has turned."

Had the P&G campaign of publicity and legal action in 1982 actually succeeded in suppressing a spate of nationwide ru-mors, or had the rumors simply declined on their own, as most such stories do eventually? With such questions in mind, the trade publication *Advertising Age* commissioned a survey in midsummer 1982 and reported the results in their 9 August issue. The SRI Research Center in Lincoln, Nebraska, con-ducted the telephone inquiry between 29 July and 3 August, calling a random sample of 1,264 people aged 18 or over.

Summing up the findings, *Advertising Age* headlined the story "P&G rumor blitz looks like a bomb." The campaign to fight the Satanism rumor, *AA* wrote, "was largely unnecessary and ineffective in reaching people who might believe the rumors."

While the total number of those surveyed who were *aware of* the Satanism rumors was substantial (32 percent in the whole nation, 42 percent in the South), the percentage of these people who actually *believed* them was minimal (only 3 percent in the nation, 5 percent in the South). Of these few individuals who said they believed the rumors, fully 94 percent admitted that they were buying about the same quantity of P&G products as before, while 5 percent of the believers were buying less, and 1 percent were buying more than ever. There was also evidence in the statistics that many people who did not believe the rumors had only learned about them from P&G's publicity efforts, while some who did believe them had never become aware of the publicity campaign. But the most surprising finding of the survey was the extremely low recognition rate among those questioned for Procter & Gamble products: fully 79 percent of the respondents said they could not name a P&G product, another 6 percent claimed they "never buy" P&G products, and even among those who said that they *could* name such a product, an unspecified number of them incorrectly named a product made by a competitor instead.

The general conclusions suggested by the SRI survey seem to be that P&G was reaching the wrong people with its rumor-fighting campaign, that brand recognition of P&G products was poor anyway, and that anyone actually trying to organize a boycott of P&G products would have a very tough time beating the odds that the right people would get the proper message. Anything can happen with a rumor, in other words, but what usually happens is that bad rumors simply disappear in time. As one grocer quoted in *Advertising Age* put it, "I think it's ridiculous. If they'd keep quiet, it'd go away."

Procter & Gamble, however, stoutly defended its actions, claiming satisfaction with the *Times* and *Tribune* stories and other publicity and stating its intention to carry through with the lawsuits to the end, even though one defendant had vowed to make P&G prove in court that it does *not* support devil worship. The only thing P&G said it was not going to do that had been suggested was to allow a company spokesman to appear on the "Phil Donahue Show"; as long as they avoided this, it could still be said in complete truth that no company official had ever been on that program. P&G officials did, however, appear on "Good Morning America" as well as on various local news and interview programs, and in autumn of 1982 Procter & Gamble cooperated with ABC-TV's "20/20" on a segment of the 18 November program titled "Dueling with the Devil."

Although the rumor story wasn't exactly hot news by then, "20/20" did a respectable job of summing up the years-long bout P&G had endured with the Satanism claims. Interviews were taped with both academic sociologists and corporate spokespersons as to causes and effects of rumor-mongering. Most interesting in the "20/20" report to a folklorist, however, were the individuals (evidently all from California) whom the program had located who were still concerned or afraid about the alleged devil-worshiping company. Those people interviewed on camera said they felt threatened because the symbol was unexplained, because it appeared on many different products, and because the company was not willing to change it even when it was causing problems. Their attitude seemed to be that if the mystery trademark was really innocuous, then why was there so much fuss being made about it.

A folk reaction to the recognizably folk attitudes shown on "20/20" is nicely demonstrated in a letter to the editor of a Texas newspaper. The following comments appeared as part of a letter published in the *El Paso Times* of 28 November 1982:

> ABC News Magazine's (20/20) article on the rumor concerning satanic implications of the Procter and Gamble logo truly gives cause for concern. . . .

      If this logo causes fear in your heart, it only shows a lack of true Christian faith. If people are living with Jesus Christ in their hearts, they have no need to fear Satan, either real or in the form of a company logo. . . .

      There are so many real threats to our world, including real satanism, that it is sad when people must scratch this deep and stretch their imaginations this far to find a "cause" to defend.

The fear of "real Satanism," of course, is an important theme among the various fundamentalist Christian beliefs held by many people to whom the Procter & Gamble trademark stories seemed plausible. Although no organized church group of national influence was ever identified as having spread the trademark rumors, many versions of it did travel from person to person via individual church bulletins, letters to editors of religious publications, and especially through callers to Christian radio talk shows. And most of these sincere, believing folks felt that they had sufficient scriptural authority to back up their suspicions concerning Procter & Gamble.

The "mark of the beast," for example, is described in a lurid and cryptic passage in the book of Revelation (13:16) as a sign that will be applied by a seven-headed monster during the last days of the earth upon "all, both small and great, rich and poor, free and bond . . . in their right hand, or in their foreheads." The final verse (18) of book 13 of Revelations specifies this mark as being "the number of the beast . . . six hundred threescore and six," although as The Revised Standard Edition points out, some ancient authorities give the number as 616 instead.

Biblical scholars have puzzled over this enigmatic reference for centuries, usually assuming in their attempts at interpretation that the figure must be a coded reference to a proper name, just as the name "Jesus" may be made to yield the "perfect" number 888 by certain substitutions of numbers for Greek or Hebrew letters. With a bit of further juggling, some commentators maintain, 666 can be equated with the name of the emperor Nero, a conclusion evidently supported by analyzing 666 via "Pythagorean numerology" as the sum of the figures from one through thirty-six, and then comparing the results to other supposed references to Nero in the New Testament. In the face of such ingenious arguments, the authoritative Interpreter's Bible commentary on the passage remarks, "The verse . . . has been given far more attention in popular thinking than it deserves."

The figure of the antichrist, which strict constructionists of the Bible have been trying to identify as an actual personality in the world since the founding of the faith, is alluded to in Revelation and mentioned (among other places) in the second book of John, verse 7: "For many deceivers are entered into the world, who confess not that Jesus Christ is come in the flesh. This is a deceiver and an antichrist." Proposed identifications of this diabolical figure—a primeval opponent of God made incarnate—have ranged from the Pope of Rome (according to Martin Luther) to witches, monstrous births, and (perhaps not too implausibly) to Adolf Hitler.

The juxtaposition of these same Biblical themes in modern fundamentalist Christian lore has occurred in other rumors and legends as well, thus probably giving further apparent support to the Procter & Gamble story among true believers. A persistent tradition, for instance, which was also disseminated widely by means of anonymous printed handouts, is that the Internal Revenue Service mailed out a number of Social Security checks recently with instructions to recipients that they must show an identification consisting of "a mark in their right hand or forehead" in order to cash the checks. In a variation of this story the IRS instructions asked that the recipients verify that the number on the checks corresponded with the number tattooed on their hands. It was either stated or implied in these documents that the mark referred to was the number 666. Supposedly, when contacted about this matter, the IRS explained that such a procedure was actually not to be instituted until 1984, this dating being an obvious reference to George Orwell's novel set in a future dictatorial state.

The IRS, of course, for all its image problems at tax time, has nothing whatever to do with issuing Social Security checks, nor does it have any interest in placing marks upon citizens. But this tradition may have gained some credence from yet another popular story that claimed that certain Social Security card numbers containing the same feared numerical sequence were also instances of the "mark of the beast." More distantly related to such rumors are such other fundamentalist folk claims as that Madalyn Murray O'Hair (or "Madeline Murray O'Hara" as the scare-notices urging letters to the FCC call her) is petitioning the government to end religious broadcasting in the U.S., or that since 1919 there has been a list of "Communist Rules for Revolution" serving as a master plan for the ultimate takeover that contains such items as these: 1) "Corrupt the young, get them away from religion. Get them interested in sex. Make them superficial. Destroy their ruggedness," and 9) "By specious argument cause the breakdown of the old moral virtues, honesty, sobriety, continence, faith in the pledged word, ruggedness." Clearly, one message here is that "if you're rugged, you're right." But experts on the history of communism have dismissed these "rules" as an obvious fabrication, not to mention being a license to identify virtually any behavior (like insobriety or an interest in sex) as being part of a worldwide communist plot.

Even the "seeing things backwards" notion in the P&G rumors has its counterparts in other lore. Simple reversal, of course, is an ancient mode of working magic, so that either reciting texts from the end back to the beginning or performing actions in the order opposite to "normal" is believed to have power to cause supernatural things to happen. (To cure the hiccups nowadays, for example, you may be advised to drink water out of the opposite side of a glass.) Similarly, in a "Black Mass" or witches' sabbath, every word and gesture was supposed to be done in reverse, as a mockery of God and

His ways. Thus, it is not much of a leap of reasoning to suggest that to see something in reverse or to hear it in reverse may be a way to reveal its true hidden message, hence the national mania in recent years to prevent or to identify supposed "backward masking" of Satanic messages supposedly recorded in reverse on rock records. (My favorite news reports on this issue were those that described the Arkansas House of Representatives' 1983 debate on a backwards-masking bill during which a number of legislators occasionally spoke backwards!)

With all this sort of thing going on—or at least alleged to be going on—it was hardly too bizarre for belief that a big company might show its true colors by means of coded antireligious markings or of prophesied symbols that were designed to be viewed backwards in a mirror. Furthermore, the significant passages in the Bible were there for anyone to read. Add to the oral testimony of fellow fundamentalists the printed handouts signed "A Good Christian," and then look and see for yourself the "Satanic symbol" emblazoned on dozens of familiar products, and it is no wonder that people started calling Procter & Gamble. (Their toll-free consumer services number appears on every package.)

To the credit of leaders in the fundamentalist Christian movement in the United States, many of them denounced the rumor-mongering, refused to disseminate the wild stories, and even joined Procter & Gamble (whose advertising support of certain TV programing they had at other times criticized) in fighting the stories. An article in the Christian magazine *Charisma* for July/August 1982 articulates this reasonable stance taken against modern fear rumors. Calling this frame of mind "The Christian 'Chicken Little Syndrome,' " author Richard Schneider described his own careful debunking of the IRS/-Mark of the Beast rumor for a friend of his. Although he acknowledged that "Certainly, it is wise to keep a careful eye out for anything that might impinge on the Great Commission," Schneider warned against reacting too quickly to unfounded claims and stories, even if they come from a source such as "a friend from church." He admonished, "We know that '666' is the 'mark of the beast.' But I wonder if the beast isn't already using it to throw us off the track." In conclusion, Schneider suggested that rumors were probably "spawned by the father of lies," an idea that ought to give a giant corporation something to *really* worry about the next time one of them has to fight a negative series of rumors.

7

Absolutely, Positively, Brand-New True Urban Legends

There are times when a novel story that someone tells you for true is so absolutely reasonable, so positively plausible, so perfectly in tune with things as they really are in the here and now that you never doubt for a moment that it is an actual account of something that happened just recently. Sometimes these thoroughly credible tales involve some feature of modern technology upon which we depend heavily but about which we understand little; or they may describe quite believably a problem with government bureaucracy at any level of the same kind that we occasionally have to tangle with ourselves. Yet another validating feature may be the mention of well-known persons' names. But usually these stories are simply so full of the realities of everyday life—the fears, the fads, and the frustrations—that they need no further verification than just their own inner logic along with a customary statement like "I heard this from a friend of a friend of mine. . . ."

This chapter gathers a group of absolutely, positively, brand-new *"true"* urban legends, which are distinguished from most of the earlier examples in this book only by their currency and by the unusual degree of faith with which some modern folk hold to them. I have grouped them here also because they seem to be the stories that people tell me just *after* I have demonstrated for them that some old favorites are widespread legends, but just *before* these people part from me, somewhat sad, yet wiser in the ways of modern folklore. "Now here's something," they'll often say, "that is just as remarkable as one of your legends, but it really is true!"

"The Jogger's Billfold"

"Now here's a story," the interviewer said on the telephone, "that is just about as funny as one of your legends, but it really is true!" The call had come from a Toronto, Canada, radio station, and I had just told the news reporter a few stories, answered questions about others, and tried in general to explain my research in modern folk legends. These comments had been tape-recorded for a later broadcast, and the interviewer wanted to tell me just one strange-but-true story before hanging up. I listened willingly, for I never refuse a piece of potential folklore, even if it comes to me via a disembodied voice of a stranger through the crackle of static on the long-distance lines.

Her true story was about a jogger in Central Park in New York City. He had been running along early one morning at his customary pace and surrounded by streams of others out getting their prework exercise, when suddenly another jogger passed by him on the path and bumped him rather hard. Checking quickly, the jogger discovered that his billfold was missing from his pocket, and he thought, "This can't happen to me; I'm not going to let it happen." So he upped his speed a bit, caught up to the other jogger, and confronted him. "Give me that billfold," he snarled, trying to sound as menacing as possible, and hoping for the best. The other jogger quickly handed it over, and our hero turned back toward his apartment for a shower and a quick change of clothes. But when he got home, there was his own billfold on the dresser, and the one he had in his pocket belonged to someone else.

I hated to tell her that this was just a new aerobic variation on an old commuter theme. How old? For starters, here's a version from the "My Favorite Jokes" section of *Parade* magazine, 3 September 1972, as told by comic Gus Christie:

> This is supposed to be a true story. A man, we'll call him Mr. Jones, is riding to work on the subway in New York City and there's a guy who keeps bumping into him. After awhile Jones gets apprehensive and thinks, "This can't be what I think it is!" He checks his wallet—and it's gone. "That's it! Nine o'clock in the morning and I get mugged in the subway. Things are really getting bad." He grabs the guy, shakes him hard, and say, "All right, cough up, give me that wallet!" The guy is petrified and he hands over a wallet. So Jones goes off to work and when he gets to his office his wife calls and says, "Honey, you left your wallet on the bureau this morning."

This must have been a hot story in the fall of 1972, for the popular radio personality Paul Harvey told substantially the same version on 18 October, as noted by folklorist Linda Dégh of Indiana University. Dégh had a particular interest in the plot because when she heard Paul Harvey tell it on the air she remembered that some twenty years earlier in Hungary her middle-aged uncle had told a comparable tale as a personal experience:

> Once, when he came off a ferry boat and made his way through the crowd he felt someone's hand in his pocket, taking his gold watch. Grabbing the hand of a man he yelled, "Give me the watch!" The man immediately obeyed. After awhile, feeling his pocket, Uncle Peter found two gold watches therein.

Furthermore, some years after hearing Uncle Peter's story, Linda Dégh heard a "trustworthy, middle-aged gentleman" tell as a personal experience a variation of the same story in which the supposed victim of thievery pursued his assumed antagonist through dark streets until he cornered him in a doorway and retrieved the watch. When he later discovered that he had two watches, the man went to the police to report the fact, and arrived just as the real owner of it, who had managed to recognize his assailant, was filing suit against him. It almost seems as if folklorists are natural magnets for tellings of this legend as an absolutely true experience.

However, folklorist Ernest W. Baughman found his version in a newspaper, and on the basis of that evidence assigned it Motif number N360(a) in his index under the general heading "Man [meaning "Person"] unwittingly commits crime." Baughman's source was the Indianapolis *Sunday Star* for 3 March 1946 and involved a woman having a meal in a restaurant with an acquaintance she has just met on the train. When the woman returned to the table from the restroom and the new friend then went to the restroom herself, the subject of the story discovered that a fifty-dollar bill she had brought with her was gone. She peeked into the other's purse, and there was a fifty, right on top, so she simply lifted it and said nothing. And I'll say nothing further about how the story ends; it should be obvious.

Even though the plot is now no surprise, it is worth quoting just one more version of the unwitting-crime legend from England simply to savor its fairy-tale opening scene and the charming touch of British dialect at the end. Besides, this is the oldest text that has been reported yet of the story. It was told to folklorist Katharine M. Briggs in 1912 by a friend from London, then published in Briggs and Tongue's book *Folktales of England* (pages 101–2), and variations are well known all over Great Britain:

An elderly brother and sister lived together, and one day the sister wanted to go to town to do some shopping. So her brother gave her a five-pound note, and she set out. She traveled third class, and the only other passenger was a shabby old woman who sat opposite her and nodded. Miss

M———was sleepy too, after her early, hurried start, so she dozed a little too. Then she woke up, and thought it wasn't very safe to go to sleep in a railway carriage, alone with a stranger. She opened her bag to make some notes of what she had to buy, and the five-pound note wasn't there. She looked at her neighbor, who was sleeping heavily with a big old shabby bag beside her. Miss M———bent forward and, very cautiously, she opened the bag. There was a new five-pound note on top of everything.

"Old scoundrel!" thought Miss M———Then she thought, "She's poor and old, and I oughtn't to have put temptation in her way." She wondered what she ought to do. It would cause a great deal of delay and bother to call the police, and it seemed cruel to get an old woman into trouble, but she must have her money. So, in the end, she quietly took the five pounds out of the bag and shut it up again.

At the next stop, the old woman got out, and Miss M———got to town and did her day's shopping, and came home loaded with parcels. Her brother met her at the station. "How did you manage?" she said, "I expected to find you up a gum tree. You left your five-pound note on the dressing-table."

Well, I certainly would have been up a gum tree (is that like being up a creek?) if I not been able to spot my Toronto caller's jogger story as a traditional tale. But it takes more than just a trendy running suit to conceal an urban legend from a folklorist. Besides, there has been a rather venerable tradition of folklorists being told that one as new and true, so I was expecting it to show up eventually.

"The Packet of Biscuits"

The "biscuits" in this legend are cookies, because it's another English story, as well as being another perfectly plausible variation on the unwitting-theft legend. I have not yet encountered this one in the States, so I quote a summary of three printed versions from British mass media sources of 1972–74 as given by A. W. Smith in *Folklore* (Summer, 1975); variations among these versions are indicated with slashes:

> A traveller buys a cup of tea and a packet of biscuits at a station buffet/in a dining car/at Joe Lyons opposite Liverpool Street station. The traveller sits down at the same table as a Pakistani/West Indian/African, drinks the tea and begins to eat the biscuits. The man opposite helps himself to one. Somewhat shaken at the effrontery, the traveller takes another. The uninvited companion does the same and these actions continue until only the last biscuit is left which the coloured man breaks in two so it may be shared. . . . the angry lady screamed abuse at him . . . /[or, a male traveller in the story] remained stoically silent. In both versions the denouement is the same. Each realizes that their own packet of biscuits lies, still unopened in "her purse"/on "his suitcase at his side."

Smith, noting the racial prejudice implied by the story, called attention to "the patient and indeed saintly character of the often despised and rejected." He also felt that "The Packet of Biscuits" might have an American origin, judging from the non-British term "purse," but I doubt it, since joining a stranger at a table in a waiting room or café for tea and cookies is not a very likely act in this country.

At any rate, the other reports of this variation of "The Unwitting Theft" are British. An Irish version, "told by somebody who knew the person it happened to, at the station in Belfast," was sent to me; here the traveler says to a black man who shares her biscuits, "Excuse me, but we don't do that in this country." He politely desists, and she later finds her unopened package of cookies in her bag. English folklorist Venetia Newall mentioned the story in a 1980 article as one she had heard for several years about different races and localized in Wolverhampton, "an area with a high immigrant population." As with other tellings, Newall's displays the neat structuring of events by which each party alternatively takes a cookie until the minority person politely breaks the last remaining one in half. "Share and share alike," says the immigrant to Great Britain; "You're taking *my* food," says the white traveler—and the traveler is wrong!

"The Double Theft"

The English have another favorite true story about a theft that is set up by a plausible sort of scam on a city person who then turns out to be the usual friend-of-a-friend. Jacqueline Simpson, the editor of *Folklore*, reported this one in a 1972 issue of that journal, having heard it first some four years earlier in connection with Harrods department store in London, then later concerning a leading department store in Helsinki, Finland. Her summary:

> A woman customer in the store named goes to the lavatory in the ladies' cloakroom there, and puts her handbag on the floor beside her. The lavatory partitions are of the sort which leave a gap between wall and floor, and a hand comes through this gap and whips her bag away. Before she can emerge the thief has escaped, but she reports her loss to the shop manager. She returns home. A few hours later her phone rings: "This is Harrods; a bag has been found which may be yours; please come to the manager's office to identify it." But when she reaches the store there is no bag there, and none of the staff have phoned her. Returning home, she sees her own bunch of keys in the lock, and finds the flat burgled and all her jewelry gone.

Simpson concluded with this report of a helpful suggestion from Venetia Newall, [who] "informs me that nothing of the sort can ever really have happened at Harrods, where the lavatory walls are solid; she suggests that it may have originated in America, where gaps at the base of such walls are common." Clearly this story calls for further research.

Whatever the origin of "The Double Theft" may have been, the story is quite well known on both sides of the Atlantic. American versions may include either the handbag-under-the-gap ploy known by Simpson or the variant form that was reported in *Folklore* (1973) by Smith:

> A married couple leave their car parked outside their house overnight only to find that it has disappeared, apparently during the early hours of the morning. They have scarcely had time to report the theft when the car is mysteriously replaced. In it they find a note which says, "Thank you for the loan of the car. You saved a life. Please accept these theatre tickets as a token of my gratitude." Delighted to have the mystery solved they use the tickets. When they return home their house has been burgled.

In my experience when this positively true theft story is told in the United States, if a store is involved it tends to be the finest department store in town, while if tickets are given in return for the use of the car they may range in type from symphony or ballet tickets to the sold-out and much desired tickets for a popular music concert or a championship hockey game, depending, I suppose, on the kind of loot the burglars are after.

Government Legends

When the rascals in the new really-true urban rumors and legends are government officials and workers, we know just about what to expect—boondoggling, the run-around, over-regulation, squandering of our tax money, and the like. The stories of this kind that we hear and believe merely fulfill expectations we already have that were honed to a fine edge by our own encounters with government and by news stories about waste in high places, "Golden Fleece Awards," and so on. Of course, many of the anti-government stories we read and hear are absolutely true, but that's another subject.

The recognizably folkloric stories about government are the kind that describe some absurdity or outrageous instance of chicanery perpetrated by a public agency; these are told with such a wealth of believable details that you just have to —well—*believe* them. The only difficulties are that most of the stories cannot be proved and probably never happened. We got a taste of this sort of tradition with the mark-of-the-beast Social Security check rumor mentioned in Chapter 6, but the government legends alluded to here are less incredible than that and are uninvolved with any diabolical master plan. Since the subject deserves a whole book of its own, I offer only a glance at a few sample government legends.

The late Dick Bothwell, columnist for the *St. Petersburg* [Florida] *Times,* loved such stories and gave this capsule account of a persistent one:

> An accounting firm says what government prose may lack in quality it makes up in quantity. The Lord's Prayer has 56 words, Lincoln's Gettysburg Address has 266 words, the Ten Commandments, 297; the Declaration of Independence, 300. The firm notes in contrast a recent U. S. government order setting the price of cabbages has 26,911 words.

This "Price of Cabbage Memo" story, however plausible it may seem, as Bothwell indicated to me has been around for about half a century, and was periodically reported by the press, sometimes with the variation that it was actually a French government memo on the price of duck eggs. While not all accounts of this leafy lie agree on the precise number of words in the various religious and patriotic texts, all versions do give an exact figure for the cabbage memo, usually the same one, as if that proves anything. I've always wondered who was supposed to have counted all those words, at least in the days before computers were available with word-count programs. After all, when you get it right down to "911," then presumably someone has tallied every last word.

The New Republic headed a satirical editorial on the cabbage memo, "26,911 Little Words" (23 April 1977, pp. 9–10), when the legend turned up in 1977 in a Mobile Oil Corporation "Pipeline Pete" advertisement. Mobil, it turned out, had found the story in a house organ published the previous year, and that version went back to yet another publication that had found it printed on a card someone was carrying around in his wallet. Max Hall in a case report on "The Great Cabbage Hoax" published in 1965 was able to trace numerous tellings and printings of the story in the mass media back to 1951, with oral reports suggesting that it existed in the 1940s as well. Although Hall could not establish the origin of the story, he did conclude that it may have first been applied to the Office of Price Administration (OPA) during World War II, then to the Office of Price Stabilization (OPS) in the period when price controls were in effect during the Korean War, and eventually it was told to ridicule just the federal government in general, in particular verbosity in governmental prose.

This is the pattern for many other legends about government's way of doing things. (Remember the folk saying, "close enough for government work.") According to popular opinion there are typically in government too many words and not enough action, too many chiefs and not enough Indians, too many rules and not enough review of them, and way too many government clerks, inspectors, and other minor functionaries. And while these general ideas may seem clearly enough to be true, the traditional stories that purport to give specific instances—of massive mix-ups in military orders, of other classic foul-ups in paper shuffling, of obscure offices with no present function, of government warehouses full of unneeded spare parts, etc., etc., etc.—these are mostly legends.

A story that I heard in Bucharest, Romania, in early 1981 demonstrates how an original urban legend concerning government that is based specifically on national social patterns can spring up anywhere in the present day. It is not a legend that would make sense in American folk tradition, because it involves details not found here, although the general concepts are familiar enough. The story is about some supposed inspectors of apartments in Bucharest.

According to the story I heard, two young men with some kind of official looking credentials, or perhaps wearing a badge or uniform of some kind, went around to all the apartment units in a large section of high-rise blocs in Bucharest saying that they were the city air samplers. They asked for a clean empty bottle or jar from each household in order to take a sample. Being given the bottle, they swung it around through the air, put a cap on it, labled it, and departed. After a day of such effort, I was told, the clever young men took hundreds of clean empty bottles to a bottle-return depot and collected the deposits for all of them.

This Romanian urban legend involves the universal theme of a clever deception as a way of "beating the system." Such authentic-seeming details as the national system of bottle and jar deposits, the presence of many government inspectors, and the problem of air pollution in the capital city all contribute to the plausibility of the story. Interestingly, when I used this narrative as an example of a recent legend in a lecture to a group of Romanian folklorists, there was some resistance to accepting it as a piece of genuine folklore; that is, until one man in the audience with a puzzle look on his face commented, "But I thought that really happened in my own apartment building—except that they were *water* inspectors." Had he met the young man himself? No—he heard it from a friend of a neighbor who had presumably given them a bottle.

Certainly in the United States, if not in other countries, a primary theme in legends about the government is the suppression of some secret that would, if revealed, ruin the careers of prominent officials or cause panic among the populace. This "secret-truth" kind of story may involve claims that government figures profited phenomenally from finagling during wartime or by exploiting natural resources found on public lands, or that conspiracies involving famous crimes or politicians have been left unrevealed with the facts sealed forever.

One of the most dramatic of these suppressed-truth stories that is frequently revived concerns "The Landed Martians." Supposedly a UFO from the planet Mars with a number of humanoid creatures aboard crashed in the Midwest many years ago, and U.S. Air Force personnel recovered part of the craft and its occupants, one or two of them still alive, before the rest of the spacecraft was destroyed in the resulting fire and explosion. The remaining UFO parts and the "creatures" were moved to an isolated hanger in the deserts of Arizona (Texas, New Mexico, etc.), and the men involved in the action were sworn to secrecy or lied to about the nature of their mission. Various "documents" alleged to be based on interviews with these men that piece together the true story circulate among UFO and science-fiction buffs from time to time, and I expect that I'll get some angry mail just for suggesting that this might be an area of modern legend. In fact, in the 25 July 1983 *Newsweek* (p. 21) it was reported that a group called Citizens Against UFO Secrecy had filed a petition in U.S. district court in Virginia demanding release of "one or more occupants of crash-landed UFOs of apparent extraterrestrial origin." The occupants were described as "three-foot tall, humanlike creatures wrapped in fine metallic cloth."

Another approach in the legends about government and space flight takes the viewpoint that top modern scientists have mathematically verified some aspect of religious doctrine or belief. Chief among these stories is "The Missing Day in Time," which shows up periodically in letters to editors, anonymous handouts, or newsletters of religious groups. It is such a well-known legend that NASA prints a disclaimer about it in its basic public relations pamphlet: "We have been unable to learn of any computations in the space program which revealed a 'lost day,' as has been reported."

Usually a particular scientist is named as the one who discovered this phenomenon, but I will skip the names to protect those who have already been harassed by eager inquiries. The premise here is that in order to plan space navigation properly, space scientists working for the government had to use a computer "to check the positions of the sun, moon and planets over centuries and millennia." This meant going back thousands of years as well as projecting the orbits forward into the future. But each time the scientists ran the measurements their computer would halt at a certain point and "put up a red signal." Finally they determined that there was an entire day missing throughout space in terms of elapsed time.

Luckily, the story goes, one scientist remembered from Sunday school classes long long ago something about a day when the sun stood still, and a review of the Bible soon brought forth the passage in Joshua (chapter 10) about the time when the Lord made the sun stand still. It was not enough, though, for their calculations continued to show a missing forty minutes, and even the biblical reference states *"about* a whole day." But the day was saved—I mean it was found—when the scientific team again searched the Bible (I hope they were using a concordance!), and they found the passage in 2 Kings (chapter 20) where the Lord caused a shadow to "return backward ten degrees" as a sign to Isaiah of His power, and ten degrees is precisely forty minutes, the true believers in this legend triumphantly declare, thus accounting fully for that "Missing Day in Time." Presumably, this correction is now logged into every navigational manual and computer program in present use for our space program, and if you only had the right stuff yourself you could probably get into Mission Control and see it firsthand.

"The Image on Glass" and "The Mystery Glitch"

Misunderstandings about the wonders of technology have spawned legends for generations, a process analyzed by folklorist Barbara Allen in a fascinating article in *Western Folklore* (1982) on the notion contained in many older legends that a flash of lightning may create a photographic image of a person on an ordinary windowpane or mirror. Usually, in its legend form, this belief has manifested itself in the United States in a claim that the image of a dead or dying person who lived in or was confined to a particular building was thus preserved by "photographic lightning." Often these subjects were supposed to be condemmed criminals or murder victims, and sometimes it was Christ Himself whose picture was left on the glass. Several reports of such images, some even claiming to be eyewitness accounts, appeared in newspapers from the 1860s to 1880s, as well as in oral tradition later.

Allen suggests that such legends must have been generated when popular acquaintance with the new art and science of photography with its glass plates, flash-light powder, and realistic images combined with traditional folk concepts of ghosts and spirits. Since people did not then entirely understand how photography worked (as is true now of, say, microwave ovens or automobile carburetors), then folk ideas provided believable explanations of what might happen. To quote Barbara Allen, "ordinary portraits become ghostly images, prepared glass plates become windows and mirrors, [and] the slow steady exposure to light becomes the dramatic flash of lightning." When flexible film began to replace glass plates in the late 1880s, the legends about images on glass declined. In a more general way, she suggests, any new elements in the environment may fuse with traditional folk themes and become modified by people's emotional reactions to produce legends similar to "The Image on Glass."

The modern technical wonder that we would expect to become the target for such legend formation is the computer, and I am endebted to computer whiz Dan Meilander of Brunswick, Ohio, for making me aware of one piece of the emerging folklore of that field. Meilander described three instances (a nice folkloric touch, that!) of the "Mystery Glitch"—a sabotaged-computer story—as he has encountered it during the past decade or so. All three are associated with computer centers at specific universities, which tends to support our belief in the prank as something that a typical college wag really might have thought up. Other people working with computers assure me that this tradition is fairly widespread.

Glitch story #1: Somebody tampered with the operating system of a college's computer. Every now and then it would print out, "HI! I'M THE UNKNOWN GLITCH! CATCH ME IF YOU CAN." Obviously someone had written a program that would generate a random number, wait until the system clock equaled that number, print its message, and then relocate itself somewhere else in memory. . . . We didn't have a chance of finding it.

Glitch story #2: A few years ago at . . . somebody put a machine language program into the computer there. While you were getting your printout it would suddenly print "YOU ARE PENALIZED 5 YARDS . . . OF PAPER," and it would kick out five yards of paper. They never could find it and get rid of it.

At once a pattern is apparent—a Glitch (i.e., error or problem) in the system, occurs at Random, Impossible to remove, planted by Prankster—shall we say "GRIP" is the formula for this legend? Here's Glitch story #3: At . . . there was a program like that on an old IBM computer that was due to be removed. The program was "The Cookie Monster." When you'd sign on the computer, it would say "WANT COOKIE " If you didn't key in "COOKIE" it would let you go on, but sometime later in the session it would repeat "WANT COOKIE " and if you didn't type in "COOKIE" it would disconnect you. . . .

They finally found a single board microcomputer with this Cookie Monster program on it soldered into the IBM's circuits.

Dan Meilander also sent me about three yards of paper printout explaining in great detail the various technical reasons why these mystery glitches probably could not be introduced into a computer system, but I cannot reveal here what he said since my own Kaypro II word processor, every time I try to type this information in, says "BUT IT'S TRUE, I HEARD IT FROM AN APPLE II WHO GOT IT FROM A DEC RAINBOW 100 WHO HEARD IT FROM THE IBM THAT IT HAPPENED TO." So you will have to ask your own computer, or computer whiz, why the story can't be true. On the other hand, the *Wall Street Journal* treated "The Phantom Strikes" and "Cookie Monster" as true stories in a piece titled "For Fun or Foul, Computer Hackers Can Crack Any Code" (13 April 1983), which does make you wonder.

The term "bug" in computerese for a flaw or mistake in the system is a metaphor that might suggest a literal reality in the world of folklore. At least that could explain this brief news story on a yellowed, undated clipping that fell out of a letter from one of the readers of my earlier book:

> MIAMI(AP)—Telephone operators call them "cord lice." To airline reservations clerks, they're "cable lice"—mysterious bugs, at home inside computer equipment, that leave nasty bites but are so tiny no one can see them.
>
> There's good reason the critters are invisible, says a University of Florida insect expert. He says they don't exist.
>
> "They're delusions," says Professor Philip Koehler, an entomologist and expert on mites.

Would anybody really believe in such things as "cord lice"? Sure they would. I can report that I once saw the secretary/receptionist of a high university executive sitting with her telephone mouthpiece inside a paper bag on her desk because some prankster had called her, impersonated a telephone-company official, and warned her that they were going to blow the lice and dust out of the line that afternoon at such and such a time and she should prepare herself for a bit of a mess.

Burt Reynolds's Telephone Credit Card Number

Celebrity rumors and legends, like government legends, deserve a separate study, since both categories involve possibly true tales that are very difficult to distinguish from fantasy or from stories that were deliberately planted or leaked for publicity purposes. And both kinds of legends have to be traced through a complicated maze of unorthodox sources, both oral and written, and both popular and folk. If anything, the stories involving celebrities are even harder to prove or disprove than those about government goofs and lapses.

For example, did Mrs. Leon Spinks (wife of the boxer) or did Mrs. Nat King Cole (widow of the popular singer), as persistent traditions maintain, ever reward a kind stranger who helped her when her car broke down on a freeway with the gift of a pair of tickets for the next fight (or show) or with a new Cadillac? Perhaps they did, since it's a fact that Elvis sometimes impulsively presented people he barely knew with expensive gifts, and Howard Hughes may or may not have willed a fortune to Melvin Dummar and the Mormon church after being picked up as a hitchhiker. Also, tickets to upcoming shows are standard freebies handed out by celebrities and their agents.

Rock music performers and groups are natural subjects for rumors and legends, such as the complicated "Paul is dead" stories that haunted the Beatles for a time,* and the apocry-

---

*In the spring of 1983 designer Calvin Klein telephoned *Women's Wear Daily* to deny the rumors that he was ill, undergoing treatment in a European clinic, or that he even was dead. The fashion trade journal debunked the story in a front-page article on 10 June.

phal gory stories about various rock performers who supposedly have killed kittens, chickens, or other small animals on
stage during a show. Another familiar theme of celebrity legends concerns the beginning and end of a performer's career:
Did Buddy Holly really leap on stage during an Elvis Presley
show and thus gain his first national notice? And how many
other musicians could possibly have *almost* boarded that fatal
airplane with Buddy in 1959; several make the claim, I am told,
thus circulating legends about themselves that connect them
with the legendary Holly.

Movie stars provided the prime grist for the gossip mills in
the past, but television seems to have taken over lately, even
when the subject of a rumor or legend may actually be a film
idol. Which brings us to Burt Reynolds and "The Tonight
Show," those being the particular celebrity and the specific
setting that became extremely prominent in an American
urban legend during the past few years.

"The Tonight Show Starring Johnny Carson," to cite the
full name of the popular late-night talk show, surely qualifies
for the clichéd claim "a legend in its own time" for the durabil-
ity of its host, the general predictability of its nightly format,
and the reliability of its high ratings. This long-long-running
program is a phenomenon of television programming. But in
folklore "The Tonight Show" is best known for things that
never quite happened—stories that were not told, guests who
never appeared, and especially for risqué quips that Johnny
didn't make. I have been involved in misconceptions of this
sort myself, when people have asserted—in good faith, but
completely in error—that they saw me on "The Tonight
Show." (Probably they dozed off near the end of Johnny Carson's program and woke up for part of the NBC talk show that
follows it, "Late Night With David Letterman," on which I *have*
appeared.)

In Chapter 3 I mentioned an alleged telling of a legend on
"The Tonight Show" by Truman Capote, which the Carson
staff says they "cannot verify." There are other guest/host

exchanges described by people who think they remember seeing them on the TV show, or else heard from someone else who thinks they saw them, that draw the same neutral response from Carson Productions. (A persistent one mentions Farrah Fawcett.) Probably the best known of these nonevents involves Mrs. Arnold Palmer, who supposedly uttered an unintentional sexy pun to which Johnny allegedly replied, "I bet that made his putter flutter." (You're not going to get the whole story *here,* because I don't want anyone suing me!) At any rate, in this respect Johnny seems to have inherited the reputation of the earlier talk-show wit Groucho Marx, whose raciest alleged punchline was "I love my cigar very much too, but I take it out occasionally."

What does all this have to do with Burt Reynolds? Well, not much, actually, except that the Reynolds legend concerns something that Burt did not say on "The Tonight Show" with (or without) Johnny Carson, but which a great number of people seem to think he said.

In late 1981 a story that had earlier been told about actors Steve McQueen, Paul Newman, or Sammy Davis, Jr., began to circulate once again, but this time with Burt Reynolds as the hero. Supposedly Reynolds had won a million-dollar lawsuit which bonanza he decided to share with all his fans and friends. Often it was said that it was a libel suit that he had brought against the *National Enquirer.* He is said to have announced on "The Tonight Show" (on which he is a frequent guest) that until a given date anyone could charge long-distance calls to Burt Reynolds's telephone credit card number. Of course, Burt never won such a suit, and Burt never made such an offer, but somehow a fourteen-digit credit-card number was circulated, and many thousands of dollars worth of calls were charged to it by people who believed the legend.

The variations in the Burt Reynolds legend were typical of modern folklore. Some said, for instance, that it was the *New York Times* that had published the story as truth. Others thought it was Johnny Carson himself who had made the offer and that he had won the judgment in the form of a million dollars' worth of calls against AT&T that he would need help in order to use up before the time limit. In the Midwest one number that was circulated belonged to a tiny telephone company in Louisville, Illinois, which reportedly got more than $100,000 worth of calls billed to it before the story was squelched. At least in Utah the credit card number was sometimes said to be that of Robert Redford, who is a resident of this state and something of a local hero, even beyond his international film fame. The distribution of the actual numbers in use seems mostly to have stemmed from college and underground publications and thence to have passed into oral tradition.

Burt Reynolds and his aides denied the story, newspapers ran stories debunking it as a hoax, and AT&T spokespersons issued the usual statements to the effect that it would be all the other uninvolved telephone users themselves who would pay for the calls, one way or another. Evidently the company reasoning was that if Ma Bell was dumb enough to accept fraudulent calls, the innocent consumer should have to pay. Actually, of course, whenever illegal credit card calls are made, they are billed back to the actual caller whenever possible. Naturally, none of the statements that were issued or the stories that were published gave the numbers in use, but still these have continued to circulate and to be used for some two years since the legend first attached itself to Burt Reynolds.

A news story in the Boulder, Colorado, *Daily Camera* (31 December 1982) mentioned, "Dozens of Boulder people are among the thousands nationwide who were told by 'a friend of a friend' that they can make free long-distance telephone calls by using the credit card number of a magnanimous celebrity." Probably the holiday season when many people make long-distance calls plus the presence of the state university in Boulder encouraged the rumor. But you can't help but sympathize with a local woman facing a $200 phone bill who is quoted in the story as saying, "It doesn't seem fair because the telephone company hasn't deleted the number and they've known about it for so long."

But in Portland, Oregon, the *Oregonian* quoted a man who said he had been told by a telephone-company employee that the story was true. *Oregonian* writer Dan Hortsch in a story published on 16 March 1983 revealed this:

> A reader, Milton E. Evans of Portland, said that after seeing news reports on the latest incident [of unauthorized free calling], he called the business office of Pacific Northwest Bell to give the company names of people he knew to be using such a number. However the fellow at PNB had not received the word that the story was a hoax.
>
> "He was a firm believer," Evans said. "He said, 'Oh, yes. Johnny Carson announced it on his TV show.'"
>
> Astonished, Evans persisted and suggested that the gullible telephone company employee read what his colleague in another department had had to say about the credit card story.

And the calls continue, with a recent report being from the *Boston Globe* of 21 March 1983: here individual phone bills up to $400 were run up by people who took the story to be true. Appropriately enough, on April Fools' Day 1983 in Provo, Utah, a local man was quoted in the news media as saying that he and his family had run the phone bill up to $125 making calls on Burt Reynolds's credit card number until they realized that it was a phony. He had learned the number from someone in his former Mormon church ward in California, and, as he said, "We trusted them 100 percent."

Yet another version published recently in the "Helping Hand" column of the Wilmington, Delaware, *Evening News Journal* (20 April 1983) drew a most sensible reply from the newspaper:

> Someone told me that several weeks ago Johnny Carson said on his show that he had won a large settlement in a lawsuit. Since he didn't need the money he had set up a

special phone number and people could bill their long-distance telephone calls to it until June.

I'm wondering if you could tell me if this is true? I have, in fact, billed some calls to that number.

—We hope you didn't talk long—or far. . . . That story is a hoax . . .

If you stop to think how many viewers he has and multiply that by the amount of money each would spend normally on long-distance calls in three months time (let alone what they would spend if they thought the calls were *free*) you would realize it just isn't possible.

The moral of this whole telephone story is that if you're going to reach out and touch somebody, don't expect Burt Reynolds to pay for the call. And, incidentally, Burt isn't Tom Selleck's father either; that's just another rumor.

"Dial 911 for Help"

While I am on the subject of telephones, I'll bow out of this book with the last "new" urban legend that was alluded to but not explained in Chapter 1, the one about the 911 telephone emergency number. Writer Jerry Johnston of the Salt Lake City *Deseret News*, who has had his consciousness raised by some of my earlier writings about urban legends, called my attention to this one in early 1982. As he put it, "I don't know if the thing is true or not, but it has all the earmarks of an urban folk tale." Here's his story—name removed to protect the gullible—as it appeared in a letter to the editor of the *DN* on 22 February 1982:

For some time I have read articles about the Emergency 911 line. I'd like to see it written Nine One One, for the following reason:

A family had the number posted by the phone and they had practiced a fire drill so everyone knew what they were to do. The father was to take the baby and the other two smallest children out while the mother was to call the emergency number and then take the two school-age children and leave. [Question: What ever happened to women and children first?]

When a fire woke them one night, the father waited on the neighbor's lawn holding the three frightened children, but his wife didn't come out. By the time someone heard his screams and came to hold the children while he ran back in to get her, it was too late to reach the two older children and they died in the fire.

The reason? In her hurry to call the emergency number, she couldn't find an eleven (911) on the dial. She tried again and again. By the time she thought to call the operator, the whole house was in flames and she was led screaming and hysterical from the home. . . .

A true incident?—Then where are the news reports on it? A legend?—Then what are the traditional themes in the story and where are the variants. Well, look at Ernest Baughman's motif J2259*(f) about foolish behavior involving telephones and numbers, as it appeared in an example published in *Hoosier Folklore Bulletin* for June 1943, during the national craze for moron jokes. Isn't the germ of the idea for "Dial 911 for Help" here?

> The little moron got up in the middle of the night to answer the telephone. "Is this one one one one?" says the voice. "No, this is eleven eleven." "You're sure it isn't one one one one?" "No, this is eleven eleven." "Well, wrong number. Sorry to have got you up in the middle of the night." "That's all right, mister. I had to get up to answer the telephone anyway."

Tastes for oral narratives may change, and fads in jokes and legends may come and go, but some great old themes of stories are just too good to let die. (I don't make them up, folks, I just study them.) The more things change in folklore, the more they stay the same.

APPENDIX

A Sampler of Urban Legend Texts

In order to provide the reader with a frame of reference for appreciating the "new" urban legends contained in this book, here are sample texts of several types of legends discussed in *The Vanishing Hitchhiker.* They include most stories from my first book that are mentioned or alluded to in this one, without any of the historical, comparative, or analytical material that was presented there. I have selected texts that illustrate a true oral style as well as the journalistic form in which urban legends may appear, and I give one British version as a contrast to the American ones. All of these texts originally appeared in the sources cited, but none was included in *The Vanishing Hitchhiker* itself, to which the reader should turn for more background material and further texts of these and many other urban legends.

"The Vanishing Hitchhiker"
(A traditional version)

There were these two boys going from Winchester to Lexington. They were going to a prom. There was this girl in a formal on the road, and they picked her up in a Model A roadster. It was cold. Each of the boys danced with her. She danced good, but her flesh was cold. They started home but saw her again on the street and picked her up. She was cold, and they gave her a coat. They took her to her house down this hill and left her. They left his coat too, but went back to get the coat and told her mother that he left his coat. Her mother told them that she was dead and buried. She then took them to the family graveyard where she was buried. They found the overcoat hanging on the tombstone.

(No. 363 in William Lynwood Montell, *Ghosts Along the Cumberland: Deathlore in the Kentucky Foothills,* Knoxville: University of Tennessee Press, 1975, pp. 127–28. Collected in Monroe County, Kentucky, in 1969 from a man born in 1905, this version combines the motifs of meeting the ghost at a dance with meeting her on the road, but it lacks the characteristic "portrait-identification" motif at her home.)

"The Vanishing Hitchhiker"
(A modern version)

HITCHHIKER NO GODSEND TO POLICE

LITTLE ROCK (UPI)—Reports of a mysterious hitchhiker who talks about the second coming of Jesus Christ then disappears into thin air from moving cars has sparked the imaginations of highway travelers and mystified the state police.

"It sure is a weird story," Trooper Robert Roten said Friday.

Roten said the state police had had two reports—both on a Sunday—that a clean-cut, well-dressed hitchhiker had disappeared from cars traveling along highways near Little Rock.

Efforts to find someone who actually saw the "highway apostle" proved fruitless. But Little Rock apparently is full of people who know someone who knows someone who had it happen to them.

One such woman, who emphasized she could not verify the story, heard about the hitchhiker from a woman she rides to work with. That woman had heard it from another woman whose parents supposedly were involved in the incident.

Lowering her voice, the woman told the story thus:

"The girl said her parents and another couple were coming from Pine Bluff. They picked up this neatly dressed man because he looked like he needed transportation, you know. He discussed current events—he knew about the [Iranian] hostages—and all of a sudden he said, 'Jesus Christ is coming again' and disappeared.

"They stopped the first trooper they saw and told him, 'you're going to think we're crazy' and told him about it. And he said, 'no, you're the fourth party that's told me about it today.' "

Roten said he checked with police districts all over the state and found only the two reports in Little Rock.

(National wire service story published in the *Salt Lake Tribune* on 26 July 1980.)

"The Death Car"

It was advertised in a newspaper in Boise, Idaho, that a 1971 Corvette was selling for $75.00. The advertisement was small and inconspicuous—not too many people noticed it. Anyone interested must appear in person to see the car— brand-new condition.

When someone checked it out, they found the reason for the unbelievably low price being asked. It seems the car was being sold by the mother of the college-aged boy who the car had belonged to. It was on the level. The only reason the car could not be sold was the fact that the son had committed suicide in it, and the car had not been found with his body in

it until after about ten months. The body had decomposed to
the point that the horrible smell could not be taken out of the
car, and no one could stand to be near it for any length of time.
The mother still has it on her hands.

(Collected by my student Kristen Jensen in October 1971;
deposited in the University of Utah Folklore Archive.)

"The Hook"

We were sitting around and it was like about 12 o'clock at
midnight at a slumber party about two years ago [when this
story was told].

Once there was a couple and they were dating and they
went out to a . . . they were out in the middle of the woods by
a lake, parking. And they were making out and they had their
radio on. There came a flash on the radio to beware that on
the outskirts of the town there was a man with a hook on his
hand who had escaped from a prison and to beware because
if they saw anybody with a hook hand that he was dangerous.
And so they sat there for a while, you know, and the girl started
getting scared. She looked over and she locked her door and
he locked his door and he said, "This is really ridiculous getting upset about it." And she said, "Well, you know, I'm kinda
scared about this thing." So they sat there for a while and she
said, "Listen, let's go into town." And he said, "No, no let's
don't worry about it, don't worry about it." And she said,
"Listen, I'm getting kinda scared, well, let's go into town."
And so he goes, "OK." So he takes . . . he takes her into town
and when they drive up to her house, he gets out and he goes
over to the side of the door, and on the door was a hook.

(From Danielle Roemer, "Scary Story Legends," *Folklore
Annual* 3 [1971], p. 13; collected from a nineteen-year-old
woman in Dallas, Texas.)

"The Killer in the Backseat"

Dear Ann: I tell this story to everyone I meet, but I hope that by telling you, others will get the message.

A lady friend of mine got into her car to do some errands. She was in a hurry but had to stop for gas.

The young attendant asked her to step inside his office because something was wrong with her credit.

Reluctantly, she got out and followed him. Once inside he asked her if she was aware that a man was crouched down in the back seat of her car. My friend nearly fainted.

Moral: Check your back seat before you get into your car. These days it is easy for an experienced rapist or mugger to open a locked car and hide in the back seat. Spread the word, Ann. —I live in California.

Dear California: Consider it spread—and thanks for the tip. (Ann Landers advice column, 31 July 1982.)

"The Baby-sitter and the Man Upstairs"

Okay, there was this lady, this baby-sitter, and she was baby-sitting these two kids and she kept on getting these phone calls, and the first phone call said (Audience: "Oh, I know this one!"), "You had better get out of your house in ten seconds or else I'll come down there and kill you. I'll kill you." And then she got another phone call which said, um, "You better get out of your house in nine minutes or else I'll kill you," and then she didn't really believe him or anything, and she kept on —don't do that! And then, so he did that about three times, well, so then it got down to—three, and then she called the police, and they trans—okay, they called it again, and the police were tracing the number, and the lady, and they said, they called her back and said, "Lady, you better get out of your house, because the man, because—(Audience: "Uh-uh, they said, 'You better get out of your house before I kill you!' ") Because the man's upstairs—" (Audience: "There's a murderer upstairs.") Before he was downstairs, and he slit the children's neck.

(From Elizabeth Tucker, "The Dramatization of Children's Narratives," *Western Folklore* 39 (1980), p. 195. Tape-recorded from a storytelling session at a Girl Scout camp in Indiana in October 1976. This version displays some typical confusions of oral transmission, especially in a group-participation situation. The assailant's calls are coming from the extension telephone in the same house.)

"The Microwaved Pet" (A)

Question: What is the most outrageous court case you know of? (Asked at Boalt Hall School of Law, University of California.)

Answer; from Sheldon Siegel, third-year student: Have you heard of the cat in the microwave case? This is true, I think. This is what I heard. A woman or a man or someone's cat got wet and they put the cat in the microwave to dry it off and the cat exploded and the door to the microwave flew open and injured the person. The person sued the microwave company for a defective latch on the door and won.

(From "Question Man, by Conti," *San Francisco Chronicle,* 30 January 1983.)

"The Microwaved Pet" (B)

I was amazed by your article "Is SAT a Dirty Word?" (Education, July 19). Intelligence is more important than memory. I've known people who knew every general involved in World War II but didn't have enough common sense not to dry their dog in the microwave . . .

(From a letter to the editor in *Newsweek*, 9 August 1982.)

"The Dead Cat in the Package" (A)

THERE'S A MORAL FOR THIEVES HERE, SOMEWHERE

Jeanne Baker of Middleton [Massachusetts] swears this story is true.

If it isn't, don't tell me. I've had too much enjoyment from it to want to forget it and besides Jeanne Baker isn't the kind of person to make things up.

According to Jeanne, it all happened to two friends of a woman with whom she, Jeanne, works at Autoroll in Middleton. . . .

The two women were driving through Danvers on their way to do some last-minute Christmas shopping at Ann & Hope at the Mall when a cat suddenly darted out in front of them and under the wheels.

They immediately pulled over to the side of the road and attempted to assist the badly injured animal. One woman went to nearby houses in an attempt to locate an owner or summon more help, but no one was home.

When she got back to the car, she learned the cat had died.

What to do. Rather than leave the poor beastie there by the

side of the road, the two women decided to continue on to the Mall and dispose of the remains in a dumpster they were sure they could find.

They took one of their shopping bags out of the car, scooped up poor pussy, put both bag and cat in the trunk of the car and proceeded on their way.

Upon their arrival at the Mall, they removed bag and contents, then put it on top of the trunk while they sorted out their returns or whatever inside the car.

Suddenly the looked up in time to see a woman march smartly by the car and snatch the apparently unguarded holiday shopping bag.

They looked at each other, then at the woman, and decided why not, let's follow her and see what happens.

They got out of the car, locked it and nipped briskly along into the Mall in time to keep an eye on the thief.

They followed her into a lunch spot and were lucky enough to find seats themselves as the woman sat down and gave her order, then reached into the bag to take a look at the loot.

The woman suddenly snatched her hand out and began to scream when she saw it was covered with blood.

She then collapsed on the floor and her hysteria stopped only when she fainted.

Workers immediately summoned medical assistance, and the woman was quickly revived. But her distress continued and the emergency responders prepared to put her on a stretcher and take her to the hospital.

But the thief continued to scream, "The bag, the bag."

So a kindly bystander picked up the shopping bag, put it on her chest and said, "Don't worry, lady, here's your bag."

And the ambulance men carried her away.

(From the column by Fredrika Joy in the *Tri-Town Transcript* of the North Shore Weeklies group, Ipswich, Massachusetts, 29 December 1982, p. 6.)

"The Dead Cat in the Package" (B)

MAYBE THERE IS A MORAL FOR EVERYONE,
NOT JUST THE THIEF

Sorry, folks. It really was too good to be true.

Friday night while the rest of you were dining and dancing the old out and the new in, I was skimming through a book from my host's coffee table during courses.

I wish I hadn't.

Or rather, I wish I'd read it the week before.

Isn't it interesting, chirped my hostess, you'll identify a lot of the stories, added my host.

And so I did.

Entitled "The Vanishing Hitchhiker" and written by Jan Harold Brunvand, that little book was a collection of "American Urban Legends and Their Meanings."

It had been a holiday gift from a friend down south and we all got to talking about some of the "urban legends" and sure enough, although we had grown up in different parts of the country, we'd all heard them. . . .

While giggling and chuckling my way through those tales, as we all exchanged memories of when we'd heard the very same stories, I came to the chapter entitled "Purloined Corpses and Fear of the Dead" and read the stories relating how the corpse of a grandmother who had died during a trip was stolen along with the car when the family went to report the death.

I also read "The Dead Cat in the Package" and the shoplifter which related almost word for word the story Jeanne Baker in Middleton had been told and which I repeated in this column a week ago. . . .

At least no one can accuse us here of failing to do our part in continuing the communal re-creation of oral folklore. . . .

(From Fredrika Joy's column in the *Tri-Town Transcript,* 5 January 1983, p. 6.)

"The Runaway Grandmother"

Here's a BUM story which may or may not be true. . . .

Way it goes, this large family decided it would be fun to vacation deep in the heart of romantic Mexico. So dad packed the whole gang, including grandma, aboard their station wagon and took off.

Had a fine time. But then, unexpectedly, granny died. What to do, what to do? It appears that when a United States citizen dies in Mexico, there is quite a bit of red tape and expense involved in getting the body home.

Wishing to avoid all this delay, the family simply wrapped grandma up and concealed the body atop the car with camping equipment.

Then a mad dash for the border followed. After six hours or so they just had to have a break and stopped at a roadside restaurant for food.

When they came out, somebody had stolen their station wagon—and their granny. Neither has been seen from that day to this!

(From Dick Bothwell's *BUM (Brighten Up Monday) Stories,* St. Petersburg, Florida: Great Outdoors Publishing Co., 1978, p. 13; originally published in Bothwell's column in the *St Petersburg Times.*)

"The Solid Cement Car"

A foaf who is a Readymix driver suspected his wife of infidelity. One day, he made sure that she thought he was going to be miles away, and then drove past his house. Sure enough, the bedroom curtains were drawn, and outside stood a brand-new Triumph convertible. Sickened at this display of opulence, our driver had a brilliant idea on the spur of the moment —he drove round the block and prepared his load of cement. Then he returned, positioned his lorry, extended the chute, reversed the barrel and filled the Triumph convertible with Readymix. As he packed up to drive away, a foxy little man came out of his house, climbed on to a bicycle, and pedalled briskly away in the opposite direction.

(From Rodney Dale, *The Tumour in the Whale: A Collection of Modern Myths,* London: Duckworth, 1978, p. 40.)

"The Cat and the Nude Man"

This is the best kitty story I've heard in a while.

A friend of mine says a friend of hers was sleeping on a mattress on the floor of a living room with a picture window covered with curtains. Kitty comes along and pisses on his head. The half-asleep enraged man picked up the cat, and without thinking, threw it at the window. Claws extended, kitty landed on the curtains and pulled them down, at which point Mr. Sleepy Head jumped up, stark naked, and tried to put everything to rights, much to the shock and amusement of several schoolchildren walking past.

(Story received on the computer network USENET, 21 July

1983. This is just one of several urban legends involving people getting into embarrassing scrapes while nude or nearly so and often involving a pet cat as well.)

"The Nude Surprise Party"

JOKE A DAY KEEPS THE BLUES AWAY
HUMOR HELPS IN DEPRESSED REAL ESTATE MARKET

When life—or the real estate market—is down, there is always somebody to pick it up. . . .

Darrell J. Winrich, chairman of the board, Winrich, Kase & O'Connor, Investment Counsel, Newport Beach, also participated [in a two-day conference of the Society of Industrial Realtors].

President "Reagan's intentions are good," he said, "but I don't think we will be willing to live with the pain." That reminded Winrich of this:

Two men were visiting and one said to the other, "Say, how is that gorgeous secretary of yours?"

"Oh, I had to fire her," the other replied.

"Fire her? How come?" the first asked.

"Well," the second said, "it all started a week ago last Thursday on my 49th birthday. I came down for breakfast and my wife never mentioned my birthday. A few minutes later, the kids came down and I was sure they would wish me a 'happy birthday' but there was not one word.

"When I arrived at my office, my secretary greeted me with, 'happy birthday,' and I was glad someone remembered. Then, at noon, she suggested that it was a beautiful day and that she would like to take me to lunch to a nice intimate place in the country. We enjoyed our lunch and a couple of martinis and then, on the way back, she said it was much too nice a day to return to the office and suggested that I go to her apartment, where she would give me another martini.

"That also appealed to me and after a drink and a cigarette, she asked to be excused while she went into the bedroom to change into something more comfortable.

"A few minutes later, the bedroom door opened and out came my secretary, my wife and two kids with a birthday cake, singing, 'Happy Birthday.' And there I sat with nothing on but my socks."

Like Reagan, suggested Winrich, "his secretary had good intentions but her execution left something to be desired."

(As reported by Ruth Ryon, Times Staff Writer, in the *Los Angeles Times*, 7 March 1982, Real Estate Section, pt. 8, p. 1, and widely reprinted.)

BIBLIOGRAPHY

Aarne, Antti, and Stith Thompson. *The Types of the Folktale: A Classification and Bibliography*. 2nd revision. Folklore Fellows Communications, no. 184. Helsinki: Suomalainen Tiedeakatemia, 1961.

Af Klintberg, Bengt. "Folksagner i dag," in *Harens klagen: Studier i gammal och ny folklore*. Stockholm: Norstedts, 1982. Pp. 151–88. [In Swedish, with illustrations; a good survey of types of urban legends, mostly in Europe. Previously published in *Nordisk folktro*, 1976.]

Allen, Barbara. "The 'Image on Glass': Technology, Tradition, and the Emergence of Folklore," *Western Folklore* 41 (1982): 85–103.

Baer, Florence E. " 'Give me . . . your huddled masses': Anti-Vietnamese Refugee Lore and the 'Image of Limited Good'," *Western Folklore* 41 (1982): 275–91.

Baker, Ronald L. *Hoosier Folk Legends*. Bloomington: Indiana University Press, 1982.

Baring-Gould, Sabine. *Curious Myths of the Middle Ages*. 2nd ed., rev. and enl. London, 1867.

Barnes, Daniel R. "The Bosom Serpent: A Legend in American Literature and Culture," *Journal of American Folklore* 85 (1972): 111–22.

Baughman, Ernest W. *Type and Motif-Index of the Folktales of England and North America*. Indiana University Folklore Series, no. 20. The Hague: Mouton & Co., 1966.

Beatty, Jerome, Jr. "Funny Stories," *Esquire* (November 1970): 44–50. [Includes "The Clever Babysitter," "The Solid Cement Cadillac," and "The Nude Housewife," among other apocryphal stories.]

Bennett, Geoffrey. *Nelson the Commander.* New York: Scribner's, 1972. [Information on shipment of Lord Nelson's body home in a cask of brandy.]

Bettelheim, Bruno. *The Uses of Enchantment: The Meaning and Importance of Fairy Tales.* New York: Knopf, 1976.

Bondurant, Sidney W. and Stephen C. Cappanari. "Penis Captivus: Fact or Fancy?" *Medical Aspects of Human Sexuality* 5 (1971): 224, 229, 233.

Bothwell, Dick. *BUM (Brighten up Monday) Stories.* St. Petersburg, Florida: Great Outdoors Publishing Co., 1978. [Columns reprinted from the *St. Petersburg Times.* Includes "The Elephant That Sat on a VW," "Cruise Control," and several urban legends discussed in *The Vanishing Hitchhiker.*]

Briggs, Katharine M., ed. *A Dictionary of British Folk-Tales.* 4 vols. Bloomington: Indiana University Press, 1970.

Briggs, Katharine M. and Ruth L. Tongue, ed. *Folktales of England.* Chicago: University of Chicago Press, 1965.

Brunvand, Jan Harold. *The Vanishing Hitchhiker: American Urban Legends and Their Meanings.* New York: Norton, 1981.

Buchan, David. "The Modern Legend." A paper given at the Annual Conference of the British Sociological Association, April 1978. Published in A. E. Green and J. D. A. Widdowson, eds., *Language, Culture and Tradition.* University of Leeds and University of Sheffield, 1981. Pp. 1–15.

Chambers, Robert. *Traditions of Edinburgh.* Edinburgh, 1825.

Child, Francis James. *The English and Scottish Popular Ballads.* 5 vols, 1882–83. Folklore Press ed. New York: Pageant Book Company, 1957.

Clouston, William A. *Popular Tales and Fictions.* 2 vols. Edinburgh and London, 1887.

Cross, Wilbur L. *The Life and Times of Laurence Sterne.* New York: Macmillan, 1909.

Dale, Rodney. *The Tumour in the Whale: A Collection of Modern Myths.* London: Duckworth, 1978.

deCaro, Rosan Jordan. "Sex Education and the Horrible Example Stories," *Folklore Forum* 3 (September-November 1970): 124–127.

Dégh, Linda, and Andrew Vázsonyi. "The Memorate and the Proto-Memorate," *Journal of American Folklore* 87 (1974): 225–39. ["Uncle Peter's Gold Watch" on p. 229.]

Dickason, David H. "Swallowing Snake Eggs," *Hoosier Folklore Bulletin* 2 (June 1943): 22.

Dickson, Paul, and Joseph C. Goulden. *There are Alligators in Our Sewers and Other American Credos.* New York: Delacorte Press, 1983.

Donaghey, B. S. "The Chinese Restaurant Story Again: An Antipodean Version," *Lore and Language* 2 (January 1978): 24–26.

Dorson, Richard M. *Land of the Millrats.* Cambridge, Mass.: Harvard University Press, 1981.

Editor. "The Poisoned Dress," *Hoosier Folklore Bulletin* 4 (March 1945): 19–20.

Ellis, Bill. "De Legendis Urbis: Modern Legends in Ancient Rome," *Journal of American Folklore* 96 (1983): 200–208.

Farmer, J. S., and W. E. Henley. *Slang and its Analogues.* Original edition, 1890–1904. New York: Arno Press reprint, 1970. [Phrase, "to tap the admiral."]

Fine, Gary Alan. "Folklore Diffusion Through Interactive Social Networks: Conduits in a Preadolescent Community," *New York Folklore* 5 (1979): 87–126. [Discusses the Pop Rocks legend.]

Fitzgerald, Percy. *The Life of Laurence Sterne.* 1896 ed., 2 vols. New York: J. F. Taylor & Company, 1904.

Giarelli, Andrew. "Telling Tales," *New Jersey Monthly* (August 1982): 39–43, 88, 90.

Gould, George M. and Walter L. Pyle. *Anomalies and Curiosities of Medicine, Being an encyclopedic collection of rare and extraordinary cases, and of the most striking instances of abnormality in all branches of medicine and surgery, derived from an exhaustive research of medical literature from its origin to the present day. . . .* First published in 1896 by W. B. Saunders. New York: The Julian Press, 1956.

Greenberg, Andrea. "Drugged and Seduced: A Contemporary Legend," *New York Folklore Quarterly* 29 (1973): 131–58.

Greig, Francis [pseud.]. *Heads You Lose and Other Apocryphal Tales.* New York: Crown, 1982. [Twenty stories, mostly urban legends, rewritten as "what might have happened that *first* time."]

Haines, Francis. "Goldilocks on the Oregon Trail," *Idaho Yesterdays* 9 (Winter 1965–66): 26–30.

Hall, Max. "The Great Cabbage Hoax: A Case Study," *Journal of Personality and Social Psychology* 2 (1965): 563–69.

Hartikka, H. D. "Tales Collected from Indiana University Students," *Hoosier Folklore* 5 (June 1946): 71–82.

Hartley, Lodwick. *This is Lorence: A Narrative of the Reverend Laurence Sterne.* Chapel Hill: The University of North Carolina Press, 1943.

Himelick, Raymond. "Classical Versions of 'The Poisoned Garment'," *Hoosier Folklore* 5 (June 1946): 83–84.

Hippensteel, Faith. " 'Sir Hugh': The Hoosier Contribution to the Ballad," *Indiana Folklore* 2 (1969): 75–140.

Hobbs, Sandy. "The Folk Tale As News," *Oral History* [University of

Essex, Dept. of Sociology Oral History Society, Wivenhoe Park, Colchester] 6 (1978): 74–86.

Hochsinger, Gloria. "More about the Poisoned Dress," *Hoosier Folklore Bulletin* 4 (June 1945): 32–34.

Interpreter's Bible, The. Vol. 12. New York and Nashville: Abingdon Press, 1957.

Jacobs, Joseph, ed. *Celtic Fairy Tales.* London: David Nutt, 1892.

Jacobson, David J. *The Affairs of Dame Rumor.* New York: Rinehart, 1948.

Kerr, Kathleen. "The Dog and Fingers: A New Urban Belief Tale?" *Tennessee Folklore Society Bulletin* 47 (Summer 1982): 66–70.

Knapp, Mary and Herbert. *One Potato, Two Potato: The Secret Education of American Children.* New York: Norton, 1976.

McConnell, Brian. "Urban Legends in Fleet Street," *Folklore* 93 (1982): 226–28.

Montgomery, Jim. "Rumor-Plagued Firms Use Various Strategies to Keep Damage Low," *The Wall Street Journal,* 6 February 1979, 1, 22. [Satanism, Pop Rocks, wormburgers, and other corporate rumors, plus how companies fight back.]

Napolitani, F. Donald. "Two Unusual Cases of Gunshot Wounds of the Uterus," *New York State Journal of Medicine* 59 (February 1959): 491–93.

Newall, Venetia. "The Black Outsider: Racist Images in Britain," in *Folklore Studies in the 20th Century: Proceedings of the Centenary Conference of the Folklore Society,* edited by Venetia Newall. London: Rowman and Littlefield, 1980. Pp. 308–13. [The packet of biscuits story is given on p. 311.]

Opie, Iona and Peter. "Certain Laws of Folklore," in *Folklore Studies in the 20th Century: Proceedings of the Centenary Conference of the Folklore Society,* edited by Venetia Newall. London: Rowman and Littlefield, 1980. Pp. 64–75.

Orso, Ethelyn, G. "The Choking Doberman Legend," *Louisiana Folklore Miscellany* 5 (1983): 49–50. [Contains the Louisiana text partially quoted in Chapter 1.]

Palmer, Kingsley. "Modern Oral Traditions Amongst Overland Travellers," *Folklore* 85 (1974): 164–68. [Various third-hand reports of terrible incidents supposedly happening to European overland travelers to India, Nepal, and beyond: "robbery, violence, sexual assault, or immorality."]

Poulsen, Richard C. "Bosom Serpentry Among the Puritans and Mormons," *Journal of the Folklore Institute* 16 (1979): 176–89.

Reaver, J. Russell. " 'Embalmed Alive': A Developing Urban Ghost Tale," *New York Folklore Quarterly* 8 (1952): 217–20.

Reilly, Robin. *The British at the Gates: The New Orleans Campaign in the War of 1812.* New York: Putnam's, 1974. [Disposition of the body of General Pakenham.]

Ridley, Florence H. "A Tale Told Too Often," *Western Folklore* 26 (1967): 153–56.

"Rock it to Me: Feeding a Candy Craze," *Time,* 1 May 1978, p. 44. [Pop Rocks.]

Roth, Cecil, ed. *The Ritual Murder Libel and the Jews.* London: Woburn Press, 1934.

Sanderson, Stewart F. "The Folklore of the Motor-car," *Folklore* 80 (1969): 241–52.

———. "The Modern Urban Legend." The Katharine Briggs Lecture No. 1 delivered 3 November 1981. London: The Folklore Society, [1982], 15 pp.

Shorrocks, Graham. "Further Aspects of Restaurant Stories," *Lore and Language* 3, pt. A (January 1980): 71–74.

———. "Notes and Queries. Chinese Restaurant Stories: International Folklore," *Lore and Language* 2 (July 1975): 30.

Simpson, Jacqueline. "Another Modern Legend?" Letter to the Editor in *Folklore* 83 (1972): 339. ["The Double Theft."]

———. "Rationalized Motifs in Urban Legends," *Folklore* 92 (1981): 203–7. ["The Robber Who Was Hurt."]

———"Urban Legends in *The Pickwick Papers,*" *Journal of American Folklore* 96 (1983): 462–70. [Identifies prototypes for pets baked into pies and other stories.]

Smith, A. W. "Yet another modern legend?" Letter to the Editor in *Folklore* 86 (1975): 139. ["Sharing the Biscuits."]

Smith, Alan. "The 'Double Theft'; A Variant Form," *Folklore* 84 (1973): 166–67. [Also mentions "The Severed Fingers."]

Smith, Paul and Georgina. "Query" [for Chinese restaurant stories]. *Lore and Language* 6 (January 1972): 15. [Responses appeared in *Lore and Language* 7 (July 1972); 8 (January 1973); and 9 (July 1973). See also items in this bibliography by B. S. Donaghey and Graham Shorrocks.]

Thomas, Gerald. *The Tall Tale and Philippe D'Alcripe* [includes a translation of *La Nouvelle Fabrique des Excellents Traits de Vérité*]. St. John's, Newfoundland: Memorial University of Newfoundland in association with The American Folklore Society (Monograph Series No. 1; Publications of the American Folklore Society, Bibliographical and Special Series, vol. 29), 1977.

Thompson, Stith. *The Motif-Index of Folk Literature.* New enlarged and revised ed. 6 vols. Bloomington: Indiana University Press, 1955–58.

Thomson, David. *Wild Excursions: The Life and Fiction of Laurence Sterne.* London: Weidenfeld & Nicolson, 1972.

Toelken, Barre. *The Dynamics of Folklore.* Boston: Houghton Mifflin, 1979.

Trahant, Yvette L. "The Oral Tradition of the Physician," *Louisiana Folklore Miscellany* 5 (1981): 38–47.

Train, John. *True Remarkable Occurrences.* New York: Clarkson N. Potter, 1978.

Tucker, Elizabeth. "The Seven-Day Wonder Diet: Magic and Ritual in Diet Folklore," *Indiana Folklore* 11 (1978): 141–50.

Wachs, Eleanor. "The Crime-Victim Narrative as a Folkloric Genre," *Journal of the Folklore Institute* 19 (1982): 17–30.

Ward, Donald, ed. and trans. *The German Legends of the Brothers Grimm.* 2 vols, 1816, 1818. ISHI ed. Philadelphia: Institute for the Study of Human Issues, 1981.

INDEX

229